VENOM

OTHER BOOKS AND AUDIO BOOKS

BY K. C. GRANT:

Abish: Daughter of God

Abish: Mother of Faith

VENOM

a novel by
K.C. GRANT

Covenant Communications, Inc.

To Kartchner's crew:
Go Mexico '94!

Cover image *Back Lit* © Xyno. Courtesy Istockphoto.com
Cover design copyright © 2012 by Covenant Communications, Inc.

Published by Covenant Communications, Inc.
American Fork, Utah

Printed in the United States of America
First Printing: January 2012

18 17 16 15 14 13 12   10 9 8 7 6 5 4 3 2 1

ISBN 978-1-60861-142-3

Acknowledgments

As usual, it would be impossible to complete this book without the help of so many people. My sincere thanks to my readers and the evaluators at Covenant for all the early comments that made me head back to the computer for another look. And to Samantha Van Walraven, my editor, for your attention to detail and your thoughtful comments. I especially thank my family for being so understanding and patient and for being the best cheerleaders in the world. To all the marketing staff at Covenant, I appreciate your continued support and trust as always. As far as my research aides for this book, my thanks to retired Special Agent Lew Rice, author of *My Life on the Front Line*, and former Police Detective Mark Arrington for their insights into the world of law enforcement and criminal activity.

Chapter 1

"WHAT?"

I stared at the bill in front of me in disbelief. "This is impossible! I've never had a credit card balance this high before!"

The overstuffed chair behind me luckily caught my fall, since I was still focusing on the offending paper in my hand. It had been a rough Monday. Roger Mellon, the five-foot-four, one-hundred-sixty-pound, thirty-five-year-old divorcé with the dubious title of being my manager, had none-too-subtly made advances at me again as I'd struggled with the new copy machine. Then I'd had to squeeze into a cramped elevator and stand next to a man who would have benefited from the deodorant ad I was working on. The final insult had come when the deli shop messed up my order and I'd ended up with a turkey on rye instead of the Monte Cristo sandwich I'd nearly fasted all day for.

And now this.

I double-checked the envelope to make sure I hadn't received Britney Spears's invoice by mistake. Nope. *Samantha Evans* it read in accusatory print. But when had I ever shopped at custom boutiques? And unless I'd spent a recent day at a spa and then blocked it from my memory, someone had had a day off on me. At least I was familiar with the businesses, some of them local San Diego hot spots for the rich and pampered, but certainly nothing that I could indulge in on my wages. One day I might be a copywriter or even a manager for Phizer-Lewis Advertising, a prestigious agency I'd been with for almost a year now. At the present time though, I was still just a lowly grunt paying my dues.

After a quick breath to sustain myself, I muttered out loud, "I can handle this. I'll just call the credit card company and tell them my card's been stolen."

Just to make sure I had all the facts, I went to retrieve my purse and looked in an inside pocket where I kept my *important* cards. Drat. My credit card was still intact along with my work ID, my library card, and a Ben and Jerry's buy-one-get-one free coupon. Now I was confused. Reaching for my cell phone, I punched in the customer service number from the back of the credit card. After a few moments of elevator serenades and mastering the "push one for this and two for that" directions of the monotone hostess, I finally came in contact with a live person who read verbatim: "Hello and welcome to Bank First USA, where *your* business is our *first* concern. I'm Joanie, and who am I speaking with?"

I told her, along with the indisputable fact that someone had access to my card number.

"All right," my server replied in the pleasant, yet detached, way that only a hired hand can employ. "If you'll give me your security password."

"Shakespeare."

"Thank you, Ms. Evans. Now, will you repeat for me what the problem is?"

"Well, I just got my bill, and there are some charges here for . . . almost a *thousand* dollars that I know nothing about! I checked my purse and found my credit card, so somehow they must just have my number. I've bought a few things on the Internet lately," I explained, "but some of these unfamiliar charges are for local businesses, so I don't know what's going on."

"All right, Ms. Evans," the representative continued as if she'd just been told something mundane—like the weather was sunny. "I'll transfer you to a supervisor, and he should be able to help you."

Why didn't she just do that in the first place? They must get paid according to how long they're on the phone "helping" customers. So I repeated my story to the supervisor, who appeared only a tad more interested in the situation, as if I'd added to the story that there was a possibility of showers later this evening.

"Ms. Evans," he drawled in a tone that leapt from paid employee to patronizing parent, "thank you for finally notifying us. I have your bill in front of me and see that some of the charges go back almost two weeks. Responsibly reporting a stolen card within the first twenty-four hours is imperative in stopping this type of identity theft, you know."

I sucked in a quick breath and exhaled before responding evenly, "But my card hasn't been stolen. As I said, it's right here in my purse. I don't know what's going on."

Was it just my imagination, or did I actually hear him snort?

"Well, give us a few days to research this, and we'll get back to you. In the meantime, we'll put a hold on your credit card until we can decide if we're able to reissue you a new one. Was there anything else I could help you with?" he added.

"No." I sighed. "I'll wait for your call."

Hanging up, I realized that days, maybe weeks could pass before this was resolved. My frustration neared anger. I'd been a customer of theirs since high school, and my balance had never reached this amount before. Weren't they supposed to have people who monitored this sort of thing? If a person who usually only had charges from places like Walgreens and Barnes and Noble in the amount of a few hundred dollars suddenly started living the lifestyle of the rich and famous, shouldn't some pencil pusher over at "Bank First USA, where *your* business is our *first* concern" *be* concerned?

"Great." I stood up, looking out the window. "What do I do in the meantime?"

The day *had* been sunny and, with May on our doorstep, the temperature along the San Diego county coast had already climbed into the seventies. I realized how lucky I'd been to find this quaint little upper-story apartment so close to the beach. Between my roommate Terri's income and the remainder of my student loan money, I figured I could hold on until a promotion came and I finally started seeing a decent paycheck.

My thoughts snapped back to the problem at hand. What if the bank called and said they wouldn't cover the charges? If they found me responsible for the bill, would I have enough money to fly home in July for the big 2008 Evans reunion? It almost sounded like they were thinking of taking my card away permanently. Could they do that?

It then occurred to me that this might be something I should alert the local authorities to as well. I picked up the phone and started calling, but the process sent me into déjà vu as they shifted me around to a few departments before someone could finally help me. I found out that *help* meant different things to different people. I told my story again, and I imagined the female officer humoring me and writing all of it down.

She asked me for some personal information, and then she added, "I suggest you obtain a credit check monthly for the next three months and report any changes to the appropriate party. Is there anything else I can help you with?"

"Uh, I guess not." I sat there, dismayed. "Is that it?"

"Ms. Evans." Her tone was weary. "Do you have any idea how many calls of this nature we get every week? We don't have the manpower to investigate every one of them. If any other threats to your identity occur, you're welcome to give us a call and we can add it to your record. Naturally, we'll forward this on to the DA's office. But I'm afraid there's nothing else we need from you."

Flipping my cell phone shut, I wrapped my arms around myself, not feeling the slightest bit reassured. In fact, I felt unsettled, vulnerable. Violated. What good was law enforcement if they couldn't enforce the laws?

I turned away from the window and stared at the empty apartment. With all of that "taken care of," I was left with only the dilemma of what to make for dinner before Terri got home. I could offer her the choice of a now-soggy sandwich or whatever else I could scrape up. We'd used to take turns making dinner until I realized that Terri's idea of cooking was mac and cheese or takeout dumped in a pot. Even after the day I'd had today, I realized I was in the mood to cook something after all. It would help take my mind off of things.

As I peered into the darkened corner of a cupboard, I realized that in spite of all her faults, Terri was an acceptable roommate, even if she was a little "flower child–ish" for my taste. Even though Terri was older than me by about five years, she seemed to appreciate my tendency to be the dependable one. She also *never* judged me—not that my lifestyle was worthy of much scrutiny. Terri worked by day in a secondhand clothing store she co-owned, where she sold apparel that artisans referred to as "antique clothing." Then at night she hung out at some of the nearby clubs. Since she was unable to supply me with a consistent schedule, I often had leftovers when I decided to cook.

While I stood debating over the stove, the apartment door opened. It was Terri, actually home and bursting in with her usual *joie de vivre*. She was wearing a bright purple peasant dress and unwrapped a yellow print scarf from around her neck as she said, "Hey, roomie! Cooking tonight? Great! What are we having?"

Terri's thoughts revolved around two things, men and food. Probably in that order.

I answered from the kitchen area a few feet away, "Well, there's a soggy turkey on rye or," inspiration dawned on me as I continued to look at the shelf, "pasta with Alfredo sauce, garlic bread, and a slightly wilted garden salad, all made to order."

"With mozzarella melted on the garlic bread and lots of fattening ranch dressing?" she anxiously questioned.

"Of course." I tried to eat my bread minus the cheese and salad with dressing on the side, but sometimes my love for food got the better of me. Terri had a consistently healthy appetite, which she naturally carried around with her, along with a few extra pounds. But nobody seemed to notice the pounds because of her carefree attitude and positive spirit. The fact that she had hair that bordered on red and curled into untamable tresses halfway down her back was also good for distraction. Terri was anything but average . . . inside and out.

"Dibs on the pasta," Terri pronounced as she flopped into a chair, holding the back of her hand to her brow. "Aye, and what a day I've had today!"

I stifled a chuckle. Terri thought she was Barbra Streisand and Bette Midler reincarnated into one person, and it didn't help to mention that they were both still alive. To hear her sing would almost convince anyone that she was right. I couldn't help but smile when she lapsed into her Yiddish dialect when she was in the mood for drama, which was often.

"I'm all ferclumped because Javier hasn't called me for three days!" she lamented, hands flinging about. "I shoulda known betta than to get involved with an *artiste*! He's dumped me. I just know it. I shouldn't have given in so easily. My grandmother always said, 'Why buy the cow when you can get the milk for free?' But with a man like that and those hands when he plays the drums, *oy gevalt*! I'm all undone!"

I knew what was coming next.

"One of these days, Sam, you'll know what I mean."

I let Terri get away with calling me Sam because she considered me a friend, even though I thought it verbally drained me of any feminine aura I was trying to maintain in this age of equality. I also usually let her get away with a few unwelcome comments like that because . . . well, just because.

Unfortunately my roommate only vaguely understood the whole concept of morality, which was why we really didn't socialize together that much. Once, I'd broken down and went to a club with her after she said they had some incredible Tango dancers from Argentina doing an exhibition. What a mistake! Even though the atmosphere and performance had been full of

Spanish flair, the dancing had been far from BYU ballroom standards, and it had only taken a few moments with the alcohol flowing freely before someone had tried to hit on me. Suddenly, an unexpected drink had shown up in front of me—most likely as a token payment for a good time ahead. I had smiled politely and refused, but I could see by the look on the waitress's face that she was thinking the same thing I was: "What's a girl like that doing in a place like this if she's not looking for a good time?"

It was a different world.

At times like that I was glad for my religious foundation. I attended the local ward, where I was a Relief Society teacher. Bishop Fosse and his wife were great. They were an older couple with children in the process of marriages and missions—a description that fit the majority of the attendees. That didn't mean the ward was completely devoid of young male influence because we did have the neighboring UC San Diego students attending. There were a few guys who I went out with now and then, but I avoided any serious entanglements. Strangely enough, with my sincere thanks whenever I *was* around Terri's friends, Terri treated the topic of religion and my conservative lifestyle with a certain respect. In fact, I almost wondered if Terri did have a little more respect and curiosity for my religion than she cared to show.

I thought about trying the old "golden question" routine from my mission days on my friend but knew I wouldn't get far with the effort. I'd heard the sentiment stated before: "Thanks, I've got things pretty much under control. I believe in God and think He wants us all to be good people. I don't hurt anyone, and I like who I am. What more could I need?"

Not everyone was ready. I would just bide my time until it felt right. Of course, I was good at waiting for the perfect moment. The only problem was I had the sneaking suspicion that sometimes those perfect moments passed me by without my even knowing it.

Chapter 2

Looking across the table at my roommate slurping down pasta like tomorrow was the end of the world, I wondered what life looked like through her eyes—if Terri ever doubted herself or felt regret. Probably not. She was the epitome of confidence. I would never forget the day Terri interviewed me for the apartment.

"Can you pay the rent, share the phone bill, and handle your own food expenses?"

"Yes."

"Do you have a problem with gays, Jews, African-Americans, people of any other ethnic or religious background?"

"No, not really."

"Are you okay with the fact that I often stay out late, do yoga on the living room floor, and have to have the tissue paper unroll from the top?"

I stifled a laugh. "Yes. I am also very partial to that type of tissue etiquette."

After that, I received a hearty smile and approval to move in immediately. It had been an interesting few months since then, but even though Terri had her moments, I was coming to realize that she was a genuinely good person underneath the makeup, hair, and unbridled personality. You really had to see it to believe it, and it was hard to explain to others, especially my parents.

Cross my heart, I *had* tried, according to my parents' wishes, to find out before I moved about any families or single LDS women who needed roommates. But I didn't have any real luck. Of course, I had neglected to tell them about the Brody family with seven children who said they had converted the garage into a studio apartment with a small kitchenette. Seven children! I knew I would become a nanny to those children in a matter of minutes, and that was the last thing I wanted.

Naturally, my choice of roommates wasn't the only decision where I'd fallen short with my parents. Graduating from the University of Utah with a degree in advertising hadn't been their first pick of the draw either. Why couldn't I be a teacher or a nurse? That way I would either have the perfect job for impending motherhood or, even better, be in the vicinity of future medical practitioners! They didn't understand how, when I was younger, I was often more entertained by the commercials than the actual programs on TV. But I had also realized the negative influence advertising could have as well. So maybe in a small way, I could put my two cents in and contribute positively to the profession that created the laughter and tears that had affected me all those years.

While I was in school proclaiming my independence, the silent blows had come. My older brother had graduated with his engineering degree a few years ago and was accepted to law school right on cue. He was now living in Virginia with his perfect wife and two small children. My younger brother was currently enrolled at dental school in Nebraska, and his wife had baby number one on the way. And my younger sister, Karen, who was on the verge of graduating from high school, had been named sterling scholar in dance and needed her own phone line to handle the tidal wave of phone calls from testosterone-laden admirers.

It's only fair to admit that my parents had stood beside me last year *until* I told them I was accepting a job offer in San Diego.

"Where? Oh sweetheart, it's so far away!"

"Mom. Dad. It will be okay." I'd tried to reassure myself as much as them. "It's a beautiful city, I hear, with lots of history and parks. Plus, I'll be by the ocean."

"Of course, we're sure it's a wonderful place to visit. But, Samantha, there must be some options closer to home. We'd get to see you more often, and there would be more, well . . . *opportunities.*"

I knew that was another way of saying "eligible men." So I countered with, "Did you have this conversation with Kurt when he went off to Georgetown or with Daniel? And I suppose it's okay that Karen's been submitting applications out of state."

"No, but, sweetheart, that's different."

"Because you believe in them and not me? I'm going. And that's final."

Naturally I had hoped time would prove who was right and who was wrong. The months passed, and I dreaded the weekly phone calls from family as I tried to sound upbeat yet reveal as little as possible. But in my mind, I could hear the conversations that must be going on back home.

"And Samantha. What news from her?"

"Well, she is still unmarried and living in that beach city with the most dead-end job she could find. Oh, and did we mention that her roommate is a heathen and completely wanton?"

Okay. So maybe they didn't sink that low, but I was sure disappointment had given way to subtle meddling.

"Samantha? Well, from what we hear, she's waiting for a big break at that advertising firm she works for. She isn't currently seeing anyone, though we do have a family in our ward who just moved in and has a son. He's going to be a doctor and is attending BYU!"

You're just jealous because everyone has a life and you're circling the drain.

Oh, did I mention the antagonistic voice in my head? I usually try to ignore or dispute it, even if it does have a good idea every now and then. This time, I chose to ignore.

I knew I was struggling with the way my life was going, but I was determined to have my parents remain oblivious to this fact. Sure, living in a quaint apartment in San Diego and working for an advertising firm sounded glamorous on the surface. The reality was, my workday was mundane, my social life all but nonexistent, and any titles before or after my name seemed to be fading away in front of my very eyes.

At least Terri's appetite was consistent. "Could you pass me some more garlic bread, please? I'm dying here!"

Leave it to my roommate to put hunger before introspection.

"Excuse me, but if you don't come back to planet earth and tell me if there's more pasta, you may find me wasting away, and then who will tempt you with Monte Cristos from the Tavern?"

Monte Cristos were my all-time weakness and one of the ways Terri made up for her errant behavior. I could starve myself all week if I knew Terri was stopping on her way home from work to pick up one of those luscious sandwiches layered with meat and cheeses between French toast and the most mouth-watering raspberry jam on the side.

"Okay, okay. Yes, there's more pasta, and since when were you wasting away?"

"Oh, dahling," Terri purred, "it's purely *meta*physical wasting—the rest of me isn't going anywhere."

As I checked the remaining Alfredo sauce, Terri pounced on my thoughts once again. "Where are you, roomie? Even I'm noticing you've been kind of distracted all evening."

"Oh." I paused, not wanting to let Terri in on all of my self-doubts. Then I came up with a topic I knew would distract her. "You'll never believe what happened to me today." I redirected the conversation to my most recent dilemma. "I opened my credit card bill today and, well, look at this."

I retrieved the bill from my bill organizer and showed Terri.

"Whoa, honey! Someone's moving up in the world."

"But that's just it," I explained. "You know me. These aren't my charges. Somebody's using my credit card number."

"Uh-huh. Isn't that the way of things? You do all the work, and somebody else does the living for you. What are you going to do?"

I rehashed my phone call to the credit card company and then the police, with their less-than-helpful attitude. "The bank is supposed to call me in a few days. In the meantime, this card's on hold."

"Oh no!" My companion feigned a horrified expression. "What will the booksellers of America do? How will they survive without your shopping sprees?"

I scowled. "Hey, thanks a lot for the support. So I like to read. Maybe," I retorted in an attempt at a comeback, "*you* ought to try it sometime."

"Touché. I couldn't even make it through the first chapter of that last one you lent me. What does *wuthering* mean anyway?"

Disguising my own ignorance, I shoved another bite of bread into my mouth. Terri looked pensive as she twirled the last of the pasta around her fork. "Seriously, sometimes I think you hide behind those books. You go to work for the Establishment, where they treat you as if you didn't have two bright ideas to rub together. Then you come home, cook me dinner—for which I am *immensely* grateful, I must say—now, where was I? Oh yes, cook me dinner and then keep your nose behind a book until you go to bed—and then you get up and do it all over again." She let out an exasperated sigh. "What brought you here anyway, Sam?"

Feeling defensive and no longer hungry, I stood and walked over to my thoughtful spot at the window and, in a response more emotional than coherent, said, "I'm here because I want to be. I fell in love with California during my mission, and I couldn't think of a better place to live. I think San Diego's a nice place. As for my job, well, I like what I do . . . some of the time. And they're going to notice me and offer me a better position; I know it. I'm actually getting to work on branding techniques with the copywriting department, and just last week I was asked to deliver some storyboards on a new campaign to Mr. Phizer's office. I think they're starting to appreciate my abilities."

"It's about time," muttered Terri under her breath.

Ignoring her, I continued, "As for my social life, well, I've been busy. There isn't a lot of time and opportunity to meet new people around here. I still have faith that things will work out when it's time."

"Hmm. Sam, I don't mean to razz you here. You're a great girl, probably the best I know. It's strange how this *faith* of yours sure sounds like another word for *excuse.*"

Terri's accusation stung.

My faith had always been something of great value. I believed Heavenly Father loved me and wanted what was best for me. I had felt His guidance throughout my life, during my school years, my mission—life had seemed so simple then.

"Well, babe." She stood up. Apparently Terri was going for a hit-and-run. "Dinner was great. I gotta go. Javier might be waiting for me at the club."

"Thanks for the enlightenment about my pitiful life," I tried to joke. "I guess I'll turn in early and do a little reading."

"Well," Terri said with a hint of encouragement, "at least you're consistent! Ta-ta!"

Ugh. Glancing back at the table, I somehow knew I'd get stuck with the dishes again.

Stacking the dirty plates into the sink and running the hot water, I heard Terri's in-need-of-attention Chevelle pull out from behind the apartment. Steam drifted up and coated the window above the counter. I reached a finger out and traced through the condensation and found that I had drawn a heart.

"What's wrong with me?" I groaned out loud, throwing a dish into the sink and splashing water all over my front. I was used to feeling talented and smart and occasionally sure about what I wanted from life. Only now, as I found myself looking at the reflection that stared back at me from the rinse water, there was a detached sort of feeling about myself, as if I had lost my former identity somehow. So what if my features were nice and even and I had a naturally slim figure that did elicit momentary glances from an occasional male admirer. This was little consolation, considering most of my weekends were spent in the pages of a book.

Yeah, the type where somehow the plain girl ends up with her dream guy.

I'd hardly call myself plain.

Ah, such vanity.

It wasn't completely unwarranted. In the fog of the window, my hazel eyes looked luminous, and I couldn't see the small bump on my nose that

I'd inherited from my mom. Even the uneven lengths of my brownish-blonde hair—which only *slightly* resembled the dishwater below—had finally grown out from a bungled attempt to look like Posh Spice. Sure, the style had shown off my high cheekbones and long neck, but I'd felt too exposed without the safety of falling hair about my face almost like a permanently attached security blanket. Only now the added weight made it hang limply in silent protest, and I often found myself brushing it away.

At first I was glad that Terri was gone, leaving me alone with my thoughts. Even though I had the privacy of my own room, some of my roommate's phone conversations could wake the dead, let alone leave the living with anything less than a feeble ability to concentrate. Now the silence seemed deafening as my doubts continued to close in on me.

So what do you do now? Throw in the towel? Go back home to Utah where your parents can line you up with every eligible man in the Beehive State?

You'd like that, wouldn't you?

I felt as if I were free falling from a tall cliff. Not knowing what to do wasn't a comfortable feeling in life. Neither was not being in control. Was I really that badly off or just panicking because things were a bit up in the air at the moment? Maybe time would take care of my job and relationships.

Since when did you get so complacent?

Shooing away the voice like an intrusive insect, I abandoned the remaining dishes, grabbed my running shoes, and raced out the door and down the back stairs until I came around to the front of our blue-and-white clapboard apartment. The path to the beach was only five blocks away. There was a slightly pinkish hue from the setting sun and a cool breeze that made me glad I had worn long pants instead of cut-offs. (Of course, the real reason for that decision was that it had been days since I'd shaved my legs.) When I arrived at the seaside promenade, I passed mothers with strollers, tourists, and in-line skaters who could obviously relate to the joy of being outdoors. Blood began surging through my veins, and I felt the tingly, prickly feeling of muscles and tissues waking up. Breathing deeply, I realized how much I loved everything about the ocean. From the squawking of seagulls to the tang of sea air, I was hooked from the first moment I'd seen it.

I still remembered that first trip our family had taken when we were kids. We'd loaded up into the family station wagon to make the eleven-hour ride—I don't know how my parents did it. Of course, there were only three of us at the time, and we'd made a few stops along the way in Las Vegas and Barstow. Thanks to the laxity of seatbelt laws back then, we'd quickly turned the car into our own playground, hopping back and forth over the seats and trying to invent games to keep us entertained. Our favorite was sitting in the backward-facing rear seat and pretending we were the crew of a starship and the yellow lines whizzing by us were phaser fire as we pelted the oncoming enemy's ship.

And then, just when I'm sure my mom was ready to abandon us at the nearest convenience store, we'd arrived.

Stumbling toward the glittering horizon, I felt as if I'd come to the end of the world and all that was left was the brilliant mirage wavering in front of me. All my siblings had cared about was digging in the sand and picking up shells and seaweed. I'd wanted to get lost in sunset and sit and watch it forever. That day I'd vowed the ocean would carry me to every corner of the world. Only, here I was already twenty-five and I had never left the country.

I ran as far as the next turnoff and then decided to head back to the apartment before it got too dark. Even though I seemed to be in good company, I hadn't gotten over my sense of vulnerability being alone at night. With fresh endorphins feeding my brain, I knew I didn't want to give up on my life here and go home. If things didn't work out at Phizer-Lewis, there would be openings at other companies.

Oh, and what kind of reference would you get? Never missed a day of work and didn't drink any of the coffee?

Thanks a lot. Well, I'd have to cross that bridge when I came to it, but I was sure of one thing now: this was my life, and I needed to start being the one in charge of it.

Chapter 3

TUESDAY BEGAN WITH THE COMMOTION of several DJs' voices coming over my radio alarm. With a slap of my hand, I silenced them. I was a little groggy, since Terri had returned the night before and started a party that didn't end until around one o'clock in the morning. Each time the front door would open and close, I'd optimistically try to drift off to sleep until I'd hear the muted voices and occasional outburst from the duo or trio that still remained. Finally, the last visitor left, and I must have slept some because if I hadn't slept, I wouldn't have had that dream.

I could remember it as clearly as if a movie had been playing in my head. I was back on my grandparents' ranch, riding Diamond at a speed only realized in a fantasy world. Bareback on the prickly horsehair, I could feel the power and potential beneath me. Faster and faster we galloped across a meadow that was part familiar to me from days past and part strange, as if I were in a foreign land. I was overwhelmed by the desire to fly and be free! Finally I let go of the reins and let my arms soar up, reaching toward the sky. Then just as we passed through a grove of trees, I saw a mist up ahead. Nearing the darkness confirmed my worst fear . . . that horse and rider were headed straight toward a cliff! The dream took on a nightmarish quality as I realized the horse was no longer under my control. My hands tried to grip the reins. But the reins had disappeared.

The precipice was near enough that the rocks took on individual forms. Faster and faster we surged, until I seemed to fly forward through no choice of my own. Terror gripped me as the weightless feeling of free falling overtook my senses. My hands flailed for contact with any solid surface. I grazed the rough surface of the cliff wall. A jagged rock. It held. Barely. But my hands quickly grew weak until fear almost consumed me.

"Reach out." The voice spoke in a whisper, as if unaware of the gravity of my situation.

I struggled to climb back up to the ledge, which was moving farther and farther away.

"Reach out."

A second time! There was nothing to reach out to!

"Let go and reach out."

Too weak to argue, I dropped. A formless hand appeared and slowed my descent.

My restless night made me wake up earlier than usual, so I dressed and then ate breakfast in blissful solitude, knowing it would be hours before my roommate could force herself awake and stumble through her morning routine in a less-than-pleasant, hungover state. Just as well. I needed to concentrate on finishing up so I wouldn't have to face the worst of morning rush-hour traffic. As I left the apartment, I thought once again how nice it would be to have some grass or a flower garden behind it instead of eroding asphalt. But then I'd have to be responsible for it. The downstairs tenants (whom I knew only through an occasional thud or slamming door) wouldn't make more than a half-hearted attempt at anything besides dumping their own trash, and even then the garbage can seemed to end up on the curb at such a precarious angle that a strong breeze could send it crashing to the ground, spilling its foul contents everywhere. Somehow I was always the one to haul it back to its platform.

Fortunately, my faithful Honda sputtered to life, and I got to work in record time. Feeling optimistic, I was even able to temper my envy of the Mercedes and Jaguars that graced the parking structure. One red sports car even flaunted its owner with a vanity plate on the back: *KAT'S KAR.*

Hmm. A bit too flashy for my taste.

The offices of Phizer-Lewis Advertising occupied almost the entire third floor in the easternmost wing of a postmodern building on Kettner Street right by the Pacific Highway. A prime location. In fact, if there were times I wasn't running too late, I often drove along the scenic coastal road instead of braving the freeway. Once you passed through the massive glass doorway to the structure, an elevator and adjacent stairway funneled an assortment of workers to their various occupations. I took my usual spot with the rest of the "herd" in front of the sliding elevator doors and then hesitated, choosing instead to walk up the stairs.

Between two classic pillars, a less-presumptuous door imprinted with the names of the company's founders marked the entrance to my world for the next eight hours. I gave a casual nod to the secretary seated at the gilded reception desk on the right but found her already too immersed in a barrage of telephone calls to give a response. Instead, I looked above her at the ten gold Cleos that stood suspended on the mirrored wall behind the counter.

One day, I thought. *One day.*

My work space was down an open hallway lined with similar cubby holes privatized with dividers depending on either the employee's need for privacy or their position in the company. Mine was out in the open with several neighbors, which left us subject not only to all the commotion and conversations of the others but also as easy targets for any number of tedious tasks and errands that had to be run.

Ensconced in my cubicle, I checked my e-mails. Nothing too exciting was on the screen today: a generic letter to all employees from management that, in order to conserve power, computers were to be shut off at the end of the workday. Another from Rachel in accounting with her urban legend of the week. It was while I was deleting and moving files, however, that I felt the sudden presence of someone behind me. My suspicions were confirmed as two hands came to rest on my shoulders and Roger's familiar and very unwelcome voice whispered almost in my ear.

"To work early, Samantha?" He chuckled.

Hasn't this Neanderthal heard of sexual harassment?

Thank you for finally being on my side!

I looked around the room and realized that, aside from a few occupied workers scurrying a safe distance away, I was one of the few early birds.

"I think I could get you a shot at a permanent position on the copy-writing team," he said without disguising the leer in his voice. I was so astonished by his words that I spun around in my chair and found myself face to face with him. Now I was trapped between him and my desk. He grinned as if aware of my predicament. "I've got some pull with management. Maybe I could put in a good word, and maybe . . . you could return the favor."

I sat there frozen, my hands gripping the arms of the chair. Roger was so close that I could see the beads of sweat under his nose and tell that he was not very fastidious about oral hygiene. I struggled to contain my revulsion and think how to get away.

"Uh, Roger." I flung my hand over my mouth. "I think I'm going to be sick!"

He lurched back as if I'd Tasered him. If I hadn't been shaking so badly, I would have laughed as I rushed to the ladies' room. Luckily it was empty, with only the sound of my footsteps echoing on the tile floor. Alone, I felt safe venting. "What a jerk! He'd better not follow me in here," I fumed, "or I'll have to find a new use for the hand dryer!" But my empty threats hung silently in the air, and I found tears welling up in my eyes. *How do I keep getting into these situations? Why won't he just leave me alone?*

Then I heard a voice outside the restroom door and dashed into one of the stalls. Though I was curious to see who was coming in, I decided to step back until I could make a graceful exit. I could only see the back of the woman at first, but her perfectly styled blonde hair and tailored suit gave her away as one of the upper brass. She was talking on her cell and waving her hands dramatically. Great. This could take forever, but I realized I'd have to stay put . . . or think of a way to explain my blotchy eyes and tearstained face. I leaned up against the adjoining stall and instead worked on stifling a sneeze while she continued talking on her phone so loudly that it was impossible not to overhear.

"I'm doing the best I can," she complained. "Convincing them from this far away and under these circumstances hasn't been easy." A pause. "I know! Don't you think I know? But I believe I may have worked something out. I'll be in touch."

I had just slunk away into the recesses of the stall and was wondering when she was going to leave when that sneeze I'd been trying to stifle finally came to fruition. The sound echoed off the bathroom walls, and I knew I'd been caught. Blushing, I opened the door, smiled timidly and quickly began washing my hands. I guess two people behaving strangely have little to talk about because she left without a word.

As I walked back to my desk, I saw that Roger was off wreaking havoc elsewhere, and my heartbeat attempted to return to a normal pace.

"Hey, Samantha," my neighbor Janice said as I returned to my desk. "I was starting to think you'd had enough of playing 'Dodge the Rodge' and quit."

"Some days it seems preferable."

"What a jerk! You'd think one day he'd just poof back into the slimy toad he is."

I smiled. "Do you have a magic wand? Maybe I should borrow it."

"I wish." Janice sighed. "Then maybe I could use it on my boyfriend. Why do guys think they only have to call you once a week when you're officially dating? Or worse, send off a quick text right before they head to the gym so they know you can't call them back."

I reached into my purse and pulled out my antiquated cell phone. "Makes me glad I still live in the dark ages of pretexting."

Janice squealed. "Yikes! You really do. Do you have to turn a crank or something to make that work?"

"It's not that bad." I shrugged defensively. "They just add features to keep you buying new phones. Technology drives me crazy."

"I suppose it can be a pain at times. Like when I opened my phone bill and saw that I supposedly called South America twice last month. Maybe I accidentally sat on my phone and let my *tush* do the talking."

We started laughing.

And then, as if on cue, my cell phone rang. I usually turned it off at work so I wouldn't draw any negative attention. But when I saw who it was, I answered. "Hello?" My voice quivered. "This is Samantha Evans."

"This is Officer Shanlon." The voice on the other line confirmed it was the San Diego PD. "I apologize for disturbing you again, but I want to give you a case number before we file your report away. That way, if there are any other incidences, you'll have something to refer to."

My frustration suddenly surfaced again. "Officer, there really isn't anything you can do?"

"Not unless you can give us something more to go on."

"I don't know what more to tell you." I sighed. "I suppose all I can do is keep my eyes and ears open and see if anything else happens."

I wrote down the reference number, and as I hung up the phone, I saw Janice's smirk had turned into a look of terror.

"How nice to know our employees are hard at work." I slowly turned in my chair and saw Roger standing there, his sweaty upper lip turned down into a frown. "'Officer,' huh? Why were you talking to the police, Samantha?" He leaned toward me. "You aren't in trouble, are you? We have high standards for our employees here at Phizer-Lewis."

If that were true, then how did he get hired? "Uh, I think it has something to do with some identity theft problems I was having. It's no big deal. They just had some more information for me."

The morning hours passed without any unusual events. I caddied and goferred as all good employees who sit at the bottom of the totem pole do. The one bright spot was getting to watch a brainstorming session with the copywriting team. Yet I was often distracted. The conference room was directly up ahead of me, elevated by a short flight of stairs and surrounded by the corporate offices with their views of the harbor. I often found myself looking longingly at the closed door and dreaming of all the important decision making that took place in there.

A hopeful moment occurred just before lunch when the company's COO, Mr. Lewis, passed me on the way to a meeting. I tried on a pleasant smile for size to express my fledgling confidence and got a brief nod for the effort then was left alone again to get back to the work at hand. The screen on my computer began flashing, a reminder about a meeting for all entry-level employees. I was full of nervous anticipation about the meeting. On the agenda, I had noticed that employee morale was going to be discussed; this had prompted some ideas of my own that I hoped to share today, which was in sharp contrast to sitting inconspicuously in the corner. There had to be some way to be singled out from the masses, and this might be a jumping-off point.

After lunch, I grabbed my notebook and favorite pen and headed for the staff area just behind the file room. The chairs had been arranged in an assembly style forum, and many of my peers were already present. I found a seat near the front of the room since no one else was quite as anxious as me. After a few more minutes, the gathering seemed complete, and Roger stepped to the front.

We spent the next half hour reviewing company policy, discussing future expansion, and listening to a droll pep talk. My mind frequently drifted off, and I realized that Roger's ears were too small for his head and he shifted from one foot to the other at least eight times a minute. Even Roger seemed distracted, absently changing the part in his receding hairline and looking at the door as if he were waiting for something. It was impossible not to fidget in my seat, but I tried to look interested until my anticipated topic came up.

"As you know," Roger said as he fumbled in his pocket for a set of note cards he halfheartedly attempted to disguise, "here at Phizer-Lewis, company morale is of utmost importance. We need to feel as if we are an army engaged in a common cause—fighting for our place in the world of advertising. It is a cutthroat business out there, where foreknowledge and determination are our weapons. We show no mercy to our prisoners. Other companies will have to step out of the way when they see us coming. We will win our accounts."

I winced. He must have stayed up all night watching a documentary on Napoleon. The surprising sound of applause echoed from the back of the room and slowly trickled forward.

"How do we do this?" he bellowed over his cards, obviously reinspired. As listeners, we jumped in our seats. "How can we present a united front when the elements of destruction seem against us?" He reached for a handkerchief and mopped his brow.

Now was my chance. I timidly raised my hand. When it was ignored, I raised it more forcefully. "Uh, Mr. Mellon? I have a suggestion to make."

He puffed out his chest and again looked toward the back of the room. "Yes, Samantha. You've been inspired. What would you like to say?"

Oh brother.

"Well, I was thinking that one of the best ways to bring people together is with the purpose of providing service to others." My words had also been carefully chosen beforehand. "I was thinking that if we could find some charitable function, such as cleaning up a local park or volunteering a few hours at a homeless shelter, we could get to know each other better outside the workplace. Even management could get involved. It would . . . uh . . . give us a different perspective on our daily jobs."

Roger ran his hand through his dwindling hair and actually had the nerve to "tsk" me. "Well, Samantha, that is a nice little thought. However, as you may not know, management"—he let his eyes wander to the back of the room—"is usually here burning the midnight oil and arriving before most of you have decided what to put in your morning coffee. I think that this company is going to progress by always being one step ahead of the competition, not pretending it's the Salvation Army." He laughed, eliciting a few echoes from the group.

I clenched my fists and felt my face flush, knowing I'd lost this battle.

Roger ended his speech and dismissed the meeting. As I received a few encouraging comments from some of my coworkers, I faced the door just in time to catch a glimpse of a tall, blonde woman exiting to the hallway. Great. Management *had* actually been here, watching me make a fool of myself.

I headed back to my desk to pick up where I had left off. Less than an hour passed before Roger approached and, without his usual insinuations, informed me, "We've got a change of jobs for you."

"What? Why?"

He shrugged. "We've got too many interns working the Right Guard account right now. They need some inventory done for another account, so go to Linda, and she'll fill you in on what we're looking for."

I was so stunned I could barely speak. "Did I do something wrong? I've been working really hard. If you'll just give me a—"

"Sorry," he interrupted, though he hardly sounded sorry. "Get your things and meet with Linda ASAP." As he walked away, I mentally drilled holes into the back of his head with my eyes, and I heard him mutter, "She'd better keep good on her promise to get me out of this pit, especially after all the favors I've done for her. Another day like today and . . ."

He thinks *he's* having a bad day!

Way to go, kiddo.

Oh, shut up.

Trying not to look defeated as I walked toward filing, I watched as a group of executives exited the conference room. It was as if a burst of confidence and energy hovered around them; they knew they were important and had a way of making you think they were too. The blonde woman I'd seen earlier particularly stood out. She was tall and slinky, and Aphrodite instantly came to mind. What was her name though? I couldn't remember, but part of me wanted to be her.

Why? Most of her probably isn't real anyway.

Just then she turned and caught my eye, frowning as if she'd overheard the voice as well. I flushed and quickly looked away.

I somehow survived the day, though my new job meant digging through dusty precomputer-era boxes and doing monotonous filing and data entry that any temp could do. What a waste. After clocking out, I trudged to my car and almost got as far as Harbor Drive before I realized that I'd forgotten my purse again. Now the tears started to flow. "How could they do this to me?" I howled. I had thought I was making a difference and that someone out there would appreciate it.

It's a dog-eat-dog world.

I know.

At least you learned not to get your hopes up.

I clenched the steering wheel as I turned around. This wasn't going to beat me. Starting tomorrow, I was going to be the employee they'd always dreamed of. I'd show up to work early again, get those ads organized, stay focused on my work—no matter how mindnumbing—and make *someone* take notice!

Chapter 4

ROGER WAS A NO-SHOW ON the office floor for almost the entire morning on Wednesday, so I was able to give my full attention to finishing my new project without looking over my shoulder every two minutes. Kneeling on the floor in the filing room, I laid in chronological order the photocopies of numerous Cover Girl ads that had graced the pages of magazines and commercials for the last thirty or so years. Cheryl Tiegs, Christie Brinkley, Niki Taylor, Alecia Keyes. While hairstyles and fashion changed through the decades, the perfection they sought didn't. As the beautiful faces of these women stared back at me, I felt intimidated by their airbrushed features and professionally done makeup and hair.

With at least two decades' worth of ads now stacked chronologically in a box, I left my "cave" and went back to my desk to examine with pleasure my day's work.

That's when I saw the conference room door open and the company's president and CEO, Mr. Phizer, along with several other executives—including the gorgeous woman I kept envying—walk out. He came down the stairs as I imagined the gods might have descended from Olympus to associate with the common folk. But this time he was walking right toward me. I straightened my back. No imagined intimidation was going to dampen the remainder of my day, and I beamed my brightest smile at him as I said, "Good evening, Mr. Phizer. How are you doing today?"

His salt-and-pepper eyebrows knit together, and he paused for a moment as if trying to figure out who I was. Then, disguising his ignorance, he responded, "Why hello . . ."

Obviously fishing for my name, I supplied the answer to let him off the hook. "Samantha Evans. I'm fairly new here."

"Oh yes," he said, feigning a returning memory. "Of course. How are things going for you today?"

"Just fine. We're hard at work down here."

"Good. Good." Then, as if remembering something else he had forgotten, he said, "You know, your name really does sound familiar to me. I think someone asked me about you."

That was unexpected. I gulped and smiled bravely.

"Well," he regrouped, "I'm sure it'll come to me. Keep up the good work."

As I watched him continue down the hall, I sat stunned. That was the most I had spoken to any of the corporate brass since I had started work and received the traditional "Welcome to Our Team" speech. For the life of me, though, I couldn't figure out where he had heard my name. Hopefully it wasn't Roger trying to get me into any more trouble.

* * *

Flopping down on the couch in my apartment, I felt tired and unmotivated, but my natural inclination toward order prompted me to sort through my junk mail and tackle the remaining work I'd brought home. A small stack of letters sat on the coffee table, and I sorted through the offers of lower APRs and "once in a lifetime" used car deals I was warned not to "pass up." I threw them away.

I sighed, prepared a snack, and tried to face the box of files I'd checked out. After a few hours, I found I had accomplished quite a bit, and my confidence started to return. I was a hard worker, and one day they'd see that. My eyes started to tear up a little. Sometimes my own emotions surprised me. Yet even more surprising was that the beautiful faces that stared back at me from the storage boxes were no longer as intimidating. After all, I told myself, they were just women who had been blessed with some attractive features that became even more so under the artful attention of a team of experts. If you took their attributes apart one by one, you'd see a slightly large nose, eyes that were too close together, and a tall, gangly body that probably plagued them all through high school. And now, here they were, plastering the pages of a magazine as an icon for women to exemplify in all their false perfection. But all my life, I'd been taught to search for what was real. An overwhelming sense of gratitude filled me.

"Dear Heavenly Father," I whispered, kneeling by the sofa. "I don't know if this is where I'm supposed to be and what I'm supposed to be doing, but I promise that no matter what, I won't forget who I am and what I've been taught."

I felt a loving reassurance come over me. That is, until the door burst open.

"Hey, roomie," Terri exclaimed with her usual less-than-impeccable timing. "What are you doing?" she asked. "Lose a contact on the floor?"

I jumped up. "Yeah, sure."

Soon the apartment was teeming with people. Javier sat next to Terri on our green and blue plaid sofa. The yellow La-Z-Boy now held what was no doubt one of Terri's many gay friends. Across the room, a dark-haired man was quite enjoying providing a lap for a giggly brunette on a chair pulled in from the kitchen area. Two more women were sitting cross-legged on the floor beside an old traveling trunk-turned-coffee table.

I knew as I walked over to the fridge for a soda that the inevitable invitation to join them would ensue.

"Hey, Sam," came the cheerful self-fulfilling prophecy from Terri, "come and say hello. Oh, and can you grab us a few cold ones?"

As I helped myself to a Jones soda, I timidly grabbed the remaining two beers in the other hand and presented myself to the group.

"Hi everyone," I said. "Well, I'm going to my room. If you'll excuse me."

It was nearly impossible to focus on my scripture study with a party going on fewer than twenty feet away from me. *Maybe I should go out there and share something with them*—I huffed—*like Alma's lecture to his son Corianton.* Then I repented of my judgmental attitude. God loved the people out there in the living room as much as He did me. It was hard not to be self-righteous, sitting here reading scriptures while a worldly party ensued just feet from my door. I heard a loud laugh and glanced over at the clock and was surprised that it was already eleven. It was way past my bedtime, especially if I wanted to get to work early tomorrow and continue to impress whoever might be watching. But first, I'd have to sneak to the bathroom and pray that it was unoccupied.

Fortunately it was, though in there I was within hearing range of the raucous party that continued. I couldn't help but overhear their conversation. They were talking about going to Tijuana the next weekend.

"Not me!" Terri squealed. "Not with all of those dead bodies they've been finding in the desert lately."

But what I heard next left my blood boiling. "Hey," someone drawled, "that reminds me. I still have some excellent weed from my last trip south of the border."

I burst from the bathroom, Crest foaming at my mouth. "No drugs here! Terri, you know the rules."

They stared at me like I was a rabid dog or something.

"We wouldn't have done it here," Terri said, duly chastened. "We can go somewhere else, right, guys?"

Sure, I thought. Then I motioned her over to me. "Terri, you shouldn't be doing stuff like that." I was still fuming.

"It's just a little pot," she said as she shrugged. "You need to lighten up."

"Drugs are drugs. Just think about the low-life dealers you're supporting."

She looked at me as if she'd never entertained that thought before. Then she laughed at her friends. "Hey, I've got a better idea. Let's go clubbing."

With an apologetic shrug, Terri pushed them out the door, leaving the apartment quiet.

I had the place to myself again and should have been glad. Why, then, was I struggling to feel at ease?

Chapter 5

I GROGGILY TURNED TOWARD THE clock and had the strangest feeling that the sun had come up earlier than usual this morning. As I stared in horror, however, I realized that last night I had neglected to set the alarm—and I had only thirty minutes to get to work.

I hastily threw on some clothes with a minimal attempt at taming my hair and blotchy face. Breakfast would have to be a cereal bar to go—which I only consumed in dire emergencies such as this one—and I prayed that the clunking noise I'd heard on the way home last night wouldn't mean a trip to the bus stop instead.

Dashing around frantically, I barely remembered my purse, but at least my car purred to life and the roads were as clear as they ever got in southern California. I was only fifteen minutes late when I arrived as inconspicuously as possible at my desk. I sat down and tried to catch my breath, fumbling around in my desk in an attempt to get organized. Then, much to my horror, I saw Roger coming toward me in an obvious huff.

"Samantha, where have you been?"

Geez, I was only a little late, and for the first time in at least three months. "I'm sorry, it's just that—"

"I can't believe I'm asking *you* of all people to do this. I'm already late for another meeting as it is, and I need this stack," he shoved a large pile of papers toward me, "copied and brought up to Mr. Phizer in the conference room. So step on it, and you might just keep your job around here," he finished before stomping off.

Regaining my composure, I hurried to complete the task, praying that at least the copier was feeling benevolent toward me. My hands felt clammy as I imagined going into the conference room and seeing all eyes turn toward me. Oh, why did I have to sleep late this of all mornings? How did I look? Had I remembered any lipstick? It didn't matter now. After the last page was collated, I rushed heavenward to the conference room.

I entered, panting, and noticed Mr. Phizer at the end of the long mahogany table, his head bent over some papers. The others I vaguely knew. Doug Lansing was the executive creative director with a polished veneer that reminded me of Cary Grant. The blonde woman I'd seen way too much of lately sat next to him and was somehow both elegant and determined in a screaming red pantsuit. (I wondered if she ever wore the same outfit twice.) Only one pair of eyes turned to look at me—and I had the distinct impression she wasn't pleased I had interrupted. I stood there fidgeting as Mr. Phizer, who seemed oblivious to my intrusion, began to address the group.

"In discussing current projects, I don't need to remind you how important the Mexico campaign will be. We've tried for years to branch out into a more international market. In light of recent . . . shall we say, *unpleasantries*, it's no wonder the Mexican tourism bureau is trying to create some positive publicity for their capital city."

Having served a Spanish-speaking mission, I was all too aware of the recent bombing near the government buildings in Mexico City. With 9/11 still present in everyone's minds, it was almost a relief to discover that it was most likely rival drug gangs that had been responsible and not a terrorist group. I shuffled my feet nervously, waiting for a break in his speech so I could personally present the papers to him.

But he continued. "Doug." The pseudo movie star looked up when he heard his name. "Do you have everything you need?"

Doug shuffled around some papers. "I'll do the best with what I've got. You've got every photographer of ours on assignment right now, but we were considering going with a local freelancer anyway. As long as the rest of the group stands, I can make it work. Especially," he smiled knowingly at the blonde by his side, "since I know Katrina will be holding down the fort while I'm gone."

They may have been on the opposite side of the room from me and hidden by the table, but I would have taken bets that he'd just squeezed her leg. "One more thing," Mr. Lansing added, "I'll need personnel to find someone to go as my personal assistant, and I want someone who speaks Spanish enough to help translate when needed."

I clenched the pile of papers against my chest when I heard what he said. It may be an unwritten rule that good things come to those who wait, but I was tired of waiting.

"Uh, Mr. Phizer?" I squeaked. While he sought out the source of the interruption, I found my power voice. "I speak Spanish." I took a few tentative steps toward him so I could deposit the papers on the table and hold out my hand. "I'm Samantha Evans. We, uh . . . talked yesterday? I've worked here for, well, a few months now. I've done copyediting, proofing, and some filing. If you need an assistant who's dedicated and motivated, I'd like to offer my services."

Finished with my rambling, I stood there waiting, wondering who this stranger was that appeared to have taken over my body lately. I kind of liked her.

Mr. Phizer pursed his lips in thought and then reached over and handed me a newspaper. I reached out and took it in my slightly clammy hand as he asked, "Can you read that?"

I sought out a news clip from the local Spanish newspaper. I cleared my throat and proceeded tentatively and then more confidently as I read about Mexico's president, Felipe Calderón, declaring war on the drug cartels. Only now he was now dealing with the horrific backlash as hundreds of people, including law enforcement officials, were being murdered in various border towns each month. Then I handed it back to Mr. Phizer. He smiled. I must have passed his test.

"Wonderful. If Mr. Lansing is agreeable, I think you'll do just fine. What do you say, Doug?"

"Why not?" He flashed me a smile of perfectly white teeth and winked. "If you're a hard worker, I'm sure I can find ways to keep you busy."

"Thank you." I flushed at his stare, wondering if I'd jumped from the proverbial frying pan into the fire. "I'll work hard."

As I left the conference room, I was still flying high but tried to resume some semblance of order for the rest of the day. I'd been given a copy of the travel itinerary and later on had a break to sit down and peruse the week's activities. Monday morning we would depart from San Diego International Airport on American flight 817 and arrive in Mexico City at 2:45 p.m., where we'd stay at the Marriott Reforma Hotel for the next two weeks. As I glanced farther down the page, I grew more excited about all the things we would see: from the thriving metropolis of the most populated city in the Western Hemisphere to jaunts to nearby archaeological sites, quaint colonial towns, and provincial villages.

I leaned back in my chair with my hands clasped behind my head. This was the life! I was going to like being paid to travel to foreign countries and soak up the sun and culture. In fact, I started thinking that there wasn't any law against me doing a little freelance work until I got my big break. Maybe I'd come up with a great story for a travel magazine or cultural newspaper after I got back. I'd heard some of them paid up to a dollar a word. The possibilities were endless. But the more practical side of me just had to jump in and burst that bubble.

Yeah, don't get too used to it. How many jobs are there that could really live up to your dreams? You'll be back in the trenches soon enough.

Oh, be quiet! You're as bad as Roger.

That evening after having rushed home from work, I went through my usual routine of opening the mail and was unnerved to see a letter from Bank First USA. Ripping it open, I relaxed when I discovered it was only a new card with my name imprinted across the front *and* a letter stating that the fraudulent charges were being taken care of!

"What a relief," I said out loud, tucking it away in my purse. "Now we can get back to business."

The rest of the mail was just junk, and I deposited it into the trash without a second thought. I wondered for a moment where Terri might be then went over the to-do list I'd worked on earlier:

Call parents
Let visiting teachers know I'm gone
Pick up guidebooks at the library
Pack
Make list for Terri: garbage, utilities bill, lock up!

I tackled the first item. My mother answered, and I felt a shiver of excitement as I explained the turn of events that day.

"Oh, darling, what a big step! Let me tell your father."

I heard the muffled voice of my mother yelling into the other room. My dad picked up on another phone in the house, and both of my parents listened as I explained my latest assignment. My father echoed my mother's sentiments that it was a momentous event but didn't let me off the hook so easily. He wanted to know the who, what, where, and when of it all. I answered as many questions as I could, trying to sound confident. Then I heard a muffled voice. "Oops. I think our home teachers are at the door. Bye, princess. Take care of yourself. Bring your phone and call us if you need *anything*. I love you. Show 'em what you can do!"

"Thanks, Big Boss," I said, calling him the nickname that had stuck from my teenage years when, on a daily basis, I'd remind him that he wasn't the boss of me.

"Mom?" I checked.

"Yes, Samantha, I'm still here."

I wanted to be a child again, when those simple assurances from my parents could be accepted on pure belief. The adult version of my faith was not quite as absolute and unwavering. "I don't know about this, Mom. This is happening so fast. To be honest, I'd actually been thinking of quitting my job and coming back home."

A reassuring voice reached out to me. "You have to do what's right for you, whatever that is." A sigh. "It hasn't been easy letting you go so far away from us. I guess I've been the most selfish. You are so much like I was at your age—with so many dreams and ambitions . . ." (I was glad my mom couldn't see the surprise on my face. When had she ever been adventurous?) "but I was scared and still so young. Marriage seemed like the answer to everything. Now, I'm not saying I would change anything; it's just that when I think of you in that big city, struggling to make it on your own, I feel a part of me there with you. I'm so proud of you."

I was flabbergasted. "You're *proud* of me?"

"Oh, sweetheart! I'm more proud of you than I could possibly say because you're still going after your dreams. I know I worry more than I should, but those are my own old fears still coming through. And we've known that you're confused and wondering if you've made the right decision."

"Has it been that obvious?"

"You just haven't seemed yourself lately. So your dad and I have doubted that things have been going as well as we've been led to believe. We've talked about what it would be like if you came home, but we have this strong impression that now isn't the right time. We don't know what it is, but there's a feeling we've both had that something is going to happen to change the way you feel about everything. Sometimes you just have to let go and let a higher power guide you."

"I know, Mom." I choked up, her words having a familiar ring. "I've been thinking that myself. I've been doing a lot of praying lately, and there are some things I have to figure out for myself," I said, my eyes tearing up. "I know I can't run away from my job and life here and just come home to let you take care of me. I need to do this."

"Then do it!"

"I'll be sure to keep in touch."

With a newfound confidence, I hung up the phone and considered what to pack. Excited again, I packed a proper assortment of toiletries, casual pants, T-shirts, a skirt and blouse, and even a swimsuit. Next I added my set of travel scriptures, a notebook, and a picture of my family taken at my college graduation. The last addition was something I'd been saving awhile. When I sent out my mission papers, I'd optimistically applied for a passport as well—not wanting to let anything prevent me from serving in an exotic location. Then I'd been called to the Spanish-speaking Fresno California Mission. Need I mention how excited my parents were that I'd been called stateside? But now it would finally serve a purpose.

Full of pent-up excitement, I decided to take another quick jog by the beach. It was just the tonic I needed. When I got back, I felt as ready as I'd ever be.

"Mexico City, I'm ready for you! I hope you're ready for me."

Chapter 6

It was incredible!

If I'd had to describe all of the emotions I was feeling rolled up into one word, it would have been *incredible*! To think that just a few days ago I was agonizing over every aspect of my life, feeling as if I'd hit the biggest dead end of my earthly existence so far and now . . . I was literally soaring, body and mind, thousands of feet over the ground below. That life could change so dramatically, so fast, was astounding. It was almost too much to comprehend, so I didn't even try. I just felt. The excitement, the anticipation of the job, the possibilities.

I scanned the inside of the plane, saw the tops of the heads of the other members of the group and tried to remember their names without looking at the notebook where I'd jotted them down that morning. Okay. There was Lin Chang, a petite Asian woman, noticeably juxtaposed by her seat companion, Mike, a large African-American who could probably bench press two of her. They were our video support team. Then I scanned the crowd behind me and saw . . . Seth? I cheated and looked down. Yep. Seth Proctor, the graphics specialist. His sandy brown hair and casual stance reminded me of Robert Redford in his younger days. Last, but certainly not least, came the surprise of the group. Instead of arriving at the airport that morning to find Mr. Lansing giving us orders, I saw Katrina Edwards standing in a turquoise pantsuit directing the expedition. Confused, I'd whispered to Lin, "Where's Mr. Lansing?"

"Stomach bug," she'd said, pursing her lips. "How lucky for Ms. Edwards, who it appears is taking his place."

At first I'd been terrified that they wouldn't need me anymore and had hesitantly approached Ms. Edwards. But she quickly reassured me that my presence in Mexico was still, as she put it, "very necessary."

My new boss had managed to secure a seat near the front of the plane, and as if my thinking of her gave her a silent cue, she stood and came walking down the aisle, smiling a perfectly white smile at the various passengers she passed. She stopped and turned toward me, her elbow propped on the aisle side seat. My seat partner was visibly salivating at her proximity.

Men.

"There will be a private car at the airport to pick us up," she said, "so stay close to the group. If you happen to become separated, though, just give me a call—you brought your cell, right?"

I fumbled around in my purse until I found it. She took one look at my archaic device and chuckled. "We'll get you a loaner after we land—I'll have Seth program in all of the group's contact information along with our itinerary. Feel free to use it the duration of the trip, even to call family or acquaintances. We want you to be comfortable."

"Thanks, Ms. Edwards," I said.

Yet another type of smile crossed her face. "Call me Kat. We're all friends here, right?" She stood and continued down the aisle.

To pass the time, I took out my travel guides. My library card had once again come in handy, and though I knew no one would probably find themselves in need of the vast amounts of knowledge I was cramming into my brain, I figured it didn't hurt to have an edge. Besides, the more I read, the more fascinated I became with Mexico. I only hoped the actual place would live up to my expectations. But why wouldn't it? I looked out from my window-seat vantage point and saw a diverse landscape pass below. I watched it for a while, and then after mountains and deserts blurred into a blanket of clouds, I closed my eyes in an attempt to block out the commotion and mechanical hum around me. Usually too anxious to sleep under such conditions, I found myself drifting off.

I was in a dreamlike state, almost as if I were a spectator backstage at a rehearsal. The people and images around me were familiar. First, my father stepped out from behind our house, held out his hands, and winked his famous wink. I walked quickly toward him but was immediately surrounded by a fog that had crept in and engulfed my surroundings. Instinct took over, and I stopped, flailing my arms in an attempt to come in contact with a solid surface. An image emerged from the mist, tall and solid, and I couldn't place its identity. I sensed it was a man. At first, I felt afraid and backed away. But then I was compelled to move toward the shadowy figure, who grew in stature as outreached hands came nearer and nearer. He came closer until we were almost touching, until I could almost discern the slant of a nose, the shadow under the jaw, almost feel a warming fire arch across the minute distance that remained, until . . .

With a jolt, the vision was torn from me as the plane hit a patch of turbulence. Dazed and momentarily displaced, I gazed out the window to see that although the cottony sea below was dissipating, it was being replaced by a smoky haze that wound like a snake through the mountainous terrain we now hovered over. I figured we were getting close to the airport, since the snake I saw was most likely pollution from the twenty million people who occupied Mexico City and its environs.

I started to gather my belongings in an instinctual organized fashion until I heard a voice over the loudspeaker. "Ladies and gentlemen, this is your captain speaking. We are about thirty minutes outside of Mexico City and will be landing at the airport at approximately 2:40 p.m., a few minutes early. You'll want to set your watches ahead one hour if you are operating on Pacific Standard Time. Until then, relax and enjoy the rest of your flight."

Still a half hour away? If the air was this thick so far away, what would it be like in the actual heart of the city? Yech. Well, no place can be perfect.

When we landed, we went out front to where a hired black sedan was waiting to take us to the hotel. I prayed that my luggage had made the journey as well. As the sliding doors opened, I felt as if I had suddenly been dropped into a vat of murky water. Aside from the considerable heat that radiated from every object, the oxygen content of the air dropped to an amount that would sustain a flea for only a few hours, possibly a little more. The Marriott Reform on the Paseo de la Reforma was a welcome sight, and I hoped we'd be allowed some time to freshen up before we tackled the project at hand.

After gathering our luggage that did end up making the trip with us, we headed our separate ways. As far as I could tell, all of us in the group were assigned our own rooms; mine had a queen-sized bed, a small desk, and a bathroom with a glass shower. It was decorated in a comforting shade of blue with several modern prints on the walls. Nice but not lavish, I thought. I deposited my bags in the corner and flopped down on the bed. *At least the bed's not hard as a rock and I'll have some privacy. Maybe I can even take a quick nap, since I could barely sleep last night.* A knock on the door shattered that immediate prospect. Shuffling over to open it, I saw the sandy-haired man, whose name I'd already forgotten again, standing there.

"Hi, uh . . ." I smiled shyly.

"Seth," he reminded me with his country drawl. "Kat just announced we're headin' out for an early dinner. We'll be meetin' up with the freelance photographer we've hired and then headin' back here for a powwow about our itinerary for tomorrow. So you'll want to be ready in, hmm, forty minutes down in the lobby."

"Sure, no problem."

He turned to leave and then looked back with an admiring grin on his face. "I hear you pulled quite the move to get to tag along with us."

I blushed, wondering if anything else had been said about me. "Usually I'm not so bold. But you'll never gain anything if you don't take a chance, right?"

The casual stance he assumed in the doorway made me think of a cowboy leaning against a fence post. He was only lacking his Stetson. "Well," he said, "we could use some new blood around here. A few words of advice. Some people around here are a little more ambitious than others, so don't feel bad if you get your toes stepped on. Of course, you've proven your own ambition, so this could be the perfect opportunity for you."

"I hope so. So far everyone's been very nice to me."

Seth nodded. "Lin and Mike, they're pretty cool. Lin has a great eye for fantasy work, but even then, she won't be able to work on more than a few simple concepts with the time limit we have. Still, it'll be enough to showcase her talents. And Mike's one of the best cameramen in the business. I won't bore you with my own inestimable abilities," he said with a wink. "So it's a great team to work with. Just hang in there, and I'll try to keep my eye on you, show you the ropes."

It suddenly occurred to me he might be flirting with me. *Nah.* "Thanks." I blushed. "I hope I can do a good job and earn my place here."

"Don't worry about it. Kat always likes to have some flunk . . . uh, I mean assistant to help out with errands and busywork. The fact that you speak the language is an added bonus. Hey, I'd better go. I just wanted to let you know you've got a friend around here."

As I closed the door, I breathed a sigh of relief. I would probably need a few friends before this trip was over.

I freshened up the best I could and headed toward the door, though glancing down at my semiwrinkled jeans and U of U T-shirt, I almost changed my mind. But I was here to work, not to impress people with my distinctive fashion sense, and everyone seemed casual enough. As I made my way down to the lobby, however, I noticed Ms. Edwards, that is, Kat, *had* changed and was now wearing a pair of tan slacks and a white-collared shirt tied into a knot high up on her stomach. The rest of the group filtered in looking pretty professional as well. Feeling out of place, I loaded up in our hired vehicle with the others for the trek to the restaurant.

During the drive, I was free to gaze around and examine the surroundings. All in all, Mexico City was pretty modern. Skyscrapers towered above with row after row of buildings and verdant parks surrounding them. The streets flowed like giant rivers with cars and bicycles, human activity, and purpose. Yet underneath it all ran a current of antiquity, as if a past civilization were masked from view, its presence nonetheless sensed. Amid the new stood the old: cathedrals from a Spanish conquest, ancient ruins from a mysterious people. They existed side by side and spoke volumes of this culture and how it came to be what it was today. This story also played out on the faces of the people. Young children frolicked in decorative fountains, and old women still carried packages deposited in knapsacks atop their heads.

I quickly noticed that the city also teemed with the poor and destitute. Beggars lined the streets and took refuge in doorways, wearing ragged clothes and hopeless expressions. Some were missing limbs, and others flaunted disfigurements. They had outstretched hands or overturned sombreros to collect the meager offerings given out of mere pity or in recompense for circuslike performances. But it was the children who saddened me the most—dirty, unkempt creatures who peered from behind adult guardians. And yet many wore cheerful smiles, as if unaware of their deprivation. A lump formed in my throat.

This feeling of despair started to dissipate when we entered Sanborn's. I had heard that there were several of these restaurants scattered throughout the city, but this one, the House of Tiles, was the most unique, known for the decorative blue and white tile work on the outside façade. There was also a shopping area where you could buy just about anything, but my nose led me to the restaurant with the others, and I inhaled all of the wonderful fragrances of the dishes being prepared. My mouth watered with anticipation. On my mission, I had learned to love Mexican food with a passion and hoped to take in many of the unique flavors I'd come to know.

The restaurant was relatively empty because true dinner or *cena* didn't begin until around eight o'clock. We were joined by those who preferred a late, though bountiful, lunch and would then wait and have a modest snack far into the evening. I was seated at the head of a large table reserved for our group and took the menu the waiter handed me. I noticed right away that my favorites were listed, and before I knew it, I was satisfying my hunger with tortilla soup and a spicy dish called *mole*, which included tender pieces of chicken bathed in a chocolate-laced sauce. I also anticipated *flan* with *dulce de leche* for dessert.

I was so intent on enjoying my food, however, that I hadn't glanced around at the others to see what they were doing. When I did look up, a few were still finishing their entrees, and I noted the usual assortment of tamales and chile verde. Lin was having one of my favorites: enchiladas with a white cream sauce instead of the traditional red one. Mike was cutting into a huge T-bone steak, which suited his massive frame, while Seth devoured the last of what must have been a chile relleno. A little sauce dripped from his chin, and when I caught his eye, I made a scratching motion on my own chin and smiled. He remedied the dilemma and gave me a thankful wink.

Kat was toying with a crisp green salad with something that might have been grilled chicken on top. It wasn't the healthy salad that made my gaze linger, however. As we'd been eating, another member had joined our party. I tried not to stare, but since he was seated next to the boss at the other end of the table, it was hard not to.

Chapter 7

I GUESSED THE NEWCOMER WAS no older than thirty. He was wearing faded jeans and a blue collared shirt with sleeves rolled up past tan forearms. His black hair was patterned after the style of a bygone day, a little longer in front so it drooped over his eyes and with slightly extended sideburns that made him seem like a mere rebel teenager in training, but it did seem to suit his rugged features. His stubble-lined chin made it look like he'd just jumped out of bed to be here. Naturally, being Mexican, his eyes were a dark chocolate brown. Embarrassed at how long I'd been staring, I looked back down at my plate. Though he hadn't been introduced, this had to be the local photographer they'd hired. Kat was seated as close to him as conventional dictates allowed and was brandishing her fork like a sword. I tried to focus in on their conversation and tell if he already knew her or was just hoping to.

What man wouldn't?

True. Kat was at least five-feet, nine-inches and had legs that encompassed a good two-thirds of that stature. The remaining anatomy wasn't too shabbily endowed either. But silicone and Botox aside, she had to be pushing forty, and at least I had that on my side. Still, I fought to keep down the feelings of inadequacy that struggled to rise to the surface during occasions like this and tugged on the neckline of my T-shirt. I had to remember I was here to work. That was all. Then why did Terri's words keep popping into my mind: "Hey, everyone's gotta have a dream"? Of course, just being here was already enough of a dream come true, and besides, I reminded myself again, I had come here to show everyone I was a good worker.

Okay, back to the real world.

I'm already there.

As I self-consciously slurped up my last bite, we were informed by the boss that a meeting would occur back at the hotel. The bill was spirited away. Corporate funds, I surmised. As we gathered our things, I had enough time to buy some guides in another section of the store. I was determined to know as much about this place as anyone else did.

As we drove back to the hotel, Kat announced we were meeting in her room. I don't think Kat left our new addition's side as we rode up the elevator to the fourth floor and went down the hall. My jaw dropped as she opened the door to her room. It was at least three times the size of mine. A king-size bed was the focal point on the left, with a sitting area to the right consisting of a love seat and two arm chairs. There was a luxurious bathroom that I could see through the half-open door with—sigh—a full tub and vanity area.

"All right, everyone," Kat directed as she passed around a series of folders, "let's get down to business. We've only got two weeks to gather enough footage to wow the execs. You each have until tomorrow to read through these packets—study the demographics, what each division's relative costs will be. You'll also see your individual responsibilities laid out in these media planners, so I won't go into too much detail. Lin and Mike—" she now directed her attention to us as individuals—"I want you to use as many AV tools as you can. I'm thinking a 'video diary' that could be turned into a montage with running dialogue or music. Maybe both. Enough to show them we'd be up to the challenge of full media spectrum if we get the account. Seth, you'll handle the graphic and computer layouts once we have the raw material to work with. And," she said as she smiled generously, "of course we need to introduce our most prized acquisition, *Dah-veed Ayala*."

I wonder how many times she practiced that.

My boss now perched herself on the edge of the armchair and physically singled out the recipient of her comment with her full attention. "A few of David's credits include the covers of many top Hispanic magazines. He's also worked with *National Geographic* and is responsible for the new Cancun Breezes resort campaign—just some of the reasons we were so lucky to have secured him on such short notice."

I rolled my eyes, since it was Kat's hand on our newcomer's shoulder that was doing all of the securing at this particular moment. Was it just my imagination, or did Mr. Ayala seem to be a tad uncomfortable under so much direct verbal attention? Unaware of his discomfort, Kat continued.

"He will be supplying Seth with the actual print work, on which the rest of us will be basing our storyboards and mockups. Be prepared to burn some midnight oil. And because Mr. Ayala is most familiar with the locations we will be using, I'll turn the time over to him with our itinerary for the next several days."

He took his time getting up and feigned a cough into his closed fist before saying in a heavily accented voice, "Thanks for that *modest* introduction." I noticed how his mouth twitched as if trying to stifle a grin. "And please, everyone call me Dave, not *Dah-veed*. I have spent the last two days looking at various settings, and I think I have—how do you say?—narrowed it down to the few best. It is important to make a good first impression."

I tried to focus on what he was saying, which was difficult because of his heavy accent—not to mention the fact that every time his dark eyes caught mine, I had an out-of-body experience.

"So this will be our schedule through Sunday. Tomorrow we'll head to some of the more famous landmarks in the city. I've chosen the Zocalo and National Palace, then UNAM and some surrounding architecture should take up most of the day. And for an evening shot, the Torre Latinoamericana. You'll see the remaining sites outlined, from the Museo de Antropología to Teotihuacán. Sorry, my English isn't always so good, but I understand that you have a translator who will be helping us if I struggle."

I was going to have to stop acting like a love-struck teenager every time he turned to look at me. Forcing a serious look onto my face, I listened to the questions the others raised as they worked out some specifics in a group conversation. Unfortunately, I was too new to the process of working with a team to feel comfortable asking questions but had learned enough about advertising that I was forming ideas about how I could contribute.

"All right, everyone," Kat ordered as the powwow seemed to be winding down. "Let's get some rest, and we'll meet downstairs at seven in the morning."

The party began to disperse, so I detached myself from my hiding spot. I walked with as much grace as I could muster past the photographer, who was still in an intimate-looking conversation with Kat. Just as I reached the door, I heard Kat call me.

"I almost forgot." She sashayed toward me and took my hand, placing in it the new phone she'd promised. "Spend some time tonight learning how to use it. And make sure it's with you at *all times*—we want to be able to get in touch with you *always*."

I stared down at the gleaming black iPhone in my hand. "Uh, thanks. I will."

By the time I reached my room at the end of the hall, I at least knew where the power button was. Now I just needed to figure out how to make a call. As I tried to use the key card to get my door to open, I heard a voice at my side. It was Dave.

"It looks like we're all on the same level."

"Uh, yeah. Looks like it."

That was smooth.

"So," he continued in English, "let me guess. Your silence in there indicates that you're the true—how do you say it?—brains behind this whole operation."

I smiled. "I wish. No, I'm just the gofer who fortunately could speak a little Spanish. Otherwise, I'd be back at the office pushing papers and pulling files. I guess I'm pretty lucky to be here."

"Not lucky," he said with a wink. "Just pretty."

He continued down the hall toward what must have been his room. I finally got my door open, but for the life of me, I couldn't remember what my name was.

* * *

Afraid my flustered state would affect my ability to set the alarm, I also set the backup I had brought. But I couldn't sleep at first. I couldn't get him out of my mind. Okay. So he'd been flirting with me. I had to remember that to a Latino, it was second nature. I'll never forget the time in college when my Argentinean roommate set me up with her boyfriend's friend. After dinner, he'd taken me up on a bluff overlooking the city and told me how the moon was hiding behind the clouds because it was jealous of my beauty.

And don't forget your mission.

I know. But that first guy hadn't really been seriously proposing to me, though the love song the other one had written me was memorable. Besides, aside from what I realized was just an offhanded comment, *Dah-veed* had spent his entire time huddled up against my boss.

Then why even bother?

My inner voice was right. He was a stranger. This was work. Besides, I'd made up my mind long ago that having a similar background was the key to any successful relationship. What could we possibly have in common?

I waved thoughts of him away. Instead, I tried to focus on the reason I was here. I studied the information Kat had given us until my brain started to melt. Needing a break, I took out some of the books I'd brought. One contained a brief chronological history of the pre-Columbian cultures of Mesoamerica. Familiarizing myself with it could be helpful with my work as well, I reasoned, so I started to study.

With my religious background and familiarity with the Book of Mormon, I thought more strongly about how the remnants of historical and cultural life I would be seeing were tangible proof of Nephite and Lamanite existence here as explained in the scriptures. I somehow felt more in tune with the presence of these enigmatic figures and the stories they had carefully preserved so they could be brought forth in my day.

First, I read, was the Olmec period, evidence of which extended from around 1200–400 BC. I tried to think of how this correlated to Book of Mormon history. I recalled the story of when King Limhi sent forty-three of his people from the land of Nephi to find Zarahemla, but instead they found a deserted land covered in bones and the record of the Jaredites. The Babel reference in that account coincided with the time period of the Olmecs. I glanced back at the scholar's guide and then at the scriptures at my side. Were these people one and the same?

Next, I read about the period of Teotihuacán, the city ruins we would be visiting in a few days. The inner structures of this colossal layout were supposed to have been built sometime between 150 BC and AD 200. A brief glance at the Book of Mormon timeline revealed this was around the same time as a great migration of Nephites from the land of Zarahemla across a narrow neck of land into a land that was northward. The coincidences here were eye opening.

As my eyes moved to the section on the Maya, I found my vision a bit blurry. Though I wanted to stay up and study more, a yawn confirmed my exhausted state, and I found myself drifting off.

Chapter 8

Looking at the clock, I realized it was six in the morning. I'd need to finish getting dressed and get a fast bite to eat before meeting the others in the lobby. I wondered if anyone else would be downstairs. After a quick check of the neighboring rooms, I found out where Lin was staying.

"Hi there," I said shyly. "Are you going down to breakfast?"

"I rarely eat breakfast," she responded. "But you'd better get down there before Mike hits the buffet, or there'll be nothing left. I was just double-checking my equipment. You're welcome to join me, and then we could head down together."

I was glad for the opportunity to get to know some of the other members of the group better and accepted her invitation. I noticed a single empty chair in the corner and was relieved to know I wasn't the only one who had been given a more modest room. This one wasn't much bigger than mine and seemed even more cramped with the various cameras and equipment lying around. I sat quietly for a moment, wondering who would break the ice. Lin was the one to take charge.

My first impression of Lin had been that of a very astute and cautious person, but before I knew it, she was talking to me like I was an old friend. I found out Lin's great-grandparents had moved to the States from China, and her father had served in the U.S. military almost all her life, reflective of the great love he had for his grandparents' adoptive country. It hadn't been easy, and prejudice often resulted, but he had risen in the ranks, and I could tell she was proud. "He was so anxious to fit in that even our names became Westernized," she explained. "In China, I would have been Chang Lin. So," my hostess now questioned me, "how long have you been with Phizer-Lewis?"

"Only a few months," was my pitiful response. "I guess that's not very long, compared to the rest of you."

"I'm only going on a year myself, thanks to Mike getting me the job. But he's the veteran of the bunch—six years now. So where do you hail from?" she asked, veering the conversation back to me.

"Uh, well . . . " I struggled to describe the suburb where I'd lived all my life. "It's really just a small town, about thirty minutes south of Salt Lake City."

"Oh yeah." Lin was gracious enough to add, "Weren't the Olympics there?"

"That's right. Back in 2002."

"So do you come from a big family? I'm an only child myself."

I smiled and found myself telling her about my family, and though I tried to remain neutral, I'm sure she caught the tinge of envy in my voice when I talked about their *perfect* lives. "I'm sure my time will come." I blushed. "It's just hard to be patient waiting for that big break."

Lin's packing now became a little methodical, but she didn't say anything right away. "So," I felt a deliberate shift in the conversation when she did finally speak, "you were kind of a last-minute addition to our group, just like Kat?"

I shrugged, not knowing how to answer. "I know. I'm still surprised at the way it worked out. I guess I was just in the right place at the right time," I finished optimistically.

I wasn't sure what exactly I'd said wrong, but Lin seemed to step back behind her business veneer again. "Well, we'd better get something to eat."

After a quick breakfast that consisted of little conversation, we reunited in the lobby at ten minutes to the hour, where Mike was already waiting for us. Kat and Dave were nowhere to be found, but Seth soon arrived and told us the two of them had gone on ahead and that a van was ready for us down in the parking garage. I scowled, wondering how my boss's leaving without me fit into my job description, but piled obediently into the outdated green hunk of metal with the others.

I immediately spotted Kat and Dave when we arrived at the wide-open area adjacent to the National Palace called the Zocalo. I remembered from the guidebook that it was the second-largest public square in the world and began development shortly after the first Spanish conquest. Though originally a public area of execution, today it hosted a variety of activities and mercantilism, all with Mexican flair, and a huge national flag as the focal point. We started on the south side of the square near the Old Town Hall, adjacent to, not surprisingly, the *New* Town Hall. As we made our way around to the east side, we saw the impressive reddish-stone structure of the National Palace. It had been built by Cortés on the site of the Aztec ruler Moctezuma's, not *Montezuma's*, own palace—a little presumptuous, I thought, and probably intentionally so. With all the renovations over the centuries, it had grown into an impressive building.

We walked toward the large central doorway. I was particularly anxious to see the giant fresco by Diego Rivera, one of Mexico's renowned muralists. It was supposed to tell the progress of the Mexican people, from ancient times through the modern industrial age. When our group arrived at the gate, however, we saw a disappointing sign that informed us that because of recent threats, tours were no longer being given into the palace. As I stood staring at it, I found Seth at my side.

"Too bad. I guess that bomb really spooked the government."

I frowned. "And rightly so. Just imagine how we would feel if someone had managed to smuggle in a weapon so close to *our* president. President Calderón must have been terrified, especially since he hasn't been in office for very long."

"Some would say he 'fanned the flames,' as it were, by coming down so hard on the drug gangs here," Seth continued. "If you push too hard, someone's bound to push back."

I readjusted my purse over my shoulder. "It's only been two years, and things are bound to get better. I think he's doing the right thing. Those people need to be stopped."

Seth shrugged as if it didn't matter to him. "The drug trade is a profitable business for a lot of people in Mexico. They can work all week for a few pesos or be a mule for a few days and make enough to support their families for a year."

"The end doesn't justify the means," I stated firmly, not liking the gist of the conversation. "I really wanted to see the murals though."

Seth brightened up. "Me too. I hear that the Grand Courtyard is incredible."

This was better. "I wonder how his work compares to the work of Orozco that we'll see in the Anthropology Museum. It seems Orozco is more bold with his colors."

"In some he is," Seth agreed. "I guess you didn't see the one in Sanborn's last night." I admitted I hadn't. "Well, you would have if you'd used the restroom!" He laughed, and I joined in.

Kat wasn't acting as jovial as the two of us. She pouted like this was a personal affront and said she was going to *talk* to one of the guards.

I found out that meant *I* was going to be ordered to translate while she *chewed out* the guard. Smoothing over some of the words she used, I felt sorry for the mustachioed man who was already sweating in the sweltering heat. But no matter what we did, we weren't able to arrange a private tour for our group even with our credentials. There was nothing to do but continue to circumnavigate the square and see the *Sagrario Metropolitano* and *Catedral*. I wasn't too disappointed because I'd really been interested in seeing these popular religious sites as well.

On my mission, I had been touched by the devotion of the Latino people to their beliefs. Though it was often frustrating to attempt to teach new doctrine, their dedication to worshipping God and respecting their religious heritage had taught me a thing or two. I glanced back at the group and wondered what kind of beliefs they each might have—Buddhist, Southern Baptist, Catholic? The corner of my mouth went up in a smile as I guessed at Kat's affiliation: self-worship!

Dave quickly had his equipment set up, and I walked closer to try to see what he saw and hopefully get a few more insights into who he was.

"It's really beautiful at night when the floodlights are on," Dave said in Spanish, and I felt a certain intimacy as we spoke together in his native language. "I may have to come back later."

Wanting to show him my witty conversational skills, I jumped in. "I know. It's amazing how different things can look in the dark—so mysterious and otherworldly."

He finished the shot and then added somewhat mysteriously as well, "True. But most of the time the dark merely conceals the true nature of things." Then he walked away.

While the others focused on their work, I wandered around the nearby vendors. There was the usual assortment of items, like sombreros and maracas, but I wasn't interested in anything until I saw an old man using colored straws to make small, decorative boxes. As he broke off the straws at planned intervals, the pieces began to form a picture—this particular one was of the nearby pyramids. He looked up and smiled at me, and retrieving my camera, I asked permission to snap a few shots of him and then of an old woman nearby who was weaving a basket. She nodded but didn't break her pace. I wondered how long it took to make a single basket. Centering the scene on the view screen, I heard a voice whisper in my ear.

"Make sure you haggle if you buy anything," Seth said. "You can usually talk them down to next to nothing." Then he walked away.

I scowled. This was these people's livelihood. What did I care if I saved a few pesos when everything here was made by hand? As if in protest, I paid the man what he asked for the tiny box he'd been working on.

Soon we had the footage we needed and headed to our next destination, *la Plaza de las Tres Culturas*, or Plaza of the Three Cultures. The square took its name from the arrangement of buildings from three different periods: Aztec pyramids and temples, a Spanish conventional church, and modern buildings. It was actually designed to be this way, sort of a tribute to all of the founders of the Mexican society today. I realized that although America was said to be the melting pot of the world, Mexico had done its own share of mixing cultures.

I looked over and found my ever-present companion was back at my side. "Cool," said Seth, as he led me to a great viewing spot. "Just take a gander at that. Ain't got nothin' like that back home." Then he winked and stuck his hands in his pockets, whistling.

As I leaned over the railing to see better, I wished there was a way down to actually walk around the oldest ruins. But there wasn't any way I could see, which was probably wise considering society's tendency to show a lack of respect for such places. Just then, I heard a voice yelling out in Spanish.

"*¡Cuidado! Está desatada la baranda.*"

I turned and saw an old man in a crumpled fedora gesturing anxiously at me. It was then that I heard the crunch of the cement giving way and felt the slight movement in the railing.

Chapter 9

As I fought for my balance against the suddenly unstable brace, I felt someone tightly grip my left arm. I turned to see Dave at my side.

"Thanks!" I replied, trying to catch my breath. "I didn't realize it was going to give way like that."

Our group had gathered around to see what was going on. Seth scowled. "I guess your country don't consider it worth the money to keep up the maintenance on places like this. Talk about mixed-up priorities."

Dave frowned, and I wished Seth would think before he blurted things out. "I'm fine," I said. "Really."

Kat sighed as if the whole situation bored her. "We'd better get back to work. Try and be more careful."

I frowned as she walked away. It wasn't like I *meant* to almost fall fifty feet to my death. They really ought to put up a sign or something though. Just then I noticed something lying on the ground. Picking up the flat metal square, I turned it over and saw the words of warning imprinted on the other side in Spanish: *Cuidado!*

Be careful!

Rolling my eyes, I reattached the flimsy sign to the railing for the next unlucky tourist.

The weather held the rest of the day, so we were able to go to the other outdoor destination of the University City. As we neared the campus, I looked out the car window and saw the familiar outlines of the Olympic rings mounted outside a stadium just bordering the campus square but was unable to recall when they had been held here. It had been a real privilege for my own hometown, and I remembered how proud we'd all felt. The driver parked in a visitors' parking lot, and we exited the vehicles and felt the increasing heat of the sun. Our boss was up to true form, immediately issuing dictates and determining the run of the day. She had us all scurrying like the cockroaches I'd found in my bathroom that morning.

With a flourish of Kat's hand, we all headed directly to the central library. Its windowless, stacked floors made it stand out as the most prominent building in the full square mile complex, with a mosaic façade that depicted various historical and religious scenes. I had already noticed many frescoes and mosaics scattered throughout the campus and marveled at the artistic atmosphere that pervaded the city. Dave must have immediately found himself in his element because he seemed oblivious to the rest of us. Everyone seemed to have a role to play, but I held back, waiting to be summoned if they needed me. The work seemed to be proceeding quite well, though the oppressive heat left me wanting to find a spot of shade somewhere. But I didn't want to be too far away. Kat barked at me once for some water, which I quickly retrieved from a cooler in the car's trunk, and then I offered some to the rest of the crew as well. Lin accepted, but the men shrugged it off. Apparently it was macho to be dehydrated.

With my water in hand, I sat down under a nearby tree. Our photographer had decided to include some of the local students in the shot for authenticity this time and, with a few hand gestures, had managed to tell them what to do without my help. While I was watching our group work, one of the native students he had just finished shooting came over to me. He was quite handsome, with thick black hair and two dimples that formed when he smiled at me.

"Hello, I am Javier," he said in a thickly accented voice.

"*Hola,*" I responded back.

"*¿Hablas tú español?*"

"*Sí.*"

Our conversation switched to Spanish, and it felt good to "flex" my skills again. He turned out to be a second-year student, curious about what we were doing there. I gave him the brief explanation that we were an advertising and marketing group there to do a campaign for Mexico's tourism bureau.

"Ah." He nodded. "So our people go to your country to work and you come here to work. How ironic."

I laughed. "I never looked at it that way."

"Of course, if they are all made like that in your country . . ."

I looked in the direction of his gaze just as Kat was bending over to pull some folders out of her bag. Geez. "I'm afraid not," I said, my words dripping with sarcasm. "She's one of a kind."

"*Si*, her boyfriend certainly thinks so."

Huh? "Who are you talking about?" I asked in English then repeated myself in Spanish.

"The guy she can't keep her hands off of. The one with the camera. Women like that always have boyfriends, and they're usually young and handsome." He sighed. "How long are you going to be in town? Perhaps I could show you the city—it is particularly beautiful at night."

No way was I going to sit still and be the backup plan. Jumping to my feet, I told him I had to get back to work.

When Kat signaled us forward to make the lengthy walk to the southeast corner of the complex, I glanced over at Dave and found myself forgetting my previous promises that I was just here to work. Kat didn't deserve to win him that easily. He was struggling with a large camera bag full of lenses, so I rushed over to him. "Can I help you carry something? You look like you've got enough for at least two people."

For a moment, he simply stood there, an eyebrow raised as if determining my ability to carry his prized possessions. His six-foot frame may have towered above me, but the heat of the day was on my side, and he handed me a bag.

"Think you can keep up?" he cocked an eyebrow.

"I guess we'll find out."

I lengthened my stride to keep up with his purposefully quick pace and finally looked for a shortcut in order to reach our destination before him. A nearby campus worker scowled as I left the main path and reminded me that this area was set aside as a natural habitat for plants and flowers. I hopped back onto another pathway and somehow arrived at the sculpture first.

The sight was both stirring and confusing. In a circular pattern that must have encompassed at least an acre were rising black monoliths, almost like they were the guardians of the large pit that contained a petrified sea of lava. *Sculpture* wasn't what I would have termed it, yet . . . art was art. And I didn't wholeheartedly dislike it. As I stood there in amazement, I felt someone come up behind me and heard a riveting deep voice. "Hey, I thought you were going to take off with those. That's expensive equipment you've got there."

"Don't worry, they've been well taken care of. I think I won though."

His smile made my legs feel weak, and I gulped as he removed the camera from around my neck. His fingers brushed against the damp skin of my neck. I wasn't prepared for the way it made me feel.

"Are there really more than a quarter of a million students—" I struggled to think of the word in Spanish—"matriculated at the university?" I asked, wanting to keep him near me.

He nodded and switched to English. "I believe so, though that includes its many schools that are . . . satellites? Is that correct? You see, I need the practice with certain words as well. Where did you educate yourself, by the way?"

"At our state university. Go Utes!" I jokingly raised my fist. "It was a good school. Luckily I had a scholarship for a couple of years, and it also helped being able to live at home."

"Getting an education can be expensive," he said, setting up a shot through his camera.

"I know. My student loans are killing me. But they're not as bad as my brother's will be when he's finished—though he's bound to earn it back quickly. He's going to law school at Georgetown," I explained. "That's in Washington DC, though he lives in Virginia."

"That's a nice area."

"So you've visited America?" I asked curiously.

He nodded. "Of course. In a way, it seems like I've spent more time away from my home country than I have in it."

That explained why that student, Javier, thought Dave was an American like the rest of us. In fact, if it weren't for his excellent Spanish, I'd assume he was just a great-looking guy with a tan. "How did you come to get this job?" I asked, curious about what my own options might be. "Is there, like, a freelance group you work with?"

He slowly raised his camera and looked through the lens before answering. "I have my connections. Do you like working for this company?"

"So far. Though I'm not exactly sure where I'll end up." Realizing anything I said might get back to Kat, I added, "Of course, I'm glad for the opportunity, and I'll do whatever it takes while I'm here. I guess you have to be ambitious to get anywhere in life," I added, quoting Seth.

Though he was still looking through the lens, Dave's countenance suddenly dropped as if something he was seeing made him sad.

* * *

It had been a long time since I'd had such an active day, and by the time we arrived at the Latin American Tower, I was ready to call it quits. But we got there just in time for the last elevator ride up. I glanced across the crowded compartment and tried to pick out Dave's head from among the crowd. It wasn't easy. His black hair blended in, though Kat was right next to him and stood out like a blonde angel ascending to heaven. Why did she have to be so perfect? I sighed.

The shivering elevator made me want to clutch a side rail, and I breathed a sigh of relief when we approached the top of the forty-third floor. We exited to the observation deck, and I took in my surroundings.

From here, we had an excellent view of most of the city, and I recognized several of the familiar landmarks we'd seen that day. But this twilight view gave me the impression of shimmering stars dancing on a sea of mist below. Though the weather was calm, even the slight buffeting of an occasional errant breeze caused the building to sway beneath our feet. I turned to see Lin at my side.

"I wondered how this building compared to the Sears Tower back in my hometown of Chicago," she said. "It's not as tall from the ground up, but because Mexico City is built on a marsh, the total weight below the ground is the same. That makes it the heaviest, if not the tallest, building in the Americas."

"Wow," I said, genuinely interested and glad she was being friendly again. But it didn't take long for my attention to wander. Dave and Kat had come around the corner, and I watched them instead.

He doesn't even know you exist.

Good. Because I'm not interested, I lied.

"It looks like Kat has more than the job on her mind," Lin whispered conspiratorially in my ear. "They seem totally engrossed in each other. So do you know Kat well?"

"Not at all," I answered honestly. "I just met her right before the trip."

"Oh really?" she said casually as I fought to look at the city skyline instead.

Hoping to get some idea of how long we'd be, I excused myself and found out from Seth that we were still going to swing by the Palacio de Bellas Artes and catch it in the floodlights. We could even return to the palace and do the same. Trying not to groan, I followed the others on the stomach-churning ride back down.

The short walk to the arts center was fascinating, if brief. The usual commotion of a large city surrounded me, this time with a different feel and flavor. Numerous kiosks selling anything you could imagine still lined the streets, along with the aforementioned beggars. One quite ragged fellow was sitting on the curb, "eating" fire for his compensation. I couldn't help but ask if it burned.

"*No, mi hija,*" he replied with a semitoothless grin. "*No me quema.*"

We arrived shortly, and Dave quickly set up his tripod before the remaining light faded. Mike and Lin fell into sync, while Kat stood like a benevolent tyrant, overseeing it all. I kept to the background, hoping I wasn't the waste of money I felt I was. With slight hesitation, I walked over to Kat. "Um, I was wondering if there was anything I could do. Can I help set up the shots? Or take down any notes for you?"

"What?" she replied, as if finally aware of my presence. "Oh, you want to help. Well, here are some pesos. Could you be a dear and get us all some coffee. We've got a few more hours to go, and I'm sure we could use a little pick-me-up."

Well, you got what you asked for.

If I want your advice, I'll ask for it.

I dutifully complied, though it took almost three blocks of walking to find a little shop that was still open to fill my request. Not familiar with the habits of coffee drinkers, I ordered a couple black and the rest with cream and sugar. Then I picked out a fruit juice for myself and prayed that they had some sort of contraption I could carry them back in. They did, so I walked out with my hands loaded and tried to get my bearings to find my way back to the shoot. But when I arrived, the group was no longer there.

I quickly set down the coffee and pulled out my new iPhone from my purse.

Actually, I panicked first then managed to regain my senses enough to pull up and activate Kat's number on the phone. When she answered, she directed me around the corner of the building to their new location, and I acted as if it had been no big deal—that I'd *expected* to return and find myself abandoned. Acting cool and collected, I held out the carrier while the crew made their selections from the drinks. I noticed that Dave took one of the plain black coffees, and I wondered why I should be surprised. It made sense that he drank coffee and probably had a beer or two—maybe more. I doubted if anyone even noticed I hadn't gotten one for myself.

By now I was *really* tired and ready to go back to the hotel. My sinuses had grown steadily more clogged from the foul air, and I hoped

I wasn't getting sick. If only I had an active role to play, it might instill me with a little more energy to stay alert—especially since the others had the benefit of caffeine circulating through their systems. I stifled a yawn and watched Dave perform what was probably another photographic masterpiece. Curious about what he was seeing, I took my own camera out of my purse and lined up a shot, only to realize that all of those extra lenses and gadgets he was using must have had magical powers because all I could see was the hazy outline of the building in the near darkness. Fiddling with a few settings, I only managed to set off the red-eye feature, which acted like a strobe light in a discotheque. Dave turned around and frowned. I tucked my camera back inside my purse and slunk away.

"Call the hotel and arrange a massage for me an hour from now," Kat ordered, suddenly at my side. "And let them know to forward any calls for me directly to my room, regardless of the hour."

I nodded and scrambled to find my phone again, hoping I could remember how to pull up the calling list. Fortunately Kat's attention was already back on the group, so I had plenty of unsupervised time to fumble with the device and look proficient. At least now I knew how much longer we were going to be. But I still wished there was a nice massage waiting for *me* back at the hotel. I'd be lucky to get a cockroach-free shower. Ah, the perks of power.

Dream on!

I ignored the barb and scurried toward Kat, who was signaling for me again.

Chapter 10

By that next day, rain drizzled from the sky, which forced us to go to the Museo Nacional de Antropología in the northern section of Chapultepec Park instead of Teotihuacán. Kat wasn't happy about that; she was pretty obsessed, I'd learned, with sticking to the schedule.

The museum housed a variety of exhibits representing the different cultures that existed throughout the Mesoamerican Empire. Our first stop was the Central Patio, which I realized upon closer inspection was a huge stone "umbrella" borne on a column of carved stone. It towered a good two stories over our heads, and water cascaded down the sides, forming liquid curtains that were then pumped up and recirculated. I could see the artistic appeal of this location, but a thought had started to form in my mind about how we were going about the campaign. All through my mission, I was constantly amazed by the generosity and genuine concern of the Latino people I'd come in contact with in California. They loved their country but had been forced to leave it in order to find better lives for their families. All of these buildings and tourist sites were great. But we needed to show the heart of this land: its *people*.

However, everything had been planned and laid out, so I tried to be content going with the flow, even though Kat seemed to be bouncing off the walls. After a few hours, we'd all been verbally chastised for some minor infraction. What did it matter if we couldn't go to Teotihuacán as planned? We were still working. I tried to steer clear of her, which was easy, considering I had very little to do.

As we walked across the ground level, we came to a section entitled *Sala Mexica*. This exhibit said it represented the Aztec period of history, with the brief rise and eventual fall of Tenochtitlán, the area that was now Mexico City, to the Spanish conquistadores. I stopped in front of a diorama encased in glass. Miniature human figures stood in groups or squatted on the ground in front of blankets laid out with representations of all kinds of goods.

"Amazing, isn't it?"

I turned to see Seth at my side, grinning at me like a little boy. "This is a model of an Aztec marketplace. I think most of us believe that because the ancient Americans had not discovered basic Eastern technologies, like rifles or gunpowder, they were a backward and uncivilized people. That was hardly the case. At the time the Spanish conquerors first saw Tenochtitlán, they were amazed at the size and well-ordered nature of marketplaces like these. One soldier recorded that more than twenty-five thousand people came to this market every day but that every fifth day a market was held that drew more than fifty thousand."

He sighed. "It was a land of wealth when the Spaniards arrived. Ripe for the plundering."

I stared at him in disbelief. "What the Spanish did here was unconscionable. They stole whatever they wanted, destroyed whatever was meaningless to them. And for what? A little wealth? That's not worth the destruction of a civilization."

Seth chuckled. "Maybe you're not as ambitious as I thought. That's good. Keep your noble principles. So," he turned to face me, "tell me about yourself."

I was stumped for a moment and then rehearsed almost verbatim what I'd told Lin the day before. We continued across the room as we spoke, and I glanced at the ancient relics as I passed. Stone statues and tools graced one window. In another, I saw something that resembled a stone box. When Seth stopped in front of a curious sculpture, I stood next to him and studied the gigantic round stone with a flat surface and strange markings all over it. Toward the center was a figure with a protruding tongue and large, painted eyes. Compasslike markings headed out from all angles in a circular pattern.

"That's an Aztec calendar stone." I pointed. "If I remember correctly, they had this belief that their present world had been preceded by other worlds, which had been destroyed by natural catastrophes."

"How do you know all that?" Seth asked, an impressed look on his face.

I remembered because it so closely resembled my own belief that the world had once been destroyed by flood and would one day be cleansed by fire. And if you took into consideration that earthquakes had literally transformed the Nephite world at Christ's death, it was no wonder the Aztecs thought that way. But I merely ended up saying, "I've been studying in my *Baedeker's Guide*."

"Tell me more."

"Well," I said sheepishly, "they thought their world was the final world and gave this calendar the name Stone of the Fifth Sun. It was believed to have begun after the gods assembled in Teotihuacán and one of the gods gave himself as a sacrifice, which in turn gave rise to a new sun. Then other gods sacrificed themselves, and their energy was transferred to the sun."

"Cool. So it was all about the transfer of power—about who could become the, well, top dog."

"I suppose," I shrugged.

"What are you two so engrossed in over here?" Kat walked over, and I couldn't tell whether the look on her face was approving or disapproving. "I'd think you were over here hatching plans, which is odd, considering there's so much work to do."

"Actually we were discussing Mexican history." Seth straightened up. "But you're right. We'd better get some work done."

I watched as Seth strolled away, hands in his pockets as he whistled. Kat folded her arms across her chest. "You two seemed pretty cozy over here."

"Oh no," I protested, afraid she'd think I was being a slothful worker. "We were just talking."

"I don't mind. It doesn't hurt to mix a little business with pleasure." I followed her gaze and found my own eyes resting on Dave as well.

* * *

The rain kept up the remainder of the afternoon. It gave the group plenty of time to deal with the technical side of things back at the hotel but left everyone feeling anxious that there was still so much groundwork to be done. That is, everyone who *had* work to do. After a few hours alone in my room waiting to be called upon, I was climbing the walls. I thought maybe pacing up and down the hall until someone came out and gave me something to do or some errand to run would help.

My efforts paid off.

"I thought I heard someone out here wearing out the carpets," Seth joked as he stood in the doorway to his room. "Bored?"

I raised my hands in defeat.

"Want to see what I've been workin' on?" he drawled, gesturing me into his room.

At first I was a little hesitant, but it would only be for a minute, I reassured myself. Though his room was a little bigger than mine, there was a sense of disorder about it that made me feel like I was walking into a closet. His idea of unpacking seemed to include laying everything out in plain view to be ready at a moment's notice. Clothes were thrown haphazardly over the only chair in the room, while the desk was cluttered with papers and computer equipment. He was as bad as my brothers.

"Sorry about the mess. One of these days I'll be rich enough to hire a personal maid to follow me around," he said.

I smiled as he turned his laptop to show me. Unfortunately, I had to sit on the corner of the bed to view it. But I was instantly impressed by what I saw. He had already compiled several of the pictures we'd taken just that day into a collage, clustered around the bold title: *Mexico Rediscovered*. The layout was eye-catching and would be doubly impressive when it was accompanied by some well-crafted copy. How I longed to be the one to put words to it!

"It's great." I sighed.

Seth frowned. "If you were any more enthusiastic, I'd still be insulted."

"Oh no! I really mean it!" I struggled to undo the damage I'd done. "I'm really impressed. Have you always been interested in art?"

"Ever since I was knee-high to a grasshopper." He chuckled, exaggerating his accent. "Of course, there weren't many art museums where I lived, just outside of Laredo, Texas. I couldn't wait to get out of that border-town dump."

I caught a glimpse of that side of him I wasn't sure about again. "Was it really that bad?"

He snapped out of his anger. "No worse than a lot of places, I suppose. So tell me more about yourself. Did you always have dreams of becoming a filing clerk?"

I knew he was just teasing me, so I slapped him on the arm. "Ha-ha. No. My goal is to get offered a position as a copywriter. I just have to be patient until that happens. *If* that ever happens."

"There's a lot of competition. But if you're good . . ."

I thought I was good. Who knows, maybe I wasn't.

"What would you do with this?" he pointed to the computer again.

"Well," I stammered, caught in my own doubts. "I . . . I would try to make sure we capture the . . . well, essence of Mexico. There's more to Mexico and this city than what's on the surface. There's an air of antiquity and struggle just below the surface."

Seth pursed his lips as if considering my train of thought. "Go on."

I grew animated as I thought he might be catching my vision. "You know, we should be seeing beyond just the buildings and museums, the historical sites and ruins, and let the world know what's really here. I think we should start by focusing more on the people."

"The people?"

I frowned, realizing I'd suddenly lost him. "The people here are genuine," I said weakly. "If we could somehow capture their struggle but then also show that through the ages they somehow keep rising above it—these landmarks we're shooting are proof of that."

Seth got up from the bed. "You're not a very good judge of character. Most of the people here would rather cheat and rob you than point out the beauties of their country. I think things are going just fine the way we're doing it. Maybe you ought to stick with getting coffee."

I struggled to push back the tears that his stinging words had caused to spring up. I didn't know what to say.

"Hey, I'm sorry." Seth came and sat down beside me. "Sometimes my big mouth gets the better of me. I guess where I grew up, I didn't have much of an affinity for Hispanics. Come on, forgive me."

I didn't have time to speak or react before he started to massage my neck. His hands were strong and his movements sure as they cupped my shoulders and caressed my throat. If I hadn't been tense before, I certainly was now! And unsure of what to do.

I was still reeling from the new side Seth had let me see of him. He had been so nice to me up until now, and I had come to think of him as a friend. A million thoughts whirled through my mind as I considered that my future job could depend on the feedback given about me when we returned. I liked Seth (or I thought I did), but I wasn't sure what to make of his words or his hands on my neck. This wasn't the first time I'd felt prompted to run from a situation, and I knew better than to ignore the feeling.

"Uh, Seth, I just remembered I was going to call my family before I turn in. It's getting late, and they're in our same time zone. I'd probably better do that before they worry. Maybe we could talk some more about this tomorrow."

I'd already started backing toward the closed door and easily made my escape. As I found safety in my own room, my breathing finally returned to normal. And then I started feeling foolish. Had I blown everything out of proportion? Seth had never given me any indication that he was interested in me that way. And the world hardly condemned a back rub.

I thought you weren't a part of that world.

True. But at times like this, I wished I at least understood it better. Maybe then I'd know how to handle it. How to stand up for myself. Sure, I was bold enough in my mind, where many an insult had been retaliated with imaginary darts being thrown at my nemeses. But I still struggled to say those things to their faces. After all, look at how I kowtowed to Roger. At least I could pull myself together and really make that phone call to my parents so I wouldn't be adding a lie to cowardice. As I struggled to activate my new phone, I had to fight for composure before I entered their number. Hopefully I didn't end up calling Russia instead.

The physical and emotional demands of the day were catching up with me. My hands trembling, I waited until I heard my mom's voice on the phone.

"Hello?"

"Mom, is that you? It's Samantha!"

"Oh, Samantha darling. It's so good to hear your voice. We were waiting for you to call."

Now I struggled even harder to keep the tremor out of my voice. And the guilt. I'd been trying to act like I was tough enough not to have needed my parents these last few days, and now here I was, breaking down. "Sorry. I've been . . . uh, busy. Is Dad around?"

"He's off with his home teaching partner giving a blessing. You could call back in an hour or so, and he should be here."

"Okay. I'll try. I'm kinda tired though."

"Are you all right?"

The last thing I wanted was for them to worry about me. "Yes, Mom. I'm just a little homesick is all. For home with you. Most of the group here is really great." I tried to generate some enthusiasm in my voice. "It's amazing all the things we've already seen."

"That's wonderful! So it's all you hoped for?"

This would be the second time I'd been forced to lie in one day. "It's really amazing. The city is so huge, and there are so many people. I just feel a bit overwhelmed." I told her about our plans for tomorrow. I let my excitement over seeing the pyramids overcome the emotions that threatened to engulf me.

"We'll call and tell your brothers all about it. I have to admit, Karen's already quite jealous. She's trying to talk us into letting her do a study abroad tour this summer as a precursor to starting college. You'll have to give her some advice when you get back."

Doing something my siblings were jealous of perked me up a little. Wiping my eyes, I explained a little more about what had happened that day. "You'd probably just better relay all this to Dad," I added. "We have an early morning, and I'm already bushed."

"I will. Be safe. We're both praying for you."

As I hung up the phone, I suddenly felt as if instead of friends, I needed all the *prayers* I could get on this trip.

Chapter 11

TEOTIHUACÁN.

Even the name sounded ancient and mystical. Though the temperature in Mexico City had been hovering in the low eighties, we knew it would be considerably higher out in the treeless desert valley of Anáhuac, so we had started off even earlier than usual. Though it was only about a thirty-mile ride, it ended up being a bumpy, dusty trip on a poorly maintained road. Sitting in the back of the van, I was glad to be able to see out the side window. Lin and Mike were discussing the setup for the day, and I tried to avoid looking at Seth, who was acting as if nothing had happened last night.

Well then, so would I.

I watched the landscape change, turning brown and yellow as if bleached by the sun, as we drove along. There were strange trees that broke up the monotony alongside the recognizable maguey plant, which, I'd read, had played an important role in the indigenous people's lives. Using the leaves and stringy pulp for everything from paper to sewing implements, they had also discovered how the sticky sap could be fermented into what would become Mexico's trademark drink: tequila.

At last we arrived. Kat and Dave had gone ahead again to the site, and even though I couldn't help but notice how tight her T-shirt was and how her hundred-dollar highlights glistened in the sun like gold, my eyes quickly zeroed in on the jean-clad figure who stood pointing at the structure to our right. My stomach squeezed together like I was at the top of a roller coaster, waiting for the initial drop. I took a deep breath of the welcome fresh air and tried to quell my feelings of jealousy by looking around me. We were standing right behind the Pyramid of the Moon. It was the second largest pyramid in the complex and marked the start of the Calle de los Muertos, or Street of the Dead. We weren't, however, the only ones present. As we made our way into the complex, groups of tourists already milled around with the locals, who were trying to sell their various wares.

Kat caught sight of me and called me over. She maneuvering her designer sunglasses to the top of her head, andd I could see the frustration in her surprisingly bloodshot eyes. She must not be sleeping very well.

"Please keep everyone away from the set," she complained as if it were somehow my fault. "Explain to those *people*," now she motioned to the vendors, "that we only have a limited amount of time and we don't want to be disturbed!"

Not happy with the task, I disguised my disappointment yet again and tried to perform the request to the best of my ability. Finding that my targets didn't seem to grasp the fact that this wealthy group of Americans wasn't going to purchase anything, I distracted them instead by asking their names and about themselves and their families. They surrounded me with a cacophony of voices, all curious about this *gringa* who could speak fluent Spanish. The children were the most fun, and I even joined a few in a local hand-clapping game.

After they got bored of me and I was sure no one in the group needed me, I decided to go on a self-guided tour of the collection of buildings to my right. They seemed to draw me toward them, and I went willingly. I found myself led into a courtyard that was open to the sky and surrounded by magnificent pillars. I glanced in my guide and saw I was in the Palace of the Quetzal Butterfly. There were traces of pale pink paint on the walls, and I couldn't help but wonder what this place had looked likc in its full glory, not to mention what it had been used for. I continued and realized it was like a maze. Back under the roofed section was another door and more stairs—this time guarded by an imposing serpent's head—and the map said that if I continued, I would come upon an alleyway with still more rooms. There was even supposed to be a tunnel that went beneath the palace—sort of a drainage system. It would be easy to get lost in here. I decided it was best if I went back.

Most of the tourists were now making the climb up the slightly less arduous steps of the Pyramid of the Moon. I glanced back at the group who was still busy setting up equipment and wondered if they'd miss me. Even if I only made it up to the second rise, I'd still be able to see them if they gestured me back down.

After a few dozen steps, I about changed my mind. I hadn't been affected by the altitude, but it was quite an effort to climb these larger-than-usual stairs. I'd hate to have to run up them. I tried a few different techniques, even using my hands to brace myself at times, and was glad I persevered because the climb wasn't the only thing that took my breath away. I felt dwarfed by the immensity of the place and the ancient, reverent feeling it invoked. Which was appropriate, considering that to the residents, this was considered the birthplace of the gods.

The entire complex covered at least a good square mile to where the furthermost buildings grew hazy, like a mirage, in the distance. All along the main street that formed a north-south corridor there were small two-story buildings that, I'd learned in the informational packet we'd picked up at the museum, had been the priests' houses. It was hard to imagine what it was like back then, with multicolored stucco and sculptures instead of the crumbling gray stone that remained. I glanced above me to the summit of the pyramid and knew I'd never have time to scale it and return in time, so I had to content myself with the current view.

Down below I could see our group still at work, and it was easy to determine who was who. Dave was leaning over his bags, pulling out a panoramic lens, while Kat hovered over him like a red-winged vulture eyeing her prey. Of course, who was I to judge those who looked like they were distracted on the job? And then it occurred to me that I hadn't taken any pictures of myself yet—maybe no one would believe I was actually here. Dave was lining up a shot of the pyramid, and I wondered if it would be a big deal if he just took a quick close-up picture of me. After all, everything was digital now, and I'd even offer to pay for it, though I had no idea what a professional's rate might go for.

"Dave?" I shouted down. I guess he didn't hear me, so I shouted more loudly.

Now everyone turned and looked, and embarrassed, I mimed what I wanted him to do. He gave me a slight nod and angled the camera in my direction. I took in the view a few more minutes before I saw Kat waving the group on toward the south end of the plaza. I started back down.

It was then I noticed that one of the tourists milling around seemed out of place. Most wore T-shirts and ball caps and had cameras around their necks. This man was dressed in black slacks and a black dress shirt with long sleeves he'd rolled up to his forearms in the heat. Now that our group was moving, he started a casual pace southward as well. I continued down the steps and almost missed my footing as I continued to watch him. When our group stopped, he stopped. When they walked, he was always just a stone's throw away. I casually began to tail him and see if I could figure out why we'd caught his interest. After all, two could play that game.

The man stopped briefly and handled some wooden flutes a young boy was selling. But he kept glancing at my colleagues out of the corner of his eye. I pretended to be interested in some stone bracelets a young girl was modeling on her own arm.

"*Qué bonita*," I said, smiling down at her.

Kat started gesturing to one of the nearby priest's houses, and the group relocated to that spot, and sure enough, the strange man followed. His ruse would have been more effective if he'd brought a camera like the other tourists. He looked awkward as he stood there pretending to gaze back at the pyramid with surreptitious glances cast to his side every so often. And then, just when things could have gotten interesting, his cell phone rang. With a huff, he disappeared behind the stone dwelling.

So I followed him.

Now who's acting strange?

At least I had a camera and a reason for being there in the first place. I crept around the far corner of the house until I was within earshot—which wasn't hard because the man was hardly being quiet. I closed my eyes and tried to make sense of the one-sided conversation. It wasn't easy. His Spanish was blazingly fast. Apparently he was chewing out some employee for messing up a large order of . . . I couldn't quite catch it. But the way the man in black was going on, I wouldn't have wanted to be on the other end of the phone. He called the recipient a few more derogatory names and added a few epithets, which, fortunately, were beyond my understanding, and then he started talking about how everything would be settled in a few days but that he needed more time to determine if this latest applicant could handle the amount of products—

I felt a hand tug on the back of my shirt, and I nearly jumped out of it. I turned around and saw the young girl with the bracelets. She held them up to me with longing in her eyes.

"*Lo siento*," I tried to explain, "*pero no necessito—*"

Drat. I glanced around the edge of the house again. The man was gone.

Disappointed, I walked back to the group with my newly purchased bracelet.

"There you are. We need to see the Temple of Quetzalcóatl," Dave said, turning to me to explain a few things. "It's a bit of a walk, but there are some shots I want to get along the way, so the rest of you can go back to the cars and drive down to the other parking lot. A wind is picking up, and we'll want to get going. Tell the group I'll meet you all there."

Here's your chance. Or are you too scared?

Okay, don't rush me.

I explained the plan to my colleagues and watched the others head back toward the cars before I asked, "Can I help you carry some equipment down?"

"I keep up a pretty good pace," he reminded me.

"I can keep up." I smiled. "Unless you're afraid you'll be shown up by a girl again?"

This time I caught a glint in his eyes as a friendly smile crossed his face, and feeling like I'd been forgiven for some unknown trespass, I picked up a bag and began to walk. He started out a good stride ahead of me—but I wasn't complaining about the view. Dave was dressed in worn blue jeans and a tan T-shirt, and I got the impression that what he wore was the last thing on his mind. There was little else I could figure out about this character. When working, he was completely absorbed in his subject, but he also seemed unusually interested in the members of the group—especially Kat.

"This whole excavated region," he suddenly began talking as if the few moments of silence made him nervous, "covers about a mile and a half. The entire zone is about twice that size. Nothing is known about the builders' language or history. We do know there were different phases that occurred, four in all, causing the various buildings you see to be built. The two main structures are the Pyramid of the Moon—that's the smaller one we just left—and the Pyramid of the Sun, which is the larger one up ahead. During the third stage of growth, the population reached more than two hundred thousand, and this was the trade center of the Mesoamerican world. Then the city collapsed, though we're not sure why. By the time the Spaniards arrived, this whole area was covered in dirt."

I was impressed by how much he knew—and how well I still understood Spanish! I was also amazed that I was able to keep up, but I was panting like a sheepdog in summer. Groaning, I could feel a rivulet of sweat trickle down my back and was almost relieved that he seemed more interested in the ruins and snapping photos than in me.

"Is that the Temple of Quetzalcóatl?" I pointed to the building still far ahead of us.

"Yes. Have you heard the story of the white-bearded god?" Dave questioned. I shrugged with pretended ignorance, curious at what he would say. "Even though they're not sure if this particular pyramid is dedicated to him or just named after him, the myth goes back for centuries that a fair-skinned, bearded god appeared to the people somewhere in these surrounding areas. He had some kind of tremendous power and stated that he'd return one day from the east. That was why the appearance of the Spaniards was so shocking to the Aztecs. They thought Cortés was the return of their god, so they worshiped the invaders. It would be interesting to know how the story started—usually every myth has some basis in reality."

"That's fascinating." *More fascinating than he probably realizes*, I thought.

I turned around and saw how far we'd already walked. The Pyramid of the Moon and nearby structures looked as small as the priests' houses we'd just passed. I took out my own camera and lined up the pyramid on my viewscreen. Then I realized Dave was at my side looking at the picture I'd taken. He seemed amused.

"What?" I asked.

"Try it once more," he smiled, "but look at it differently this time."

He held up his Nikon in front of me then stood behind me with his arms on either side of my body to support the heavy piece of equipment. "Most people simply look at what they think is the focal point and shoot."

I shook my head. I didn't understand "focal point" in Spanish.

He smiled. "Look again at the pyramid." He leaned close and held up his arm, pointing slightly to the right. I could see the dark hairs on his arm and a few veins running beside sinewy muscle. There was a musky scent to his skin. "Do you see that wispy cloud right above the gnarled tree? If you pull back on the zoom lens and include them as well, it will give your eye more to focus on. Then the pyramid becomes part of the landscape, as if it were born from it."

He waited until I had a sure grip on the camera. It wasn't easy with him that close, but I took a quick breath and waited for the image to materialize through the viewfinder. There it was. This time, I shifted my view off to the left. I pushed the shutter and smiled at the result. Dave was impressed as well.

"Uh . . . thanks," I managed to stutter as I handed it back to him. "I'll try to look at things differently from now on."

I glanced off to the right side of the road and saw a mess of scaffolding and a tent-covered wall. It looked like someone had started excavating.

Dave noticed it too and motioned me over. We stood by the nearby wall and stared down into a large pit that had been dug at its base. "Why are they doing that?" I asked.

"I think they're trying to uncover more of that mural," he responded. "But from the look of things, they haven't been at it for a while."

We studied the faded colors on the wall, where the remaining picture was barely visible. It appeared to be a rendition of some battle, with the victorious warriors bringing back the remaining prisoners. "Did the Aztecs really sacrifice their captives?" I shuddered, both at the thought and the darkness of the pit.

"As far as historians can tell. Whether it was as extensively practiced as scholars used to believe is being debated. But they have found mass graves where perhaps the victims were merely thrown into the ground and covered up."

I grimaced and looked up at Dave. "Well, thank heavens those days are past."

"Yeah, sure," he said, his jaw clenching. "We'd better go."

We reached the others, and I watched as the team set up the equipment again. This gave me a chance to do a little exploring around the temple, this time making sure I stayed out of the camera's way.

The Temple of Quetzalcóatl and the surrounding citadel were different from what we'd seen so far. Sculptured serpents and masks graced its walls, and these details made up for its lack of size. I reached out and gently touched one of the figures on the façade. I wondered what they meant and what these buildings had been used for. I had read that the name of the complex itself meant "the place where men become gods." Did those ancient people also believe that through certain acts they could attain what their Maker had achieved? Of course, any pure doctrine that had once been given anciently had become twisted and perverted by the inhabitants of this enigmatic city. It was man's nature, I supposed, to sink into depravity when there were no higher laws.

I drew my hand back from the cold stone.

We were quite close to the museum and restaurant, and I wondered how much longer we would stay—and if lunch had been worked into our schedule. The number of tourists had increased, and I realized our group wasn't getting the footage they needed. I hoped Kat wouldn't take it out on one of us, namely me. But Kat was nowhere to be found, and when heavy rain began to fall, I realized our work here was done. I ran over to Dave and helped throw some tarps over the equipment before we made a mad dash to the cars. Just as we finished throwing the gear into the back of the van, Kat finally came scurrying toward us with no explanation as to where she'd been. I snuck a peek over at Dave, who now had droplets of water running down his face. He caught my eye and held my gaze for a moment before jumping into the other car with Kat.

Chapter 12

Finally, after we'd sat moping around in the rooms of our hotel all afternoon waiting for the rain to stop, Kat announced that she wanted to head out to a nearby nightclub to lighten the mood. I groaned. Nightclubs were not something I aspired to, and besides, my head was starting to ache, which didn't mix well with pulsating music and belligerent, intoxicated patrons. But I didn't want to be the odd person out, so I tried to find something appropriate to wear. I guessed my alma mater T-shirts had worn out their welcome, so instead I put on a purple tunic over white jeans and thought it flattering. Other than the flowered skirt I'd had the presence of mind to throw in just in case I found a church building or we went someplace more formal, it was as good as it got.

This time a black sedan transported us to our destination, and after it pulled up to the rain-soaked curb, I got out and looked up at the neon sign. It must have been a popular place because another sign outside declared that we should *hacer fila aquí*. I explained this was where the waiting line formed, and at first we took our place in the long line of drenched potential customers. But after a few minutes, Kat snarled, "We'll see about this." She scurried toward the front door without me and was gone for a few minutes. When she returned, there was a triumphant look on her face.

"Sometimes you just have to speak the right language," she said, rubbing her fingers together in a way that suggested money had crossed hands.

Before I knew it, we were being ushered into the chaotic madness of the dance club. I stood there not knowing what to do, since Mike and Lin had retreated to some dark corner somewhere and Seth had, at the last minute, used the excuse that he had computer work to do. After

Kat dragged Dave onto the dance floor, I found a table of my own and politely declined an order with the waitress who approached me. Then I waited for the night to end.

After two hours, I wondered if it would.

Accepting two requests to dance—the first had called me *querida* the whole time and his breath had reeked of beer; the second's vampirelike attraction to my neck still had me shaking—I finally got wise and turned the third guy down. He was a heavily tattooed man, and when he held out his hand, I politely shook my head and said in English that I didn't feel well. It was mostly true. Rubbing my temples to try and stave off a worse headache, I saw a pair of jean-clad legs walk up to me, and I groaned. "No, *gracias*," I said none too politely.

But it was just Dave. "*¿Como estás?*" he asked. I was already half deaf from the noise, so he asked me again how I was, this time leaning in near enough that I could feel his warm breath on my neck and smell the scent of his cologne. "You don't seem to be enjoying yourself too much," he surmised as he took the seat next to me.

"No," I admitted, "this isn't really my scene. My roommate back home loves this nightclub atmosphere. I prefer things a little more peaceful."

"Me too. I think your boss has more energy than me as well. Can I get you anything to drink?"

I watched as a waitress walked by to supply someone with more liquid entertainment and had to admit how enticing it all looked— amber liquid in tall glasses, carafes with pink bubbles floating to the surface, drinks the color of icicles that reflected the pulsating lights.

"No, I'm not thirsty," I said timidly at first. Then with a little more confidence in who I was, I added, "Actually, I don't drink."

His eyebrow raised, and I wondered if what I'd said implied the same thing in Spanish. The hip-hop music on the DJ's stereo changed into a ballad, and I could hear again. "So," Dave rested an arm on the back of my chair, "how do you think it's going so far? The job, I mean."

Now I wished I had something to gulp down instead of answering. I wasn't sure I wanted to chance rejection over my ideas again, so I was tempted to tell him what he undoubtedly wanted to hear. But I figured he was better at reading people than that.

"You have something to say about it, don't you?"

I squirmed in my seat. "Well, I guess I've had some ideas of my own."

"Oh? Like what?"

With some trepidation, I repeated what I'd said to Seth about how we'd been focusing too much on the things around us and not enough on the people. I braved a glance out of the corner of my eye, waiting for the dismissal of my thoughts, but there was none. Instead, he ran a hand through his tousled hair. "I never thought of it that way," he said with a half smile.

Then I remembered our conversation earlier that day and smiled back. "Maybe you just have to learn to look at things differently as well."

"I can't decide about you in my mind." He laughed just as the music got loud again.

The conversation paused, and I watched the gyrating dancers and cheering spectators, all intent on enjoying their alcohol-induced state. I finally saw Kat standing nearby with a scowl on her face. She was probably upset that the rest of us weren't in as festive a mood as she was. She came toward us, and I tried to think up some excuse to head back to the hotel by myself.

"Keeping each other company?" she asked.

Dave stood and pulled out the chair across from us. "We were just talking about work. *Si?*"

"Oh?" Kat pouted and sat down, crossing her ridiculously long legs. "Did our little assistant have some ideas? Maybe we ought to turn things over to her so they'll start going right for a change."

I doubted she was serious and suddenly felt like the brunt of a joke. "Actually, I'm a little tired. I think . . ."

And then everything fell apart as the waitress, who I thought had been maneuvering past Kat with the skill of a speed skater, suddenly lost her balance and went careening toward me. The beauty of the beverages she held diminished as their sticky, ice-cold contents rained over the left side of my body.

I was too stunned to react.

Dave had more presence of mind because he reached for every napkin in sight and mopped up the mess as best he could, but it was running down my arm, off my fingertips, and into my lap. As I stared down at my ruined clothes, the stench of the concoction finally hit me and I jerked my head upward in an attempt to avoid the unfamiliar smells.

As I did, I thought I caught a hint of a grin on Kat's mouth. If it had existed, it quickly vanished. "Oh my goodness. You poor thing." Then, turning, she berated the waitress in English. I hoped the poor girl didn't understand.

"You'd better go to the ladies' room to get cleaned up," Dave said. "I'll help deal with things here."

I stumbled through the chaos until I found the door marked *Damas*. There wasn't a handdryer in the room, so I pilfered the rest of the paper towels in an attempt to at least not feel soaked anymore. But I knew I wouldn't feel clean again until I got back to the hotel. Glancing at myself in the mirror, I groaned. I'd left my purse on the table and couldn't even touch up my make-up, which was now dripping as well. Add to the reflection hair half plastered to the side of my face and a blouse alternating between shades of light and dark purple, I looked a sight. Surely this would be my excuse to head back to the hotel.

Exhausted, I pushed open the door and decided that no matter what, I would tell Kat I was going back. I'd get my own cab and pay for it myself if I had to. When I glanced back at our table, however, I only saw Dave there. I waved some of the haze aside and couldn't see Lin or Mike in the smoke-filled room either. I finally saw Kat behind a nearby pillar. Walking as confidently as I could toward her, I stopped when I realized she was talking on her phone. I almost turned away when I heard the tone of her voice.

"I know I'm not supposed to call you, but don't worry. It won't get back to me." A pause. "I want to know if, after today, you've made up your mind." Another pause. "Yes, I know who's in charge, but I've traveled all this way—"

I bit my lip and started to turn around when she saw me. I felt as if I were in the presence of some Oscar-winning actress because, after lowering the phone and coming toward me, she started to smile sympathetically and guide me back toward the table.

"You really should go back to the hotel." Kat had been holding my purse, and she handed it to me. "Feel free to charge the cab to our business account."

I gave a sigh of relief. "Thanks. Are the rest of you coming with me?"

She cocked her head. "I think I'll have another drink." She looked back toward our table. "And I don't like to drink alone. We'll see you tomorrow."

I watched her hips sway as she walked toward Dave.

How can you compete with that?

I'm not going to, I huffed. I'm going back to the hotel.

The manager approached me on my way out to apologize, and I asked in Spanish how I could get a cab. He showed me the number on a nearby sign, and I reached for my phone, only it wasn't in the usual compartment. After a little searching, I found it wedged between my wallet and a pack of tissues. Strange.

A couple walked through the door just then, and the woman pinched her nose as she walked past me. Sure. Like they weren't going to reek like a distillery in a few hours. Irritated, I tried to scroll the application screen to call mode and instead pulled up the trip's itinerary. Apparently I had massive thumbs that couldn't initiate the correct feature, and it took me another two tries. In the process, I also pulled up the list of last numbers called. I saw my own call home but noticed another posted after it. I compared the number to the taxi sign and realized it had been a local call. I bit my lip and looked around. Then, because my curiosity usually got the better of me, I activated the redial feature.

"¿*Bueno*?" a voice said after a few rings. I said nothing but stood paralyzed by what the voice with the thick Mexican accent said next. "Why do you call again? This is not a game. Do you want to get me killed?"

I quickly hung up, trying to make sense of what I'd heard. The voice on the line had been angry, but I sensed something more: an undercurrent of fear. My taxi arrived, and I slowly got in. Driving back to the hotel gave me time to think. I realized Kat must have used my phone to make a call, and then I'd called that person myself.

Great. So what does it all mean?

I didn't have the slightest idea. But I couldn't escape the nagging thought that said that somewhere I'd heard that voice before.

Chapter 13

BECAUSE I HAD FORGOTTEN TO close the blinds, the morning sun woke me well before my alarm. Still, I felt prepared to face the day because I'd made up my mind right before I fell asleep that there were going to be no more entanglements. I wasn't about to get in the middle of some power struggle Kat had with some strange man, and she was welcome to Dave for all I cared. And as for Seth—continuing to ignore what had happened between us appeared to be the best decision because he hadn't tried anything since then.

I dressed in my usual jeans and a brown T-shirt and quickly styled my hair. There was a knock on the door just as I was finishing up, and I opened it to find Seth standing there. I tried to smile, hoping I hadn't spoken too soon.

"Hey," he said warmly, "I think you must have gotten a little more rest than the others because you're the only one I can get up. Bet a few of them will have a nasty hangover today—you were smart to have kept your drink on the outside!"

I cringed, realizing he must have heard about last night's fiasco. Something about his personality was infectious, however, and it was hard not to forgive him for something he was probably completely unaware that he'd done. So I smiled genuinely this time and silently forgave him.

"I was headed down for a quick breakfast," he said with a grin. "I thought maybe you'd join me."

I glanced at my watch. "Sure, let me just grab my purse."

We were seated on a small veranda outside of the restaurant, where the surrounding trees and walls almost blocked out the commotion and pungent air around us. Seth ordered strong coffee and *huevos rancheros* to go. There was *pan dulce* on the table already—a sweet bread formed into different patterns and dusted with sugar. When the waitress turned to me, I was tempted to order, as many women were inclined to do, something light. But then I remembered pretenses were supposed to be over for me. "I'll have the same, but with extra cheese and no coffee, please. Just a big cup of hot chocolate instead."

"A healthy appetite," Seth said approvingly. "You could start a trend." He took a sip of his coffee and leaned back in his chair, hands behind his head. "So, Sam, tell me what makes you tick."

I wrinkled my brow, partly because he'd started calling me by that nickname and also because I wasn't sure what he meant. "Well, I . . . like to keep busy but enjoy reading and—"

He chuckled. "That's not exactly what I meant. How did you come to work at Phizer-Lewis anyway? It seems a long way for someone as young as you to have come, especially considering it's such a competitive company with few chances for promotion." Then he leaned forward and though he was smiling, I felt as if I were on the other end of an interview. "Nobody at the company seems to know much about you. Do you keep to yourself on purpose? Or are you afraid of anyone getting too close—"

I started to squirm. "Hey," I blurted out, relieved. "Here come Lin and Mike."

They stumbled onto the veranda, not looking too worse for wear, which left me wondering when they'd gotten back last night. I wanted to ask if Kat and Dave had stayed with them the whole night. Seth must have been thinking the same thing but had the guts to ask. "So where's the boss? Did she have too many shots of tequila to join us?"

Lin answered, "I don't know. She didn't come back with us and wasn't in her room this morning when we knocked."

Seth scowled. "Probably already hard at work. She's the type who can survive on four hours of sleep and minimal sustenance. Makes the rest of us seem lazy."

"Could be," Lin said. "Or maybe she headed off with that hunk of a photographer. When I last saw her, she sure had him clutched tight."

I felt a sick feeling in the pit of my stomach. Maybe Kat's advances were too irresistible after all.

You knew this could happen. It's not like he showed any romantic interest in you.

I know. I just didn't think it would sting so much.

The others grabbed their bread and coffee to go, and as we went into the lobby, we saw Kat and Dave. I tried to see if she had the look of a woman in love, but her huge sunglasses kept most of her face covered, so my curiosity wasn't satisfied as we all piled into the van.

At least we were all together as we headed to the outskirts of the city to the little town of Xochimilco. Having forgotten to read up on it after last night's adventure, I took out my travel guide and caught up on how the town was famous for its flowered boats. These "floating gardens" originated back in the twelfth century when the native Aztecs used to plant their crops on the small rafts. Because of the abundance of water and the fertilizing effect of the mud they used to hold the interwoven reeds together, the crops could be harvested up to seven times a year. Now, however, the rafts were more of a tourist attraction, where visitors could sail along on the floating *trajineras* and enjoy a little mariachi music along the way.

I closed the guide and took a deep breath. Floating flowers were just what I needed to push away all of the drama of the last few days.

The little town was delightful. After we passed through the marketplace and survived the numerous vendors shoving their wares in our faces, we boarded the boat *Alejandra*. It was large enough to comfortably seat a dozen people, but we found ourselves alone, and I think just to make sure it stayed that way, Kat ordered me to pay the boatman and tell him to take off. As we propelled down the narrow canal with a long pole, I wondered if the driver ever tipped the boat over. But I quickly realized he knew what he was doing. There was little to do but sit and enjoy the ride. I was sitting next to Seth, and Dave was directly across from me, and though I could feel the warmth of Seth's body next to mine, it was Dave's veiled gaze that had me feeling unbalanced. Something *had* changed since last night. Over and over again in my head I kept repeating the mantra, "Please don't have spent the night with Kat. Please don't . . ."

Diverting my attention to the sights ahead, I watched as another boat came right up against our side. An old woman held up a variety of beaded stone jewelry, calling out in a raspy voice that they were only fifty pesos each. I did some mental calculations and realized that was fewer than three dollars. They were beautiful, and I fingered a purple bracelet I considered would go nicely with my blouse—especially after it was cleaned and pressed. I rifled through my purse and pulled out the appropriate change, only to catch Seth rolling his eyes. But I handed the money to the old woman and claimed my reward anyway.

The strains of music I'd been hearing now grew louder, and a mariachi band pulled up alongside us. We listened for a while and then I noticed that, besides me, only Lin and Dave threw a few coins into the outstretched hat. As the boat with the band drew away, excited voices replaced the music. I looked onshore and saw a wedding party sauntering along the riverside. The bride echoed the theme of our surroundings by having numerous flowers in her hair instead of a veil, and her lace train was being held by a young girl equally bedecked with blossoms. I smiled as I watched them and wished we could pull over so we could follow the procession.

Dave picked up his camera and straddled the center bench. As he \ clicked away, I realized he had noticed the group as well, and that with his attention diverted, I could look at him without him really noticing. A few wisps of hair hung in his eyes, though he was too focused to push them away. I also noticed that the sleeve of his white T-shirt had ridden up on his left arm, and there was a scar—almost like a round, puckered welt. Maybe from a burn? Seth shifted in his seat and, before I knew it, had casually draped his arm over the back of the bench seat. I leaned forward and pretended to tie my shoe as I shifted slightly away.

"Those were some great digitals you sent me last night, *compadre*," Seth said. "I'll be able to do a lot with them."

Dave kept shooting away, not glancing in our direction. "Thanks."

"You must have been up all night," Seth continued.

"Yeah." Dave put his camera down. "I started on them right after we left the club."

With a smug grin on his face, Seth extended his legs over the bench. But he wasn't the only one who was pleased. Now I was left wondering if there was more to Seth and Kat's relationship as well, a real possibility since it appeared she liked her men young. After a few more shots, Dave frowned and walked over to Kat, who had been sitting perched at the front of the boat like the queen of the Nile. I couldn't hear what they were saying, but she was playing the chameleon again, and I didn't know if she was happy or not with what he was asking.

Like magic, my wish was fulfilled, and the boat slowly maneuvered its way over to the edge, where a set of stairs led up to the elevated square. We disembarked, and it wasn't long before Dave had convinced the wedding party to pose for a few shots. He focused on the people, and I realized maybe he had listened to me last night after all. While he worked, I visited with the children who had gathered around me, trying to sell a few packs of *chicle.* I actually quite liked the gum, and at only a couple pesos a pack, I bought a few and talked with the kids for a few minutes. Apparently, they attended a nearby school, but it was a religious holiday, so they had the day off. I grinned, thinking that eight days out of ten around here were some sort of holiday. The kids back home would be jealous. Of course, the school system in general in Mexico was different from what I was used to. Once children reached high school age, they would choose from a variety of upper-division schools that specialized in one particular field, such as law or engineering, and continue their education in a more focused way. Kind of like precollege.

"*¿Uno más?*" A young boy tugged on my sleeve and grinned, anticipating another sale.

"*No. Ya tengo bastante,*" I replied, knowing he'd sell his entire box to me if he could.

Then, as a distraction, I asked if I could take their picture. This elicited some shouts of delight and some amusing poses as I snapped away. Finally, afraid I'd fill up my memory card, I lifted my hands in defeat and put my camera back in its case. Though the children groaned dramatically, it looked like Dave had finished with the wedding scene and we'd probably be moving on soon. As I waited and glanced around, the scene transported me back to some bygone time, where women carried swaddled babies on their backs or walked effortlessly with baskets on their heads. One wrinkled woman sat on the shore embroidering an edge of lace on a traditional dress. There was an ageless expression on her face, and she seemed oblivious to the commotion around her. I wondered what she thought about: her family, her children, if there was more to this life than what she'd been given?

The whines of the children broke me away from my thoughts, and I decided I could at least show them the pictures I'd taken. There was nothing more fascinating to children than to see themselves that way.

"Those are good."

I turned and saw Dave over my shoulder. He held up his own camera, and the children immediately started making silly faces and posing with few inhibitions for the camera while he snapped away; Dave even got me to join in a few of the scenes. We were both laughing, especially after one of the young boys held up his puppy for a picture and ended up with a stained front. I made it a habit to carry packs of tissue in my purse for various necessary purposes, and I handed them to the boy. I turned and caught Dave watching me intently. "So," I gulped, "are these for the campaign?"

He shrugged. "Maybe." After a few more pictures he added, "Perhaps I just want them for myself, to be reminded that there's still something innocent in the world." He replaced the lens cap and walked with his long stride back toward our group.

Back at the hotel, Kat announced she had a meeting with the executives. Her controlled demeanor had started to crack, and I could tell she was anxious about it. At least something was starting to make sense, and I attributed the strange phone call of the previous evening and her catty behavior to the fact that some big wig's assistant must have been giving her a hard time. Seth was right—this was a brutal business.

Since she never implied she wanted me along, I hoped I could have some time to myself and perhaps see some of the city on my own schedule. Though I felt like I was approaching a vicious attack dog, I cornered Kat before she took off. "Would it be all right if I did a little sightseeing on my own while you're at your meeting? Uh, that is . . . unless you need me," I quickly added.

For the first time, Kat didn't try to disguise her feelings. "No, Samantha, we don't need you."

Chapter 14

I SWALLOWED MY EGO AND hailed a cab, thinking I would start farther to the north and then begin walking in a southwesterly direction on the Paseo de la Reforma, the main thoroughfare of the city that was at least six lanes wide, sometimes eight. The lanes were divided by a wide expanse of verdant green, with spreading palms and towering pines—not to mention the flowerbeds. Busts of famous men and statues of leaders rimmed the traffic flow. By the time I'd reached the Glorieta de Cristobol Colón, the Columbus monument by the French sculptor Charles Cordier, I had begun to shrug off Kat's words. Asking the cab driver to drop me off, I stood at the base of the statue where the figures of learned monks who played a leading part in the Spanish settlement of Mexico and its integration with the native people were represented. The entire landmark was surrounded by a huge roundabout.

As I continued walking, I came across the statue of Cuauhtémoc, the last Aztec ruler. Here, the main north-south intersection crossed my path, and I felt like a small ant scurrying along. But the largest and most familiar *glorieta* was up ahead, so I bravely marched on. The Independence Monument, or *El Angel*, was a gilded angel perched atop a tall column. She looked as though at any moment she would take flight. I could tell from the map that I wasn't far from Chapultepec Park, where I was hoping to see the *voladores*.

But mostly, I was hoping to keep busy enough that I couldn't think about how things were falling apart on this trip. I had one man I was trying to avoid, another who didn't seem to know I existed, and a boss who had dubious acquaintances here and seemed to be making it her personal goal to make me feel worthless.

The day was considerably hot again, so I stopped at a nearby cart to buy a soda. I was surprised when, instead of handing me the bottle, the vendor poured the contents into a plastic bag and gave me a straw to drink it with instead. I shrugged and sipped away. When I arrived at the Park, my feet were a little tired, but I was amazed at the sights around me. The area was teeming with tourists and locals out for a casual picnic or breath of relatively fresh air. I breathed deeply myself and enjoyed the vitality around me. The *voladores* were indeed astounding. Five men stood atop a tall wooden pole, probably fifty feet above the ground. The top portion was movable and began to rotate. Then, while one of them danced atop the pole to the sound of a flute, the other four hung suspended by their feet from ropes but continued spinning. They gradually lowered themselves to the ground in a process that took all of ten minutes. I applauded when they were through and even felt like it was worth the few pesos I threw into their nearby tip basket.

I walked around for a while, smiling at the children and families around me. Then I saw a shriveled old man sitting on the ground with a tiny flute, from which echoed a haunting tune. It seemed to have no rhyme or reason to it, and I wondered if the man was sober. *The homeless here are probably like the ones back home,* I thought. *If you give them money, they'll just go spend it on something to drink.* I sighed. How easy it was to judge someone like that without knowing their true story. I drank the last sip of my soda and threw the bag away in a nearby trash receptacle then sat down on a nearby bench and retrieved the small notebook I carried in my purse.

My sketch of the old man was acceptable when it was done. I felt I'd captured his time-worn face, and looking at it, I realized how alone he seemed. Nobody deserved to be alone. I stood and dropped a few coins into the battered sombrero on the pavement. The man gave me a weary smile that I returned.

I had no idea how big the park was until I started down the Gran Avenida, then suddenly it seemed every inch of its nearly two square miles. I could see the magnificent Chapultepec Castle perched on the hill behind me—whose name meant "Hill of the Grasshopper," of all things. I'd wanted to see it up close, but the line for the tram lift was much too long. Besides, there were plenty of other sights to see. Ahead of me was supposed to be a large man-made lake, a zoo, and botanical gardens. I glanced at my watch, not sure how much I would really be able to see in an afternoon. Maybe we'd all return together and spend the good part of a day. I heard some music up ahead and saw that down a pathway to my left there appeared to be some sort of celebration. Curious, I followed the noise and came upon a group of *folklorico* dancers who were doing an exhibition for the surrounding spectators. I watched for a minute as they spun in their brightly colored costumes, tracing out the steps that had been passed down from their parents and their grandparents.

I quickly found myself pinned in by the ever-increasing crowd and realized I'd better make my escape. As I pushed my way through the sea of dark heads, I saw a figure in the distance that caught my attention. It was a man, and though he was too far away for me to say for sure, I could have sworn it was Dave.

I pushed more determinedly past the crowd, sidestepping bicycles and small children that scattered around my feet.

"Dave!" I shouted. "*Dave!*"

He didn't stop, and I eventually lost sight of him. I guess he'd decided to go sightseeing as well, though I still wasn't positive it was him. The streets surrounding the park contained a plethora of shops, boutiques, and restaurants. Worn out, I wondered if I should just head back toward the hotel. A carnival of Spanish whirled around my head, adding to my feeling of imbalance. Though quite capable of interpreting the conversations of a few, the cacophony of voices around me was a little daunting. Plus, all the walking I'd done combined with a lack of food was zapping my resolve.

I finally saw something that gave me a little hope. On the outskirts of the park was a small kiosk with smoke rising from it. Walking closer, I saw it was a cart selling *tacos al carbon*. They had the Mexican equivalent of two giant woks. One was for cooking up the tortillas, the other for different kinds of meat. I knew it was kind of like playing Russian roulette because there probably wasn't a health department monitoring these things, but the smell of sizzling steak and the aroma of freshly made corn tortillas made it irresistible.

I ordered two tacos, and the woman behind the counter rolled out a couple small dough balls and flattened them in a metal press. Then she placed them in varying positions around the outer rim of the fire-heated cauldron. She laid a concoction of meat in the browned tortillas and then offered me a choice of freshly prepared salsa and limes to season them. This was probably going to be the part that gave me a nasty case of Moctezuma's revenge, but I went for it, choosing the green tomatillo variety, which was usually milder. I took my first bite and groaned for sheer delight. I polished them both off pretty quickly.

Now I was ready to do a little shopping for some presents with the precious time I had left.

I had learned in my reading that each region of Mexico had a reputation for its artistry. When the Spanish clergy had arrived, they thought they had stumbled upon a heathen and uncivilized culture with little redeeming value, so they had trained the people to work with their hands. The traditions continued and were represented in a small part by the items I saw around me: woven baskets, bright-colored dresses, silver jewelry . . . and pottery. I stopped by a table covered with painted clay figures in a bright array of colors. A display of the nativity caught my eye, and I looked at it longingly. They were almost abstract in nature, but the simplicity of the Virgin Mary, Joseph, and Jesus figurines were very touching. It was quite pricey, however, and I figured I could probably find it for half the price in the actual village where it was made. I decided on a small wooden chess set for my dad, with figures carved based upon the *Man of La Mancha* story. There was a beautiful painted plate close by that I wanted for my mom.

Then I glanced up at the wall where some delicate handmade shawls hung. There was a white gossamer one—it reminded me so much of one my grandmother used to wear. I asked the salesclerk to take it down and draped it gently across my shoulders.

"*¿Hay un espejo aquí?*" I asked.

She directed me toward a back dressing room, and I sighed when I saw myself in the mirror. It was beautiful, and I felt tears come to my eyes as I thought of my family. Then I saw the price tag and nearly choked. But as the commercials on TV said, wasn't I worth it? It could be the only real souvenir I brought home with me, other than a few bruises on my ego. The store accepted my new credit card and even wrapped the shawl in decorative paper. I smiled with approval and had just left the store when I saw him again at the end of the street.

And this time I *knew* it was Dave.

Walking as fast as my throbbing feet would let me, I realized he was talking on the phone to someone. He was gesturing frantically with his other hand, which he then pressed to his forehead as if exasperated. I was near enough that I could hear him talking, so I started to call out his name, but he was already shouting none-too-politely for a cab. One immediately pulled over, and I stood watching through the crowd as he drove away.

When it was gone from sight, I found I couldn't move. But it wasn't Dave's improper language that left me stunned. I was still trying to grasp the fact that he had just had an entire conversation with a perfect American accent.

Chapter 15

ANOTHER CAB TOOK ME BACK to the hotel. As I rode the elevator up to my room, I felt uneasy. Maybe my overworked senses had fooled me. There was no reason for Dave to lie about something so basic—unless he had a reason. Opening the door to my room, I removed the DO NOT DISTURB sign, which I'd pretty much kept up since my arrival. When I stayed in hotels, I never liked the thought of some middle-aged woman working for slave wages coming in to clean up my messes and make my bed, so I kept my room off limits for as long as I could stand it, but I was due for a few new towels and toiletries.

Wanting to collapse on my bed, I instead carefully packed my new purchase in my suitcase, pushing it back under the bed when I was done. Then I did inventory on my purse, realizing my phone had gone dead at some point during the day. The thought that someone had tried to reach me gave me a moment of panic. So instead of a quick siesta, I freshened up and went to Kat's room to see if she was back.

I was halfway down the hall when I heard the screeching voice. Apparently someone was not in a good mood.

"Samantha!" Kat bellowed as she saw me in the open doorway.

You're really going to get it this time.

Oh, go away! Hey, where have you been all day?

"Finally! I've been calling you for hours."

I gulped as Kat unleashed her anger on me.

"Some of us came down here to work, you know. If you can see fit to take time from your own *busy* calendar, perhaps you'd like to help."

Oh great. How was I to know that today they'd *finally* need me?

Seth, Lin, and Mike were also in the room, and my face flushed as I felt duly chastised. They had indeed needed my help, so I spent the next hour revising some of the Spanish phrases in the graphics layout Seth had been working on to bring across the correct impression. I supposed Dave would have helped if he'd been around, but we never saw him. And after today, I wasn't sure what I'd say when I did see him again. At least Seth had the decency to thank me when we were done, and I was so grateful for a friend that I even ignored his hand that rested on my back most of the time we worked. As I left the room, I felt someone come up behind me. But I wasn't ready to face him yet, so I quickened my stride.

"Hey, slow down!" It was just Lin. I turned and smiled, comfortable that at least I was meeting a friendly face. "Kat was furious when she couldn't find you, but I suspect it was her meeting that upset her, not you. Where were you anyway?"

I shrugged. "I went to Chapultepec Park and then did some shopping." I was tempted to tell her about Dave, to get her opinion about his sudden lingual prowess, but changed my mind. What business was it of mine anyway? "I promise I won't take off like that again. I really did come here to work, and I'm sorry if I let you guys down."

Lin stood silently for a moment. Then, after glancing back at Kat's room, she took me by the arm and led me farther down the hall. "I like you, but I'm only going to say this once. Be careful what you get yourself into because you may not be able to get out."

I groaned. Lin must have misinterpreted Seth's friendliness and worried that I would be getting into hot water with Kat again. "Yes, ma'am." I saluted. Then more seriously I said, "Thank you for the advice. I really appreciate having you on my side."

* * *

By Saturday, I was having a hard time believing I'd only been in Mexico for six days. It seemed much longer. It made me wonder how I was going to survive another week.

Maybe you're not cut out for this business.

My annoying inner voice had returned full force that morning and was wreaking havoc on my attempt to put the bizarre circumstances of the past few days aside. So what did I care if the handsome photographer Phizer-Lewis had hired had been faking a Spanish accent? Maybe it was a hit with all of the *gringas* from America. I know I fell for it. What was it to me if our team leader was a professional flirt and made unexplained phone calls to mysterious men who spoke with threatening undertones?

This was my chance to work at my dream job, and I wasn't going to blow it.

Sometimes dreams turn into nightmares.

Enough, I scowled, ignoring the warning.

I was the first one down in the lobby that morning and repeated my mantra that I was going to mind my own business while I waited for the others to arrive. We loaded up in the van and headed toward the Southern District to see the church of San Juan Bautista along with several museums.

Seth rolled his eyes when he found out the plan. "Great. More churches."

I said nothing, accepting the fact that I was only along for the ride. Actually, the day ended up being pretty interesting. After the church, which was typical of the period and had the most beautifully carved doorway, we made our way to the neighborhood of Coyoacán. I felt like I had stepped back in time as I looked at the many Colonial-style mansions, cobblestone streets, and airy plazas. Our first stop was the Frido Kahlo museum, or the Blue House. To be honest, the only thing I knew her for was her trademark unibrow and felt kind of guilty as the tour guide led us around what seemed to him to be some sort of inner sanctum. He took us through the house she'd shared with Diego Rivera from 1929 until her death. Aside from many personal mementos, there were pictures and sculptures as well as an impressive assortment of pre-Columbian objects and folk art from her personal collection. You could tell the pride she had in her people. Her own work also manifested this sentiment: from the clean lines of young girls kneeling by sheaves of flowers—their hair braided in the traditional indigenous way—to her own honest self-portraits, there was a simplicity and yet sense of honor that exuded from the canvases.

It was also fascinating to know that the Russian revolutionary, Leon Trotsky, had also inhabited this neighborhood for some time after his exile from Russia. We next visited his home, where on the walls of his austere bedroom still remained the bullet holes of an earlier attack by the Stalinists. A plaque by the front door commemorated the revolutionary's bodyguard who was shot in the attack. I noticed Dave paid particular interest to it, as if he somehow had a personal attachment to it. Feeling as if I were intruding, I went around the corner, only to interrupt Kat in another phone call, where she was apparently trying to get some samples of something for our campaign.

I quietly backed away.

When Kat ended her call, she barked that we were leaving. Loading into the van, we only stopped a moment at the bizarre mushroomlike Polyforum Cultural Siqueiros, a twelve-sided building constructed by the famous muralist José David Alfaro Siqueiros. (I bet that was a mouthful for him as a young boy.) Nearby was the Ciudad de los Deportes, a large sports stadium that accommodated more than sixty-five thousand spectators, and the Plaza México, the largest building in the world, with more than sixty thousand conference seats. And I thought the Conference Center in Salt Lake, with a capacity of more than twenty-one thousand people, was impressive.

I thought we were headed back to the hotel until Kat suggested we stop at the nearby Ciudadela, a large open market where all sorts of local goods were sold. "The guide at the museum told me you'll get the best prices here, and I really want some souvenirs before we head home."

I wondered if everyone was as surprised as I was at this suggestion from none other than our workaholic boss, but everyone seemed glad for the break. We explored the nearly full block of open stalls. There was the usual Talavera pottery I'd admired earlier, and it was more reasonably priced. But I couldn't figure out where I'd store it on the flight home, so I walked on. I admired the leatherwork and tile-framed mirrors, the rugs, and even the kitschy sombreros and paper-mâché skeletons. But I managed to keep my wallet tucked away and wandered aimlessly until I saw a young boy, about eleven or twelve, standing behind one of the kiosks. He kept staring at me like he was expecting me to come over. I looked behind me, certain he was gesturing to someone else, and then went over to him even though I was still confused about what he wanted. As I got closer, I realized he was probably a few years older than I'd thought.

"*¿Te puedo ayudar?*" I asked, thinking he needed help.

He cocked his head and gave me a confident smile. Then he reached in his pocket and pulled out a plastic bag, its contents resembling an herbal tea packet. I stared bewildered for a moment and then realized what it was. I shook my head furiously and, disgusted, walked away.

Geez. Did I have *pothead* written across my forehead or something?

Starting to sound like my inner voice, I stopped to look at some of the pottery at a kiosk, glad the boy had disappeared from sight. After a few minutes, I saw Dave coming toward me with his confident stride, which made my knees feel wobbly.

"Not interested in anything?"

I shook my head. "There's some great stuff though. What about you? Don't you need a few souvenirs from this trip . . . maybe a present for someone?"

Why don't you just ask him if he's got a girlfriend?

He shrugged, but his eyes were serious as he looked at me. "No. That's not what I'm here for."

I guess his remark explained some of his on-again, off-again friendliness to me. Maybe he had a hard time keeping his professional edge when there were "distractions" all around him, as Kat had put it. But it wasn't as if I'd thrown myself at him—unlike some people—so the cold look I had seen in his eyes from time to time was unwarranted in my opinion.

Somehow we found ourselves walking away from the shops together, and the dissonance of a dozen conversations was now joined by the sounds of voices in harmony. In a nearby park, a group of mariachi players were strumming in harmony, and a singer was doing his Placido Domingo imitation of "Cielito Lindo." I stood there listening, enjoying the flavor of the music, when the couples around us started to dance. Before I knew it, a short, pudgy man had grabbed me by the hand and was trying to pull me into the fray.

"Oh no!" I shouted in Spanish above the noise. "I don't know this dance."

"*Está bien. Venga. Te muestro.*"

I let the stranger lead me in a simple waltz step that had been adapted to the faster-paced rhythm. He twirled me around, and I lost my inhibitions and laughed in delight. The song changed, and I was giddy as we worked through the crowd, hindered only slightly by my unskilled movements. A few times our steps clashed, and I tried to apologize between breaths. But he didn't seem to mind. When the song ended, he gave me a courtly bow and was gone.

I found Dave again and groaned at the thought of him watching. "Yikes, I bet I was awful. I probably stepped on the poor guy's feet about ten times."

He gave me a slight grin. "You weren't so bad."

Another song started, and we were suddenly surrounded by dancers. Feeling foolish, I worked my way through the twirling crowd until I felt someone take my hand. I only hesitated a moment and then let Dave lead me into the throng of dancers. As he twirled me around, I lost some of my inhibitions again and stopped wondering what it all meant, even though a part of me knew that getting too close would mean vulnerability . . . and that meant I could get hurt.

Dave's arms were strong as he guided me, and I could feel his muscles beneath the hand I had on his shoulder. Then the tempo of the song suddenly changed. I found myself growing giddy as his hand still clasped mine tightly and we worked through the crowd. A few times our feet collided, and once again I found myself stomping on my partner's feet and having to tighten my grip on him to prevent a fall. Our bodies sometimes were so close I could feel the rise and fall of his chest as he breathed. I was dizzy, excited, and scared all at the same time because part of me knew I was falling for this man I wasn't sure I could trust.

The dance ended, and the spell that wove around us was broken, but I no longer had to wonder if Dave had felt something too. The emotions in his eyes as we danced had finally betrayed him, and I thought I finally caught a glimpse of his true feelings as he let his guard down.

"That was fun. Thank you." I smiled timidly. "Can you still walk?"

He tilted his head and grinned. "I think I'll manage." When he quieted, I wondered if I'd said something wrong, but then he continued. "My younger sister was always making me practice with her. I remember one time, my feet were so sore from being stomped on by her high heels that I couldn't play soccer for days." He chuckled at the memory.

Soccer? Doesn't he mean football?

So he Americanized it. Big deal.

Between the exertion of the dancing and the way he was gazing at me, I felt flushed. "There's such an atmosphere of joviality here," I mused. "Some of these people look like they were coming or going to work, and yet they stopped to dance with strangers in a park."

Dave nodded. "You're right. There's a different mentality here versus that in the States. A need to enjoy the here and now without thinking too much beyond that. I suppose that can be a good and bad thing."

I supposed he was right. But there was nothing harmful, I thought, about what was happening here. Then I heard Terri's words echo in my head. "You ought to loosen up, Sam; have some fun once in a while." Oh, she would love hearing that she had been right. I must have chuckled because he asked me if something was funny. I told him I was just remembering something a friend had told me.

In a moment of boldness, I decided it was time to find out more about him. "You seemed to know the dance so well. Is it a favorite in the state you grew up in? I don't think you ever told me where that is."

He sucked in a quick breath and didn't explain but instead quickly said, "We should go back. They're probably looking for us."

We found the group, and I had to laugh when I saw the large wooden statue Seth had bought. It must have been hollow or he wouldn't have been able to carry it like that. Lin was showing off the beautiful silk scarf she'd come across. Wanting to be friendly, I asked Kat if she'd found anything she liked.

She smiled slyly. "The selection was a little scarce, but I came across a few things that interested me."

"Well," Seth boomed in a voice that was a little irreverent for the tone of the place, "I'm ready for some grub. Are y'all with me?"

I had to admit I was famished. I asked one of the vendors for a suggestion and was told we should go to the north end of the market where there was a group of restaurants in and around the square. We decided on one that was a little less posh than the ones we'd frequented the last few days since Kat was more inclined to have us patronize the fancy shops and restaurants in the Polanco district—the Beverly Hills of Mexico—whenever possible. But in my opinion, these family-owned establishments were where you could find the more authentic food. We found tables and sat down, menus in hand, until we were ready to order. I noticed Kat handled her tri-fold menu like it was unsanitary and, after I returned from a quick side trip, knew the restrooms would send her into anaphylactic shock. Dave must have been thinking the same thing because when I caught his eye, he gave me an amused grin.

Feeling adventurous, especially after the day before, I ordered chicken taquitos with guacamole. Seth raised an eyebrow, and I knew he was worried about my eating too much fresh produce. It wasn't the fruit or vegetable that was the problem, however; it was the water they might wash it in. But I'd survived so far and probably had a cast-iron stomach like my dad.

The guacamole was pure heaven—smooth-textured and cool, with just enough seasoning that you could still taste its earthy goodness. Even Seth seemed a little jealous. Kat was picking at her usual salad and had mellowed a little since that morning. I was glad, though, that I wasn't that uptight about keeping on schedule.

As we loading up our things in the van one last time, my stomach let out a monstrous rumble. Embarrassed, I was glad the noise of the traffic had drowned it out. As we drove along, though, it did it again. As my suspicions grew, I prayed for a quick arrival at the hotel, but we crept along at a snail's pace the remaining few miles, and time seemed to stand still as we finally spilled out of the van and filtered toward our respective rooms. I said a quick prayer in the elevator and had no sooner opened my door than my insides lurched as if there were an intestinal tug-of-war commencing.

Uh oh.

I rushed to the bathroom.

Looking slightly pale as I gazed at my reflection in the mirror a few minutes later, I suddenly regretted my daring behavior. Apparently, Moctezuma had not conquered his last victim.

Chapter 16

I wanted to die.

But I *needed* to act as if nothing were wrong so I could handle work if someone called on me. Ignoring my Girl Scout training, I was in no mood to tough it out and hoped there was a drugstore nearby where I could find some appropriate medicine to calm things down. A little wary, I realized there were probably substances I could find over-the-counter here that I couldn't get back in the States. Hopefully Pepto Bismol was part of some universal language. Praying another attack wasn't imminent, I grabbed my purse, but before my hand could even touch the doorknob, a knock startled me. I opened the door and saw Dave.

I couldn't think what to say, a result of both seeing him there and the sudden churning of my stomach again. Finally, I blurted out, "Is there something you . . . does the group need me to help with something?"

He stared down at the purse in my hand. "Are you going somewhere?"

I blushed. "Uh . . . well, I just needed to buy something." As I stood there waiting for him to talk, my discomfort increased until I felt myself breaking out into a cold sweat. Oh boy. Twitching nervously from side to side, all I could think about was getting rid of him. "Do you want to come in for a minute? I'm kind of in a hurry though."

Looking confused, he held out what he'd been hiding behind his back. "I thought you might want to see these. I just developed them, and I thought they were pretty good."

I took the folder from him and felt the spark again. Nervously I opened it and saw the pictures he'd taken of me with the children. There was the little boy who'd asked for a kiss on the cheek and the girl who'd shyly fingered the bracelet I'd been wearing. "They're wonderful," I exclaimed. "I like that you kept them in black and white—they look old, like the city around us."

"Well, they're yours. I can always make another set. I liked . . . I liked what I saw. But then again, sometimes we only see what we want to in them."

There was a look of hurt in his eyes, but it made no sense that I was the cause of it. Perhaps something was going on in his personal life: a "dear John" letter from a girlfriend or news of an ill family member. This man was a complex bundle of emotions, I realized. I also realized the door had closed behind him, and we were standing alone in the room. It was quiet enough that I could hear our breathing, and when he started to walk slowly toward me, holding my eyes fast with his, I waited anxiously to see what would happen next.

As usual, my life never played out the way I wanted it to. A cramp gripped my stomach, and I had to quickly excuse myself and rush to the bathroom as my inner voice laughed.

Just like a scene out of a romantic movie!

I would have returned the taunt if I hadn't been doubled over in pain. A few minutes later, when I could tolerate standing again, I came back out to find Dave gone.

Right person, wrong time?

"Wrong person, wrong time," I answered myself, sadly picking up the pictures he'd placed on the nightstand and glancing at them once more before grabbing my purse and trying to depart again. I didn't feel the need to tell everyone I was leaving since I was going to hurry as fast as I could. But luck didn't seem to be on my side because I reached the elevator doors just as they were closing. I glanced at the nearby stairway. We were only four flights up, and I could probably beat it since it was all downhill.

I was right. I arrived in the lobby just as the elevator doors swung open and a blonde woman stormed out. I realized Kat had been its occupant. I watched her retreating figure heading toward the revolving doors, her hair glistening like a golden waterfall down the back of a navy blue silk shirt. Shrugging, I asked the front desk clerk where the nearest pharmacy was. He told me in heavily accented English that it was less than two blocks away, so I scurried out the doors as well.

The pharmacy technician assured me that the little box of white pills he'd given me contained nothing that couldn't be sold back home. But he warned me that they were to be used sparingly and that it was better to get the toxins out of my system as quickly as possible. Well, I could accept that happening through the night, but traipsing around another landmark tomorrow with possibly no facilities in sight would be another story.

It had only taken me twenty minutes to run my errand, and I was sure Kat couldn't have missed me in that brief time, especially since she had gone off somewhere herself. This time, I let the elevator do all the work but still arrived exhausted back at my room.

"Samantha!"

I turned and smiled wearily as Lin came toward me. Clutching my tiny bag as another cramp left me speechless, I started to wonder if it really was better to let nature run its course. "Hi," I managed to squeak.

"Do you have a minute to talk?" she asked.

Not wanting to be rude, but knowing I really just needed to lie down, I asked, "Actually, can it wait?"

She stared at me through narrow eyes. "Sure. Maybe at dinner."

Food? I wasn't sure I'd ever be able to eat again. "I'm not going to go down to dinner tonight. How about first thing in the morning?" I panted.

She nodded her agreement and turned around. I whipped the door open and prayed that for the rest of the evening, this would be the last interruption.

* * *

By midnight, I had faith that I would live. Only I hadn't thought to get any bottled water from the drugstore, and I could tell I was getting dehydrated. Glancing down at my green pajamas with monkey faces that I had thought cute when I'd bought them, I realized that at this hour, I'd have to settle for a vending machine. Tiptoeing down the hall—which was absurd considering it was carpeted and I had bare feet—I finally found a machine around the corner of the next hall over. Inserting some coins, I listened as the *thud* of the bottle echoed down the corridor. I quickly purchased another and hoped no one would come investigate the strange noise. But it was deathly quiet, and I tiptoed from the vending machine, feeling confident I would make it back undetected.

I spoke too soon. Almost back to my own hall, I heard voices. Lin and Dave were coming down the corridor toward me. Panicking, I realized they hadn't seen me, and as I looked around for a means of escape, I finally settled on hiding behind the ice machine. I prayed they weren't coming to use the other set of stairs that were directly across from me. Their voices were muted at first, becoming clearer as they neared.

"I think you're on to something," Lin was saying. "She seemed agitated to me as well."

Dave's voice reverberated in a whisper. "Classic signs, huh. Too bad. I wanted to believe my first instinct."

"Yeah, well, look where that got you before." There was some muffled noise. "Don't deny it, I saw you coming out of her room. You'd think you would have learned your lesson."

"Nothing happened," Dave snapped, his voice raised. "Besides, I'm still not convinced."

Lin shushed him but not to where I still couldn't hear. "It doesn't matter, anyway. She's still small stuff. You know what you're supposed to be doing."

I could almost picture the irritated look on Dave's face as he said, "Hey, you do your job, and let me do mine. I'm not going to jeopardize anything."

I heard the sound of muffled footsteps moving away from me and was about to come out from my hiding place when Lin's voice sounded within feet from me. "You'd better not. I've invested too much in this already." I jumped back, my heart skipping a beat as my colleague stormed unknowingly past me and through the door leading to the stairwell.

As my heartbeat returned to normal, I tried to come to terms with the fact that Dave—and now Lin—were definitely hiding something. There hadn't been a single trace of any accent other than pure American speech in that conversation. Setting that fact aside, I tried to decipher their conversation. Had they been talking about Dave and Kat? Or did this have something to do with me? Lin had given the impression she'd only just met Dave, so why would she care if he got close to me? Or was someone else pulling the strings here? I knew Kat had a thing for Dave—had they hatched some scheme where he would lead me on and then dump me to prove her point that he'd never choose someone like me over her?

Of course, this all could have to do with work. Perhaps Lin had gotten Dave the job, and for some reason they wanted everyone to think he was a native. Maybe they were laughing over the fact that Kat had been so easily fooled.

Do you really believe it's as harmless as that?

I felt my fists clench. What kind of game were they all playing? Because I definitely felt like there was some kind of game going on—only, I didn't know what the rules were.

Chapter 17

THE NEXT DAY I ONLY felt half dead. Seth started teasing me that I must have been out all night clubbing, but when I cast him a dirty look, he raised his hands and backed off. "I think I ended up eating something that didn't agree with me yesterday," I explained in a low voice.

He grinned. "I tried to warn you." When I grimaced in return, he said a little more sympathetically, "Are you sure you're up to a full day? You know, I could talk with Kat, try to get you some time off."

I bit my lip, tempted. After all, it was Sunday and I could use a day of rest. But what good would that accomplish? That would only leave Kat alone with Dave. Plus, if I was here to make a good impression, I needed to be *with* the group to make it happen. But as my stomach rumbled in protest, I imagined being jostled around in the van as we made our way to our next destination. "Maybe that would be a good idea. I could use a little while longer to feel myself again."

He tipped his imaginary hat. "Shucks, ma'am. I'm here to serve."

I watched as he went over to confront Kat. She didn't seem too pleased at first, but I could swear Seth looked at me and mouthed the words, "She's harmless." After that, my boss nodded her head and Seth walked back over to me.

"All set. There are some files that need to be organized along with some stat sheets she wants copied and bound. Think you could handle that?" I nodded vigorously. "Here's an extra keycard to Kat's room. You'll find the forms on the side desk in the second drawer down." He explained briefly what they needed them for so I'd know how many copies to make and the quality level to aim for.

"Thanks. I owe you one."

"Don't think I won't hold you to that." He winked, ambling off toward the others.

I managed to get some toast and juice down for breakfast and then took the elevator to our rooms. I had to admit, it was strange being in Kat's room alone. Everything was neatly organized, not a pillow out of place. My own tendency toward organization often masked an even bigger lack of confidence, and I wondered if my boss was ever insecure about anything. Realizing I'd been standing in the middle of the room for a few minutes, I hurried and opened the drawer, found the papers I needed, and left.

The desk clerk—who was starting to get a *little* friendly—informed me of a nearby office supply store. I walked the few blocks and began making copies. I'd decided that the first page would stand out more and would set the tone for the remainder of the presentation if it were in color. I also felt like I'd done a good job of determining in what order to place the pages, starting with the market research, which I immediately followed with the net reach calculations because the ROI potential was incredible. I saved the budget analysis for last. It was a good advertising rule of thumb to sell your idea first before telling them what they'll have to pay.

Pleased with the results and hoping Kat would feel that way too, I walked back to the hotel and saw that the front desk clerk was leaning against the side wall smoking. He smiled at me. I hurried inside, as much to avoid the smoke as the admiring look on his face. Maybe he was reading too much into all the conversations we'd had.

By noon, I had the rest of the filing done and decided to break for lunch. After a quick bite to eat down in one of the hotel's smaller, though still expensive restaurants, I was at a loss for what to do next. There were nothing but game shows and *telenovelas* on the TV, and I hadn't thought to buy a book just to read—I'd supposed I would be too busy. Staring around my room, I made the decision to send out for maid service again. My "distress" had all but used up the remaining toilet paper.

But now that my stomach cramps had stopped, I realized it might show initiative if I called the group and asked if I could arrange to join them. I was feeling like a pro now as I made the call—I'd even figured out how to activate a few other applications and found out the device had GPS capabilities. Kat finally picked up on the fifth ring.

"*What?*" she snapped.

"Uh, it's me, Samantha," I stammered. "I have the presentations completed and am feeling much better, so I thought maybe I could call a cab and come join you."

I could hear her yelling instructions at someone before she answered. "No, don't bother."

Undaunted, I struggled to think like a personal assistant. "All right then. Is there anything I can have ready and waiting for you when you return? Uh . . . maybe another massage scheduled?"

She paused. "That won't be necessary. You know, I think Dave is doing some of his finest work today—it must be the lack of distractions. Well, don't wait up. It could be a long night for some of us."

I felt sick again as I hung up the phone.

Walking over to the window, I almost had to laugh at my situation. Here I was, staring out at a vibrant city, and all I could do was feel sorry for myself and mope.

Ready to pack it up and go home at last?

Not on your life, I decided as I pushed away from the window.

Trying to stay optimistic, I decided to call home again. When my mom came on the line, she seemed more than a thousand miles away, and I felt a tug at my heart. "Home" was becoming like an echo that was slowly fading, and I desperately clung to every word. But even I was not so caught up in my own situation that I didn't realize there was something wrong in Mom's voice.

I let her talk of trivial things for a few minutes then reversed the roles and asked her what was going on. She dismissed it at first, saying that she and Dad had only been busy. I wasn't convinced. When she finally let it out, I almost wished I hadn't been so nosy.

"Samantha, sweetheart. We didn't want to worry you, especially considering you still have a week left there. But your father had some tests done this past week."

"Tests?" I said in my little child voice. "What tests?"

"Do you remember that benign polyp he had removed from his colon last summer?" I remembered. "Well, they found more during his annual checkup, and this time, the doctor isn't so sure they're harmless."

My hand started to shake a little bit. "What does this mean, Mom? Where's Dad?"

I could almost feel her reaching through the phone to give me a hug. "He's just resting. Don't worry, Samantha. I'm sure everything will be fine. He's been on top of things, so even if it is the worst, it won't have progressed too far. If the tests come back positive, they'll want to do a more extensive laparoscopic search, and just to be ready, he's scheduled to go into the hospital this Friday."

When I didn't respond immediately, my mom tried to reassure me one more time, and I tried to let her strength buoy me up. Suddenly all that talk of faith and trust in a higher power seemed impossible. Would my dad be all right simply because I wanted him to? I knew better than that. I understood the uncertainty of life and that sometimes bad things happened to good people—but he was my dad.

"I wish there were something I could do," I said weakly.

"Everything you could do here, you can do there."

Again, she was right. There were no parameters set on prayers, and my love was not diminished by distance. I told her to hug Dad for me and said good-bye. But flopping down on the side of my bed, I still wanted to do something more. My dad needed to know everything he meant to me, something more tangible than the memory of my voice saying I loved him.

I fumbled around in the nightstand drawer until I found the hotel stationery. I found a matching pen nearby and poured out my heart to my dad. I wrote about the tree house we'd made when I was just seven years old and how he'd let me paint it purple because that was my favorite color. Then about the time I'd broken my arm and he'd sat up with me all night because the pain had made it difficult to sleep. And how could I forget my first dance and how grateful I was when he didn't embarrass me too much when my date—I think his name was Mark?—came to the door with a huge corsage and two left feet.

My tears started to flow, and I could barely see to finish and sign my name. Grabbing for some tissue, I folded the letter and went downstairs to the lobby to see if I could get an envelope and postage enough to mail it home. They had everything I needed at the desk, and just for fun, I addressed it *c/o the Big Boss* and handed it to the clerk, who had progressed to winking at me. He took it and placed it under the counter as if to say, "I knew you couldn't stay away!"

Then I had the best idea I'd had all day. When I asked if he could call a cab with a driver who knew where the LDS temple was, I wasn't surprised by the blank look. I rephrased it as "*el templo Mormón.*" He still shrugged but relayed the message to the cab company. When the green bug arrived about ten minutes later, I hoped I wouldn't be taken on a two-hour-long scenic drive around the city until we found it.

I was in luck. The driver knew right where it was, and it only took us about ten minutes of navigating through monstrous traffic and blind alleyways before we arrived. Fortunately, we had decided on an amount before we'd left, and I paid the driver the price agreed upon and stepped out to the curb.

Of all the temples I'd visited, this one impressed me as one of the most unique. It seemed to have grown up from the ground around it instead of being constructed by modern machinery. The adaptations of Mayan designs imprinted upon its white-cast stone made me feel as if I were walking toward another ancient pyramid. But this one had been designed to save lives, not take them. The temple itself was closed on Sundays, but the visitor's center was open, and it pulled me back into the present with its modern architecture. Walking under the building's stone portico, I was immediately overcome with a feeling of peace.

A familiar white *Christus* statue graced the foyer, and I imagined that I was in Salt Lake for a moment. The rest of the facility was also familiar: from the touch computer screens and their messages on families and temples to the photographic display that allowed the visitors to see what some of the rooms of the temple were like. I had grown up in the Church but suddenly wondered what someone seeing this for the first time would think. Then a thought occurred to me, and I stopped by the information desk to ask the worker if he had copies of the Book of Mormon in English for sale. He nodded but told me they were free of charge. I started to tell him I was a member and would happily pay for them, but he waved my protest away.

"No, sister. Whatever you need it for, it will have served its purpose."

I thanked him and started to walk away when I was greeted by a senior sister missionary.

"Welcome! I couldn't help but notice your interest in our facility. I'm Sister Remington," she said warmly. Her white hair curled just above her ears, and I thought she had a pixielike look about her. I introduced myself, and she clasped her hands together. "Oh, you're American! Where are you from?"

I told her then explained, "It's just north of Salt Lake City."

Her eyes widened as she told me she lived a short distance from there. I felt my throat clamp as I realized that, compared to the size of the world, we were as good as neighbors. It was almost as comforting as reuniting with a long-lost family member. She must have sensed this as well, because she led me over to a nearby bench in front of the *Christus* statue.

"Homesick?" she asked, patting my hand.

I nodded, too choked up to speak.

"Are you here on a trip or with a group of students? You look so young to be away from home."

I wiped a small tear away. "Actually, I'm on a business trip." I briefly told her about our group and why we were here. Sensing she was interested, I talked about some of the places we'd been this past week.

"Even though I've been here for nearly a year," Sister Remington said, "I think you've seen more things than I have! The calling keeps my husband and me busy, but we love it."

"Is this your first mission?"

"Our second, actually. But the first was stateside in Nauvoo, so coming to another country was quite daring for us."

I sighed. "I felt the same way about coming on this trip. It can be . . . scary to leave everything that's familiar to you."

"Especially when the world can be such an inhospitable place."

Her words reached down and found the frustration I'd been feeling. Suddenly I felt as if I were sitting at my grandmother's side, listening as she gave me advice. For the first time all week, I truly felt as if I could trust someone. "Sister—" I began. Then I hesitated. But with a little urging from her, my concerns started to pour out. I described Kat to her and the increasingly hostile way she was treating me. I even found myself talking about Dave and the roller coaster of emotions I'd felt between us but how I wasn't sure I could trust him. And I mentioned my dad's health issues. She smiled, obviously having known something of those types of feelings.

"I just wish I didn't feel so alone here."

Sister Remington patted my hand then pointed to the nearby statue. "I'm sure you've seen that many times living so close to Salt Lake. And now here you are, thousands of miles from home . . . and there *He* is. Sometimes you just have to let go of your fears and trust in that. And," she spread her gaze to cover the room, "everyone here is your friend, ready to serve and help you if you need it. Think of this as your home, Samantha, if only for a little while. And consider *us* your family."

I glanced up at the statue, the eyes that seemed to search for me and the arms that stretched out to me. Sister Remington was right. No matter where I was, I could always find a piece of home.

Arriving back at the hotel in time for a late dinner, I was surprised to see Mike sitting in the lobby reading an English-speaking newspaper. I waved to him and got a solemn nod in return. I had figured the rest of the group had returned as well but discovered that only Lin was in her room. Since I was beyond wanting to ask where Dave and Kat were and was glad Seth was also absent, I went straight to my room.

The door hanger for maid service had been moved, and I realized someone must have come while I was gone. The garbage had been dumped, but I was certain the towels weren't new. It looked like they had just been hung back on the rack. Gross. And even though the bed was made, the corner of my suitcase was sticking out from underneath it. With a scowl, I was tempted to call the front desk and report whoever was responsible, but my deplorable unwillingness to get anyone in trouble kept me from doing so. I could always request a few extra towels and be here to receive them myself. Fortunately, I had kept all my valuables in my locked suitcase.

My suitcase . . .

I knew I'd pushed it firmly under the bed, out of sight after I'd put the shawl inside. Curious, I pulled it out and checked it. The lock was intact, and since I couldn't remember where I'd last left the dial code, I looked inside to see if anything was missing. It seemed okay. I made a cursory tour of my room, looking for anything that indicated someone, perhaps uninvited, had been here.

Now who's getting paranoid.

I did start feeling a little foolish jumping to that conclusion. And unless I pulled a James Bond trick and slipped a hair into my door, this spy business was beyond me.

So instead, I took a much-needed hot shower.

* * *

I felt back to normal, at least physically, the next morning. My emotions were another story as I continued to worry about my dad. But by eight o'clock, I was as ready to face the day and rejoin the expedition as I would ever be. Today we were heading north to the archaeological site of Tenayuca. Sitting by the slightly open window for some air, I read in my travel guide as we drove until I knew that the name of the site stood for *Serpent Pyramid*, indicative of the numerous carved serpents that decorated the base. Dedicated to the sun god, the pyramid apparently had been rebuilt every fifty-two years in accordance with the Aztec calendar, though the entire site had previously begun under Toltec and Chichemec control. Like many such structures, scholars assumed it was probably used for astronomical observations.

After we'd parked alongside the street, I helped unload the gear and carry it to the east side of the pyramid, where numerous interlocking stone serpents lined the wall. Fortunately, we had beaten the tourist rush, and it appeared we would have the site mostly to ourselves for a while. Spurred on by that thought as well, Dave started assembling his equipment—with some unnecessary help from Kat—while Lin and Mike took off to the double staircase on the north side. It appeared that only Seth and I had nothing pressing to do at the moment.

As if through unspoken agreement, we circumnavigated the pyramid, which was still in excellent condition. The double monumental staircase was quite intact. Even though the interlocking serpents were now located on only three sides of the structure and it was much smaller than those at Teotihuacán, it had its own unique appeal. But while the latter had made me feel small and insignificant, there was a different feeling here. Something more . . . menacing. Maybe that was just because of everything that had been happening.

I walked by Seth's side, trying to decide if I could trust him with any of my concerns. Finally, I broke down. "Uh, Seth. Some unusual things are going on around here," I tentatively began, "and I don't know what to think."

"Oh really?" he asked, not breaking his stride. "Like what?"

Now I felt foolish. So what if Dave really spoke English better than he'd let on, and as far as Kat's moodiness, strange phone calls, and the confusing conversation I'd heard between Dave and Lin—what did it all mean anyway? And the last thing I was going to mention was that I thought someone had been in my room yesterday. "Well," I said, testing the water, "I was just wondering how Dave got hired to work with us."

Seth paused. "I don't know. I suppose Lansing arranged for it before the trip. Why?"

"I thought maybe Lin had something to do with it."

"I don't think so. I mean, she's only worked for the company for a year and just barely met him like the rest of us. Right? Why, do you know somethin'?"

"No." I started to backpedal. "It's stupid, really. I've probably just misinterpreted everything." We were now on the south side of the wall, and I noticed the single large coiled snake next to a small, raised platform.

"I love these serpents." Seth reached down and touched the headpiece of the coiling stone figure. "They must have been the guardians of this place, responsible for scarin' unwanted intruders away. I'm sure there were a few who didn't heed the warnin', of course, and snooped around where they weren't wanted."

"Uh, sure." I wrapped my arms around myself as if a cloud had suddenly passed over the sun. "I wonder why that one's all by itself."

My companion shrugged and said jokingly, "Maybe it had the real power, and all the rest were just backup. Well, let's go see if anyone needs our help."

Lin and Mike had now descended the stairs and were discussing their ideas with Dave. There seemed to be a few artistic differences, and though I couldn't hear what they were arguing about from where I stood, I was reluctant to get in the middle of it. After standing there fidgeting for a few minutes, I realized I could have been invisible for all anyone cared. There were a few more tourists starting to arrive, and I figured it would be best if I got out of everyone's way until someone called for me.

I went to the staircase on the north face of the pyramid, this time continuing all the way to the top. Though the view wasn't as spectacular from its full height as it had been even halfway up the one at Teotihuacán, it was still a long way down. I could see Lin and Mike brainstorming with Dave, while Kat stood arguing with Seth, her hands on her curvy hips. After a quick walk to the other side of the ridge, I noted the route Seth and I had taken earlier and could clearly make out the single stone serpent guarding the entrance.

Preparing to head back, I noticed a man walking near the giant statue. He stopped and looked around, as if confirming he was alone. Even though it had been days and he was far away, I recognized him. It was the man I'd seen following us in Teotihuacán. The man in black. Was it merely a coincidence? Acting on some impulse, I hunched down so only my head was visible above the edge of the wall. I watched as the man, convinced he was going about his business unobserved, stooped to place something inside the serpent's mouth. Then he stood and casually walked back to the parking lot as if he were a typical tourist. An uneasy feeling grew in the pit of my stomach. Time seemed to stop as I waited there, unsure what to do. And yet somehow I knew I couldn't let it go. I had to see what was there.

You're letting your curiosity get the better of you!

Ignoring the warning, I casually made my way back down the steps and along the wall to the opposite end of the pyramid until I came to the stone figure. Then, in a movement that mimicked the one I'd just seen the man make, I scanned my surroundings and stooped down to peer into the serpent's mouth. Inside was a small package wrapped in brown paper. Hesitantly, I reached in and took it out. It was nearly weightless, and I shook it, much like a child would with a present under the Christmas tree. It made no sound. I turned it over and saw on the underside that there was a small ink marking. I looked closer, and the mark came into focus.

It was the image of a serpent.

Chapter 18

EVEN AFTER WE RETURNED TO the hotel later that afternoon, I was still shaken up.

I had immediately returned the package to its original place, but I continued to feel as if it were clinging to me and wouldn't let go. I needed something to distract me from thinking about it. Of course, everyone but me had work to do. Kat said she was going to be in her room giving an update to the execs back at Phizer-Lewis and left strict orders not to disturb her. Seth had already turned his focus to the technological world, anxious to put the images of the day onto his computer's screen. Lin and Mike had a lot of editing to do—though watching them, I had my doubts it was going to be all business. Something was going on between them, but I sensed it was nothing too ominous in nature.

As I walked toward the elevator, I asked Dave if he'd gotten some good shots today. "*Creo que sí,*" was his brief reply in the affirmative.

Back in my room, I needed some kind of reassurance, so after reading my scriptures and saying a prayer, I decided to call my family. I'd just talked to my mom, but I really needed to hear my dad's voice. As I stared down at the gleaming black phone, however, I was hesitant to use it again. I realized that if Kat saw a horrendous bill after the trip, it might give her more ammo against me. I'd just use the landline and my phone card instead.

After some considerable dialing, I heard the ring tone and waited. This time my dad picked up.

"Hello?"

"Hey, Big Boss. It's me." My eyes started to mist over.

"Samantha! I was hoping you'd call again."

"How . . . how are you?

"Fit as a fiddle," he joked. "Really, I'm fine. Your mother took Karen to the store to get her a new dress for the senior dance. She'll be so sad she missed your call. How's everything going?"

After all these years, I don't know why I believed I could lie to my father. "It's going great."

"Oh, really?"

I bit my lip, not wanting to reveal too much. "I had a little *turista* stomach bug, but I'm fine now."

Wanting to spare him all the gory details, I instead told him about visiting the temple grounds, and then I told him I was going to search out a local meetinghouse for sure next Sunday. I just had to figure out where it was.

"Try the Internet, princess," my dad suggested.

"Of course!" I groaned. Sheesh. Sometimes I forgot how helpful technology could be. I was sure there was some way to access it from my phone—but that would be way beyond my skill level. I'd seen an Internet lounge downstairs just off the lobby; I could try that.

"Hang in there, kiddo. We love you, and you're in our prayers every night."

I managed to hang up before my voice choked up and then headed downstairs. The front desk had me sign an agreement form and assigned me a terminal. But what had seemed like it should be a simple search turned into nearly an hour of Googling and browsing, and I still couldn't find an address for a nearby meetinghouse, let alone a meeting time. I had come across several sites discussing the temple in the area but nothing that helped my current dilemma. Even the Church's website only contained information that had been set up by individual stakes and wards, and there was nothing listed here in Mexico City. Of course, maybe I didn't know where to look.

As I sat there staring at the blank search engine, I had a thought. I quickly typed in "David Ayala, photographer." There were a surprising number of results that came up, most of them Facebook pages. I also found out on LinkedIn that I could find a David Ayala who was a cartoonist, a fashion designer at Walmart, and even a doctoral candidate at the University of Cambridge. My parents would like that. And then finally I added "Mexico" to my search request.

Bingo!

I pulled up the website of a photography studio in the heart of Mexico City. But the webpages were nondescript, and there wasn't a photograph of the actual owner. I wondered if that was where Dave worked. Sure enough, I saw some accolades for *National Geographic* and a brief bio, some contact information, and an outline of the various services he offered. It sounded like what Kat had told us about him, but those details could have referred to a lot of people, I suppose.

Disappointed, I was about to log off when I thought of that strange package, so then I typed "serpent" and "Mexico" in the search engine. After a few seconds, more than one million results came up. I didn't have time for that, but I did briefly scan the first page. I groaned when I saw that a group of students had apparently seen a "space" serpent releasing a fleet of flashing UFOs over Tijuana and I could watch it happening on YouTube. (I thought about Terri's friends and wondered if the group had been doing a little "wacky weed" when they saw them.)

As I continued to read, the articles I found reinforced my previous understanding that the serpent symbol was very prevalent in Mexican history, as indicated by the carvings we'd seen in Teotihuacán and Tenayuca. Finding it interesting but not helpful, I moved the cursor to shut down the screen but saw something in the second-to-last entry of the page that caught my attention. In an Associated Press story titled "The 'Serpent' Evades Capture Again in Mexico," the writer explained how violence in Mexico had been intensifying in the last few years, fueled by the South American drug cartels that were trying to infiltrate the country and a major drug lord who had managed to escape arrest again. I clicked on the link to read the rest of the article and, ignoring the banners and ads that suddenly flashed at me, managed to read about several people who had been killed execution style and dumped in the desert outside of Nuevo Laredo, Mexico. A note had been attached to the bodies that stated how the "Serpent" would take revenge on all who had crossed him.

A shiver went through me.

I stared at the computer screen and felt the hair bristle on the back of my neck as if I were being watched. I shook the sensation off. The article was a coincidence. This event had happened thousands of miles away, and as I continued to read, I saw there were also threats made to a local school in Ciudad Juarez by the "Bandit," not to mention it had been "La Raza" who had claimed to orchestrate the recent bombing here in the city. There were many pseudonyms these gangs used, from jaguars to eagles, and it shouldn't have surprised me that one of them had chosen a serpent as a means of intimidation.

Still, it made me just curious enough that I decided to have the article printed out anyway. After I collected it from the printer and paid the nominal fee at the front desk, Seth waylaid me in the lobby.

"There you are!" he exclaimed, coming toward me. "Whatcha got there, darlin'?" Before I could react, he'd grabbed the papers from my hands. "Hmm. Some easy readin' for bed? Don't worry your little head at this kind of stuff. I won't let anything happen to you."

He handed the article back to me and gave me his trademark grin. "Want to see somethin'?" He didn't wait for my answer but grabbed my hand and accompanied me back to our floor. With a sigh, I let him lead me until I saw we were nearing his room again.

"Uh, Seth, I don't . . ."

But he was already dragging me forward, and I felt strangely helpless against the momentum. Like a little kid anxious to show off his latest drawing, he showed me what he'd been working on. Instead of sitting down on the bed like I'd done last time, I remained standing and leaned over, admiring the new layout.

"It's great."

His excitement continued as he explained his latest plan. "I've got some ideas to completely overhaul the city's website. With a few animated GIFs for each category and an eye-catching banner at some strategic positions on the site, we're gonna *kill* the competition."

I tried not to roll my eyes, thinking how Seth's speech reminded me of Roger. Having displayed ample enthusiasm, I tried to excuse myself, but Seth apparently wasn't ready to have me leave. I stared at the closed door, wondering how I kept getting myself into these situations.

"So, Sam." He leaned back on the bed with his hands behind his head. "You were tryin' to tell me somethin' earlier." When I didn't bite, he added, "You know I'm your friend, don't you? If you have a problem or concern, I'm here for you."

I wanted to believe he sincerely cared, but the last thing I was going to do was dish on my colleagues and have it get back to Kat. I was starting to get the feeling the two of them might be a little closer than I thought. "Thanks, Seth, but I'm fine. I think the stress of the trip is getting the better of me. I'm sure I'm just seeing shadows where there aren't any."

"Yeah, right," he replied. "So, got any ideas up there in your head for this layout? I keep wonderin' what the copywriters might do with the body copy."

I looked at the computer screen and the collage of pictures he'd used. Dave's work was fantastic, but I thought better than to praise him in front of Seth. Instead, I stared longingly at the blank window he'd left for the eventual text. There were so many things I could come up with. How could someone sitting back at headquarters capture everything I'd seen? Seth nudged me as if to tell me it was all right to dream a little. So I sat down and poised my fingers over the keyboard. Then I wrote:

Imagine a country where two cultures have blended into one—a place where a society was born from both an ancient world and a world daring and fierce in its exploration.

Realizing I'd been caught up in my own thoughts, I stopped and blushed. Seth grinned and read what I'd written. "Not bad. Someday you might just get the chance you've been waitin' for." He closed the laptop and leaned toward me, his green eyes blurring into hazy shadows.

Oh no. Not again.

"Seth, I—"

His lips were on mine. My head started to spin as I felt the warmth and pressure on my mouth increase—there was nothing timid or unsure about this kiss. He knew what he was doing, and for a moment, I was helpless to do anything about it. But that was only for a moment. When I regained my senses, I pushed him away. "Seth, please don't." I jumped off the bed and ran back to my room.

With the heavy door safely closed behind me, I felt as if I could release the breath I'd been holding. But I couldn't stop trembling and immediately wiped any trace of his lips from my mouth. Why had his kiss made me feel so . . . violated? It had been so intense, so demanding. I felt as if he'd wanted something from me and was reaching down inside me to take it. I shuddered. As if trying to replace that unwelcome memory, I started to imagine it had been someone else—someone with eyes the color of chocolate, with dark, wavy hair that often hung unnoticed over his tanned brow.

I realized a smile had crossed my face, expelling the demons from before. But I also realized I couldn't leave it at that. We couldn't just pretend tomorrow—again—that nothing had happened. Seth needed to know where I stood and that I had no interest in him that way.

Praying that somehow the "bold" Samantha would return when I needed her, I opened the door and walked slowly down the hall toward his room. My hands started to sweat, and I could feel my heart throbbing out a nervous rhythm in my neck. As I approached his room, the voices across the hall in Kat's room distracted me. She must be finished with her meeting, I thought. Then, when I heard Seth's voice as well, my breath caught in my throat. Maybe it would be best to do this later, when he was alone.

Coward.

All right, I'm going.

As I neared the room, I couldn't help but hear a portion of their conversation.

"Why do they keep playing these games with me?" Kat pouted. "Why can't they just let me know if I'm in or out?"

"They do things differently here. It's all about hype and drama," Seth answered. "To remind you who's in charge."

Kat caught me out of the corner of her eye and scowled at me. Seth's face, however, was a blank slate. "Uh. I'm sorry to interrupt, but, Seth, can I talk to you a minute?"

Seth's eyes narrowed, and a smug grin appeared on his face. "Yeah, sure. My room or yours?"

I cast him a dirty look I hoped Kat couldn't see. Unfazed, Seth sauntered past me into the hall. As I followed him, I wondered if I could undo some damage by showing my support for my boss's situation. "Kat?" She turned and stared coldly at me. "I wanted you to know that I think you're doing a great job. If the execs can't see that, they're blind."

Even though I didn't get the response I'd been hoping for, maybe she'd at least try to remember that I was on her side. That we were a team here.

After I informed Seth that we wouldn't be in *either* of our rooms, we continued to walk down the hall. I struggled to begin. "About what happened . . . it's not that I don't like you . . . I think you're really nice, but . . ."

An angry glare crossed his face momentarily and frightened me. Then it disappeared, and his characteristic grin replaced it. "Maybe if I took photographs instead of just scanned them?"

Suddenly worried that this would get back to Kat, I protested. "No, it wouldn't matter because I'm here to work. Period. Can we just let it go at that and still be friends?"

He stopped walking and leaned toward me. Afraid he was going to try something again, I tensed up. But he only pushed back a lock of hair that had fallen from behind my ear. "Of course, Sam. We'll be great friends."

Chapter 19

I WASN'T DISAPPOINTED WHEN SETH declined to join us on the next day's expedition to the Basilica of Guadalupe. He stayed behind, he said, to continue working on a new spreadsheet. "Churches aren't really my thing anyway," he said as he grinned at the group, though I wondered if I was really included in his friendliness anymore. At least his absence provided me the unique opportunity to sit next to someone else in the van. Of course, Mike wasn't exactly a bundle of excitement, especially after his better half bowed out as well. Our conversation hinged on his work—about which I received monosyllabic responses—and the weather. But his lack of pretension was somehow endearing, and I relished that there was someone on this trip who had yet to draw attention to himself, good or bad.

The Old Basilica had been closed years ago, unfortunately, after ground instability had made it inaccessible to worshippers. But the modern New Basilica, with its concrete and marble, was still quite impressive, and after a few preliminary shots outside of the old, we ventured toward the new. Following in the same direction were dozens of pilgrims approaching the Basilica on their knees in supplication. Though my own faith deemed such public displays of devotion unnecessary, I couldn't help but be touched by the sacrifice they were willing to make. But then I was reminded that most people didn't understand religious dedication.

"Why should anyone want to do that?" Kat asked, her voice tired and her words slurred. I shrugged, not sure I wanted to get into a discussion of religion. "I guess I don't understand," she continued, "why they think some unknown power is going to make their lives any better. Nothing changes unless you make it change."

"Maybe they've done everything they can," I said quietly, "and now they're leaving it up to a higher power."

Kat laughed.

I saw Dave glance at me through the corner of his eye as my boss sauntered away, and then he said, "It sounds like you have some experience with all this. Hope you weren't offended."

"No, it's all right." I shrugged. "I guess when you grow up in a religious household, you take these things for granted until someone challenges you on it. I'm not Catholic, but I understand their need to worship God and feel guided by Him. Have you"—I was starting to feel a missionary moment coming on—"ever stopped and wondered why we're here and what it's all about?"

Dave shrugged. "I think we're supposed to live good lives, regardless of religion. Maybe some people need that structure, so they join this church or that." He replaced his camera in his bag. "Of course, in a Hispanic household, it's not so much a matter of choosing your religion—you're essentially born into it. And that's that."

I was going to ask him if that's how it was in his family but decided against it. Every time I tried to get into his mind, he shut down. If I wanted to have the slightest chance of finding out who he really was, I was going to have to stay at a comfortable distance and wait for those subtle hints into his personality to unfold. And surprisingly, one did.

"Maybe if I saw Him a different way," he mused, almost reverently. "If He were someone who actually cared about me instead of a vindictive God who waited to mete out justice for my sins, I could almost understand all this." He shrugged and swung his camera bag over his shoulder. "Otherwise, it's not for me."

Naturally, everyone, regardless of religious affiliation, was curious about seeing the mantle, so we went inside. I was surprised at first that the spacious interior was devoid of the statues and pictures that were prevalent in the Catholic religion but then remembered that this was a pilgrimage site, not for an impressive nave or gilded altar but for the mantle of the Virgin of Guadalupe.

I opened my guide and read about the legend of Juan Diego, a baptized Aztec who had a dark-skinned woman appear to him and charge him with building a church on the location of the apparition. When he tried to do as he was told, however, the bishop of the town didn't believe him and asked for proof. The Virgin appeared a second time and caused roses to bloom on a hillside even though it was winter.

Gathering up the flowers, Juan Diego returned to the bishop, spread out his cloak, and not only did the roses spill out onto the floor, but they saw that the image of the Virgin had become imprinted upon his cloak.

It was this cloak that drew thousands each year to see the small church that had been built and the mantle, which now hung high in this modern edifice in a glass case and was supposedly the original miracle. To be honest, behind the thick glass protection, it was hard to determine its age or possible origin, but I had no reason to ridicule what many of the people around me obviously believed. I was just glad Seth wasn't there to make some inappropriate comment.

Leave it to Kat to fill in for him.

"All right, we've seen enough of this nonsense. Let's go," she said sluggishly, covering her bloodshot eyes with her sunglasses even though we weren't outside yet.

Usually I would have described her behavior as "moody," but today she seemed to be moving in slow motion. She also looked like she hadn't been sleeping well, though that was hardly an excuse for her behavior. I rolled my eyes—real brave since I was standing behind her—and followed the group back to the van.

Back at the hotel, I wasn't ready to let the connection go that I had felt with Dave, so I tagged beside him like an eager puppy as we made our way up from the parking garage. "I love what Seth's doing with your pictures. I'm glad you gave him the ones of the children."

"I'm surprised he actually used them."

"Maybe he's starting to see things differently too," I said, getting a smile for my efforts. I felt like an awkward teenager when he didn't respond. "Well, I'm sure you have a ton of work to do."

He nodded. "I am kind of backlogged on getting some pictures developed."

I looked at him, a bit confused. "Don't you just store them digitally on the computer or something?"

"Most of them," he agreed. "But I always save a few to develop the old-fashioned way. I'm afraid technology has taken some of the fun out of photography. There's nothing quite like being locked away in a dark room, watching the images you saw earlier materialize like magic right before your eyes."

I could understand that and wanted him to know. "It sounds like you really enjoy what you do."

Then right before my eyes, he became the sullen Dave again. "Yeah, sure."

The sarcasm in his words hit me hard, and I frowned.

A look of concern crossed his face. "Sorry. I didn't mean to make you feel bad. I guess I'm just feeling a lot of weight on me."

I nodded. "I know how you feel. Why . . . ?" I hesitated to bring him into my confidence. "Why is everyone so tense and acting so strange? I mean, we're in this beautiful country, and there's so much to see and learn. It seems like everything's going okay. This should be a great experience, and yet we're all walking on eggshells."

Dave cocked his head to one side and looked down at his feet. "Eggshells? What does this mean: to walk on them?"

I laughed, realizing it didn't work to think in English. "It means that we're all nervous and anxious, like something bad is going to happen."

A momentary frown crossed his face as well. But then Dave's eyes lit up like he'd had a brilliant idea. We'd been standing behind some giant potted plants, and now he peered around them into the lobby, like a little kid worried he was going to get caught. "Come on." He grabbed me by the hand, and we dashed toward the front doors. "There's something I want to show you that will get rid of those eggshells!"

I was still surprised at his behavior when I found myself out on the street corner and even more bewildered when he hailed a cab and we got in. "Where are we going?" I asked.

He winked. "Trust me."

We made our way up the familiar Paseo de la Reforma and onto Calle Benito Juarez. It wasn't long before Dave signaled the driver to pull over. We got out, and I followed Dave's lead as we crossed the street and went into a shop with a sign reading ESTUDIO VISUAL on the door. Why was that name so familiar? I was past guessing at what Dave was up to. A bell on the door chimed, and Dave was immediately greeted by the dark-haired, heavy-set man who'd been standing behind the counter.

"*Hola, amigo.*" I mentally began to translate the rest. "Back to rob me of more work? The favors I do for you and the organization—"

"A-hem." Dave cut his friend off by introducing me in English. "This is Samantha Evans. From the States."

"A pleasure." He leaned over my outstretched hand and kissed it. *Oh please.* He then whispered to Dave in Spanish, though I could still hear everything. "Your taste is improving. But I can't blame you. As I recently found out for myself, these blonde American women are incredible!"

I didn't miss the scowl that crossed Dave's face. "This is work. Can I use the darkroom?"

The man shrugged. "*Que lástima*. It is all yours. Make yourself . . . how do you Americans say it? . . . 'at home.'"

I glanced at all of the photographs on the wall as we went to the back room. The owner of the photography studio appeared to be a good friend of Dave's. They certainly razzed each other like friends. "So, is your friend a photographer too?"

"I've known . . . Juan for several years," Dave confirmed as we stepped into the room and he shut the door behind us. "He lets me use his studio when I'm in town."

"Oh, okay," I croaked as Dave turned out the lights. The darkness was replaced with an eerie red glow. I watched as Dave stepped across the room, and I tried to accustom myself to the pungent smell of the chemicals he was pouring into plastic bins. He gave me an explanation as he worked.

"I'll try to speak in English so you'll understand all of the steps. First, we prepare our solutions for the developer, the stop bath and the fixer. Juan already has everything mixed up accordingly." He paused a moment as he poured the last bin half full. "I'm going to print some black and whites from a set of negatives I made the other day."

The process was fascinating. Dave hardly spoke as he concentrated on the placement of the special photographic paper under the light. The image's opposite only appeared for a brief second, and I couldn't tell what it was. I found myself standing right next to him as he gingerly picked the paper up and placed it in the first bath. It was so quiet I could hear our tandem breathing. His nearness was making my heart beat faster, and I was afraid he'd hear that as well.

"Uh, what's it like to be a professional photographer?" I asked to disrupt the silence.

He released a quick breath of air. "Interesting at times."

"And have you been doing it long?"

"I suppose."

Obviously the man can't work and talk at the same time.

But I wasn't too discouraged. I realized I just hadn't been asking the right questions. There were a few questions I would have liked him to answer, but I settled on a different course. "What's it like when you see the picture appear?"

The corners of Dave's mouth went up. "When I was young and saw it for the first time, I thought it was magic. But it's real. There's a strange relationship between taking the picture with a camera and waiting to see the results. There's that moment of doubt where I think, 'Perhaps I used the wrong shutter speed or shouldn't have chosen a wide-angle lens.' But then I find trust in myself and watch . . . and wait. And suddenly. . . *es mágico*."

His head was so close to mine that his hair brushed against my cheek and I could smell the woodsy scent of his cologne. I turned slightly to look at him and found him looking back. I could swear he was leaning in toward me. Was he going to kiss me? And then I made the biggest mistake I'd probably ever made. I glanced down at the shimmering surface, and my breath caught in my throat as I watched a close-up image of the serpent statue from Tenayuca come into focus.

Dave must have thought I'd reacted that way for another reason because he jumped back as if he'd been shocked. "Uh, sorry. We'd probably better go back to the hotel."

I wanted to say something. I just couldn't think what.

As we finished up and left the room, Dave shook hands with his friend again and whispered something in his ear. While they were occupied, I glanced around the studio again and saw various framed photos and a plaque on the wall. Stepping closer, I saw that it was an award for the 2007 International Photography Award in Advertising. And below it was the winner's name: David Ayala.

Now I knew where I'd seen the studio's name before—on Dave's website! But why wouldn't he have told me this was his place?

The trip back was heavy with silence and unasked questions. We barely said good-bye as we made our way to our rooms. As I sat on the corner of my bed, wondering why Dave acted the way he did when he was around me, my phone rang. I reached into my purse and saw that it was my home.

"Hello," I answered breathlessly.

"Samantha?" My mom's voice cracked a little.

"Mom?" That was all I could get out.

And yet she knew what I was silently asking. "The tests were positive, sweetheart. But everything's going to be all right."

Why were we always trying to reassure others by saying that, when in reality we were just wanting to reassure ourselves? My words played along and hoped my heart would follow. "I know, Mom. Dad's strong. Where . . . is he?"

"At the temple. He wasn't sure he'd be able to make it there for a while."

"What can I do?" I moaned. "Should I come home?"

I heard her sigh through the phone. "No. Not yet. There's little anyone can do, and you have your work to think about. We want you and your brothers and sister to keep on living your lives. Together, your dad and I can handle this."

Of course. If anyone could take on cancer, it would be Gary and Ruth Evans. I admired their strength and courage. And their love for each other.

After I hung up, with a promise that she'd give Dad a hug for me, I stared at the hotel room door I suddenly found in front of me and thought about my parents. Love was all about taking chances and opening up. I knew that what I'd been feeling for Dave was far from that. But it had to start somewhere, and I wasn't ready to let any chance—no matter how small—pass by.

Standing in front of his door, however, I started to have doubts again. Somehow I found the courage to take a deep breath, stand up straight, and raise my hand to knock. But before my hand made contact with the door, I heard voices coming from inside. Angry voices. I couldn't make out what they were saying—or even who it was, for that matter. A man and a woman? Which would mean it could be Dave and Lin.

Or Kat.

I prayed it was the former but decided not to stick around and find out. The last thing I needed was to be caught lurking outside in the hallway. I ambled back down the hall, hoping whoever was inside would finish their argument and come out. They didn't.

My stomach suddenly growled. My side trip with Dave had caused us to miss lunch. Now my stomach took precedence over my heart, so I went down for a quick bite at the hotel restaurant, though I was going to have to find someplace cheaper to eat in the future. Kat had me all confused about what the project budget was supposed to cover, so I'd found myself paying for some of the incidentals. But I have to admit, I did enjoy the shrimp enchiladas with peach-mango salsa. And I was even brave enough to ask for some extra salsa and tortillas to take with me as a possible snack later if arrangements hadn't been made for dinner.

As I was making my way back to the elevator, I saw Kat and Dave strolling across the lobby. They hadn't seen me, but as I watched them leaving, I felt my heart drop. He had his arm around her waist. I ducked behind a large potted plant and continued to spy as they headed toward the revolving doors. Before they left, I saw Dave lean over and whisper something in her ear. Kat faked surprise and swatted him playfully on the arm.

How cozy.

New tears sprang to my eyes, and I had to wait until I could get my emotions under control before I went back to my room. Then disappointment turned to anger as I realized it *had* been a game: the times I'd caught him looking at me, the way he'd held me when we'd danced. The connection I thought we'd had this afternoon. It was all just a joke, and I'd been the brunt of it.

Bravery under extreme duress was easy when you were alone in your room. "You haven't defeated me yet," I vowed out loud. "I'm not going anywhere!"

Chapter 20

I HATED MEXICO CITY.

All right . . . I didn't hate it. I just hated some of the things it would always remind me of. Even the next day when Kat announced we were going to Chapultepec Park, I couldn't manage to muster a smile. My boss, on the other hand, looked like the proverbial cat who'd swallowed the bird. All sorts of tormenting thoughts started running through my head as I decided that only one thing could make a woman smile like that. Need I say it? Dare I say it? Could it be love?

Now I was starting to sound like my inner voice again, but that was the least of what was bothering me. Ironically, everyone was pairing off—Lin and Mike, Dave and Kat—which left me with Seth. I hugged the side of the van the best I could and stared out the window the entire time, which spared me the task of making conversation. By the time we arrived, I had grown a little more excited. I'd been hoping for a chance to see more of the park, and it was big enough that maybe I'd even be able to wander off and get lost in it, leaving all of this drama behind. They probably had vagrants who camped out here just like at home, and I could curl up in some corner and die.

Talk about drama.

I accepted that I was just feeling sorry for myself even before my conscience continued to remind me that this was still the opportunity of a lifetime. Just because things hadn't worked out exactly as I imagined them didn't mean I couldn't still be grateful.

So I determined to be grateful for the little things that day.

I was grateful for the beautiful pillared monument just south of Chapultepec Castle that honored the young men who had given their lives when the United States had invaded the castle in 1847, and I realized that how we perceive war is all a matter of which side we're on. I was grateful for the magnificent castle itself perched on the hill we were climbing. Inside, we passed through a museum housed in a circular, modern building. We saw displays illustrating the history of Mexico, from the struggle for independence to the postrevolutionary period. The nineteen rooms of the castle held fascinating exhibits, including collections of armor and maps, even handwritten plans from the Conquest period and its immediate aftermath. We saw the apartments occupied by Emperor Maximilian and his wife, Carlota, decorated in a neoclassical style with furniture they had brought from Europe. From the nearby terrace, there was a magnificent view of the city, and I stood there and let it soak in for a minute.

"Not bad being rich," Seth intoned at my side.

I frowned, hopefully not enough for him to notice. "I suppose. Of course, they're gone now, and all of this is just a tourist site."

He shrugged. "But I bet it was fun while it lasted."

I turned to see where Dave was, not surprised to see him by Kat's side. When he noticed me watching him, I turned away, not wanting to give him the satisfaction of seeing that I was jealous.

We went to the lower level and saw the Tree of Moctezuma, which was said to date back to Aztec times. I wondered how something living could last that long. North of the castle was the Lago Antiguo, a lake divided into two parts by the Grand Avenue. I found myself grateful for the tiny island nestled in the middle of the man-made lake and the beautiful Casa de Lago perched on its edge. I was even grateful for the face on the Fountain of Netzahualcóyotl that made me laugh. Though Mexico was beautiful, its economic and social struggles were evident wherever we went, and I started to understand why people were willing to sacrifice so much to have just a portion of what I had. I was especially grateful, as I thought of my family back home, that my father would have the best care that medical doctors had to offer.

When we arrived at the more forested area of the park, I felt as if I'd stepped into some mysterious world where *brujas* and other phantasms were going to leap out from behind some tree. We passed on the few other museums in the park environs, and I tried to focus on anything besides Dave and Kat walking cozily side by side and thoughts of my dad's illness.

Apparently, if we had continued to follow the small street farther to the east, we would have come to the residence of the president of

Mexico. I thought back to the bomb that had been set off during their equivalent of a session of Congress, which, ironically, was part of the reason we were here in the first place. I was glad we had a chance to undo some of the harm. It was a shame to think that the acts of a few might prevent others from enjoying these beautiful sights, especially when I had felt completely safe in the city so far. Hopefully our work here would help change that negative perception.

Ending my gratitude kick, I was grateful when we went back to the hotel so I could be alone.

* * *

I'd hoped the next day would be normal enough that I could regain my equilibrium. Leave it to Kat to shatter that expectation.

When she announced the next morning that we were headed to Toltec ruins of Tula, I pulled up the mental map that had formed from my hours of research and realized the archeological site was at least a two-hour drive—maybe more. Even though it was one of the more unique sets of ruins in this area, I thought it was a little distant to be included in our presentation on the city itself. Oh well. It's not like I was in charge, and if it made Kat happy . . . we were all happy.

I put on my university T-shirt again as I tried to remember that I was a "team" player here. It wasn't easy when at every turn, I felt like I was going to see Kat rubbing my nose into my failures. And when I saw that she was also wearing a red T-shirt, so tight it must have been painted on, it didn't help my ego either.

But then I was reminded that sometimes, even our most trivial prayers can be answered.

Apparently, Seth wanted to work on his laptop as we drove, and he decided to ride shotgun up front beside the driver and use the nine-volt jack in the car's dash. That meant I wouldn't have to sit by him. Kat then announced she hadn't been sleeping well and was going to crash on the third-row seat in the van. With Lin and Mike naturally pairing off, that left . . .

That's right!

Would it have been tacky to do a victory dance? Probably, so instead I turned to the opposite extreme and pretended like I could have cared less that I was sitting by Dave. Choosing the window seat, I acted as if watching cacti pass by was the most fascinating thing in the world.

Oh look! There goes another one!

It was a bit juvenile, but it worked for the first half hour. Then I realized I was falling into the habit of "protesting too much," which probably made him think I was purposefully avoiding him because I was hurt, and that forced me to engage him in what I hoped he thought was merely a casual conversation.

"So have you ever been to Tula before?" I asked.

After he recovered from what must have been the shock of me speaking to him, he replied, "No. It's my first time."

Okay. Let's try the weather now.

"It's sure been hot lately. Is that usual for this area?"

"I suppose."

"What will you do when the project's over?" I persisted.

"Wait until the next assignment."

I hadn't been looking directly at him until now. But he seemed so preoccupied—as attested from his nearly monosyllabic responses—that I took my chance. He was wearing a light blue V-neck T-shirt, and it made his skin look even darker than usual. And yet, where the front of his shirt dipped, I could tell that his skin tone was perhaps a few shades lighter. The edge of his sleeve had ridden up a little, and I could see that scar again but still couldn't figure out what could have made it. I moved my gaze slowly up to his face. He'd taken the time to shave this morning but had missed a spot right under his jaw line. His nose was narrow, as were his lips. Hmm, his lips looked so soft.

Oh please.

Sorry. At first glance, I hadn't disputed his local heritage. But now that I was taking each feature into consideration, one at a time, something didn't seem right. Between that and his height, it all added up to one thing: a mixed heritage. Which meant he wasn't pure Mexican.

"Seeing something you like?" The corner of Dave's mouth curled up.

How did he know? He'd been staring ahead the whole time. I could feel the heat rising in my face as I sputtered, "Uh . . . I was just . . . I was curious."

"About what?"

"I was trying to figure out where you're from."

His head whipped toward me, and a flash of discomfort crossed his face. But he quickly had it under control. "What do you mean?"

I shrugged. "Well, you're supposed to be a local photographer but, uh, you don't exactly look Mexican."

I heard a sharp inhale of breath. "That's because my mother is Mexican and my father is European." That explained just about everything. I felt like an idiot, and I started to apologize for my nosiness. "No, it's all right," he cut me off. "You're perceptive. I like that. Some people can't see what's right in front of them."

I wondered if he was referring to the heavy breather in the back seat. As I stared out the window again, I wondered why Dave was such an enigma. It was as if he were two people: one that I felt drawn toward and one that made me want to run away.

* * *

We must have driven over a rut because something jostled me back into consciousness. I guess counting maguey plants had done me in. After I remembered where I was, I realized that at some point during my nap, I'd leaned against Dave's shoulder. Was that why I'd had such a nice dream? Being embarrassed around him seemed to be my lot though.

"I hope I didn't drool," I said sheepishly.

"Just a little." There was that killer smile again. "I think we're here."

At first I thought I would be bored seeing yet another pyramid, but this site had its own surprise: giant Atlantean stone figures that guarded the top of the pyramid where the temple would have stood. Everyone got down to business, leaving me free to explore the surrounding area; that is, after I'd made a few trips back to the van because we'd forgotten some items like more bottled water. It was getting hot, and I tucked a bottle in my purse for myself later.

A group of children ran toward us, trying to sell us their wares. Kat made an unpleasant face, and I did my duty by holding up a few pesos and leading the children away from the group like the Pied Piper. Though I didn't think I'd have much use for the small wooden boxes they were selling, which, when opened, had a carved snake jump out and "bite" your finger, I bought a couple. Maybe my nephews would appreciate them. I'm sure I paid too much for them, but all I had to do was think about the poverty most of these children would probably return to tonight and found it was an alternative to taking them home with me.

Compared to the Temple of the Moon, I thought it would be a breeze to climb this pyramid, but these steps were better suited to someone seven feet tall. From up top, I could easily see the other notable features of the area: the Burnt Palace, the Ball Court, and another building that, according to my pocket guide, was also dedicated to Quetzalcóatl. There was a mazelike series of walls visible to the north of the temple, and when I noticed the sun angled in a way that mostly shaded that area, I decided it would be nice to take another self-guided tour and head in that direction. After all, Kat was ignoring me, Dave was in his work mode now, and I had no desire to stick around and see the two of them make eyes again.

As I descended the steps to the ground floor, a young boy came running up to me with his face lit up. I thought I recognized him as one of the children I'd been talking to earlier. "*Hola*," I said and then, thinking he was searching for me to sell me something, added, "¿*Me estas buscando?*"

He didn't answer but instead thrust a paper into my hands. Confused, I opened the crumpled paper and read:

The Serpent has decided to meet you.

Come to the wall, and I will give you further instructions.

I looked up to ask the boy what it meant, but he was already gone. Glancing down at the paper again, I considered that it might be just a bad joke someone was playing. Maybe one of the mothers of the children I'd been talking to thought it would be fun to tease the *gringa*. Of course, the note was in English and quite formal, not what I'd expect from these provincial people. Still confused, I folded the note again and put it in my purse. I glanced up to the top of the structure again to reassure myself the group was still focused on their work, and then, convinced I wouldn't be missed, I continued with my tour.

As I wandered around to the west side, I found myself in the Palacio Quemado. I wondered if at some point it really had been burned or if it derived its name from some other source. It had a number of large halls, colonnades, and courtyards. In the central one were two interesting statues and another painted relief, this time showing a procession of richly attired nobles. I wanted to see the nearly destroyed ball court as well, where the ancient inhabitants gathered to watch their equivalent of soccer—though it would be more appropriately called "hip ball." These athletes had the handicap of not being able to use their arms *or* their legs; instead they would propel the extremely heavy nine-pound rubber ball down the court by deflecting it with their bodies and perhaps even using a wooden stick. I couldn't find anything about it in the tour book, but I'd once heard that one of the teams—I think it was the losing team—would end up being sacrificed at the end.

Yikes. Talk about fierce competition.

I was now at the shady north side of the pyramid. The wall behind the pyramid ran parallel to the back of it, and I noticed immediately the sculptured frieze that decorated its one-hundred-thirty-foot length. Though the red and blue paint that covered it had all but faded, it was still amazing that something so superficial could have survived this long. Of course, I wasn't impressed with the theme of the wall itself. The image of the large serpent swallowing human skeletons was not my cup of tea . . . or chocolate, if that was more appropriate. This space between the wall and the pyramid was quite narrow, and as I walked down the long, closed passageway, I felt strangely alone. I came across other sculptured panels, which, due to the better quality, I guessed had been restored. There were some animals—jaguars or lions?—and they were moving along in a procession. Then I saw a human face between the fangs of a feathered serpent, and I guessed it was a representation of the god Quetzalcóatl again. Yech. As I turned away from it in disgust, I realized I *wasn't* so alone after all.

The man who stood at the other end of the pathway seemed just as startled as I did. We stared at each other for a moment, and then, with an angry glare on his face, the man stormed toward me. For a moment, I thought he was going to knock me over, but instead he pushed past me toward the open end of the corridor.

Startled, I fell back against the rough stone and tried to gather my senses.

How rude! I knew tourists visited here from all over, but regardless of what language he spoke, he could have excused himself as he passed. It wasn't my fault I'd interrupted his alone time with the ruin. Not wanting to waste more of my energy on the boorish man, I started to head back myself. I casually traced the raised figures on the wall as I walked away, but I stopped when recognition dawned on me. Though the man had been wearing a hat this time and had removed his sunglasses in the darkened corridor, I knew why he had seemed vaguely familiar.

He was the same man I'd seen following us at Teotihuacán—which also made him the man who had placed the strange marked packet in the mouth of the serpent at Tenayuca.

I pulled the crumpled piece of paper out of my purse and stared at the words again. Were all of these incidents connected? As I emerged from the confines of the walled area, I could see our group still working on the pyramid's summit. As far as I could tell, the man in black was nowhere to be seen.

There were a few other things to see in this area, but it would take too much time, and after that strange encounter, I was anxious to hurry back up the pyramid to the familiar faces of my colleagues. Ascending the monstrous steps, I walked between the enormous statues and felt like I was playing a game of hide-and-seek. I came across Seth and ducked the other way, only to have Dave come into my line of vision. A few other tourists had joined me in the game, and we smiled and sidestepped each other to get where we wanted to go. I walked to the edge, thinking I might see the man in the hat but was unsuccessful. I did see, however, as I looked at the parking lot, a tour bus pull up and a group of Chinese tourists begin spilling out. It wouldn't be as easy to lure them away from the site as it was the children. Groaning, I knew this wouldn't make Kat happy and decided I'd better be the one to tell her.

I heard her complaining voice before I saw her behind a nearby statue.

"What are you talking about? I'd never send someone else to do my job." I stepped closer, listening in. "Yes, I'm taking this very seriously." As she finished her conversation and lowered her phone, I figured it was the best time to approach her. Her eyes narrowed when she saw me, however, and then turned stone cold. "Where have you been?"

"Uh, just walking around," I said innocently. "Did you need me?"

She took a moment before answering, as if considering something. "We're almost finished here. Don't take off again. Or," her eyes narrowed, "we may just find ourselves minus one employee."

I gulped and completely forgot what I'd wanted to tell her. I guess it didn't matter, especially if we were almost done anyway. Just to be sure, I walked back to see if the tour bus had finished disembarking. With a sigh of relief, I saw them headed away from the pyramid toward the Ball Court first. At least something was going my way! I wiped sweat from my upper lip and took a swig of my water, deciding I'd better cling to my boss's side before Kat followed through on her threat.

I was putting the water bottle back in my purse when I noticed the shadow that fell across the rugged stone floor. But I never saw its owner because before I could turn, a shove sent me toppling toward the edge of the wall.

Chapter 21

I HEARD A CACOPHONY OF voices shouting immediately beneath me. I assumed the shocked tourists were giving instructions on either how to retrieve me from the ledge or brace themselves if I fell on one of them. I had faith that my screams for help must have alerted someone closer by. I held on, digging my feet into the stone support beam that had luckily been sticking out from the crumbling wall where I was hanging. I found that by pressing my foot into the stone, I could haul myself up and over the edge, somehow ignoring the fact that the backs of my arms were being scraped with the effort.

Safely seated away from the drop-off, I struggled to compose myself and found that my hyperventilating had now subsided to occasional choked sobs. Everyone on the summit had joined us, and I suddenly felt embarrassed at my show of emotion. Kat and the others were unusually silent, and it was Seth who finally broke the tension. "Shucks. I know this place is to die for, but we didn't think you'd take it literally."

My sobs turned to gasping laughter, and I wondered if my legs were steady enough to hold me up. With a slight wobble, I stood and started to move forward, only to feel them begin to collapse again.

"Hang onto me," Dave said, propping me up with his arm.

His body was warm next to mine, and I could feel the strength of his forearm supporting me. I was too shaken to remember that I wasn't sure I could trust him, and he must have been too concerned to act aloof.

"Thank you," I said.

I could still see the concern in his eyes as he answered, "You're welcome."

He said nothing to me after that but informed Kat that he thought it would probably be best if we headed back to the hotel. She protested at first; after all, it was a long trip back and we hadn't completely finished.

But then she must have realized how harsh she was sounding because she finally relented. My knee and left arm were scraped, and I winced as I tried to get into the van. Seth reached out a hand to help me and whistled. "That was close. You're pretty lucky."

I smiled wryly and sat down.

Dave sat quietly in the backseat this time, and I wasn't bold enough to turn around and see if he was watching me. Besides, Seth was impeding that effort by placing his arm protectively around the back of the seat. I wanted to tell him I was fine and didn't need to be coddled, but I let it go.

Sensing my squirming, Seth joked, "You must have a death wish. What were you doin', tryin' to see the view over the edge and lost your balance?"

"No." I tensed. "Actually, someone pushed me."

* * *

Needless to say, my words stunned the group. We drove back to the hotel in silence after that. By the time we arrived, I'd almost convinced myself that maybe I'd been mistaken, that I'd lost my balance as Seth had teased and thus had nearly toppled to my death.

Death. It was a frightening word.

Seeing me limping, Dave asked me if I was all right or if I needed medical attention. If so, he'd be happy to accompany me to wherever I needed to go. I told him I would be fine.

"Nothing that a few bandages and a hot shower won't fix." I managed to smile.

He still insisted on walking me back to my room, almost as if he wouldn't rest until I was safely inside. When I was finally alone, my bravado wavered, and I started to shake. Shock. I thought back to my Young Women camp training. What were you supposed to do? Ahh. Put your head between your legs—or was it lie down and raise your legs? My mind was too fuzzy to think clearly about what to do next. The blood on my knee stuck to my pants, propelling me into the bathroom to clean up. With that out of the way, I found I could dwell on what had happened.

I knew I'd been pushed. If some clumsy tourist had merely bumped into me, they would surely have stuck around to help me. Wouldn't they? Of course they would have. Satisfied with my logic, I next tried to determine the answers to the other questions that swirled around my mind, like, "*Who pushed me?*" followed immediately by, "*Why?*"

Since my only experience with this type of situation was an occasional TV cop show, I realized I had to come up with a list of potential suspects. Unfortunately, everyone who knew me was on top of that pyramid with me—along with a half dozen or so other strangers. And even though I hadn't seen a reappearance of the man in black, he could have been up there hiding behind one of the statues as well.

I was reluctant to make another phone call to my parents, especially in light of the confusion that threatened to swallow me. Besides, tomorrow was Friday, and I was going to call early and find out about my dad's surgery anyway. I prayed that nothing else happened between now and then so I could be there to support my dad instead of pouring out my own miserable life to them. My phone's battery was low again, so I plugged it in. It was then I noticed the strange note in my purse that I'd been handed earlier that day.

I stared at the words again. What did it mean? I felt like if I could answer that question, everything else would fall into place. But the meaning was beyond me, and thinking only made my head throb more. Angry, I threw the note into the nearby wastebasket as if somehow it was to blame for today's misadventure. Then I carefully stretched out on my bed, turning so my scraped arm wasn't in contact with the mattress. With nothing to do, I found myself drifting off into semiconsciousness. The events of the past few days swirled in my mind the way the mist rose in the nearby jungles.

* * *

I was walking in darkness, sure of nothing other than the sensation that I was being watched. My feet dragged across the ground as if held down by heavy weights. The wind swirled around me, and I coughed as dust pelted my face. Struggling to see, I could finally make out a large image ahead. It was a pyramid. It towered above me, and I felt compelled to walk up the stairs, but no matter how quickly I climbed, the summit rose ahead of me, always out of reach. Then I heard a screeching noise. I looked up and saw a large eagle flying through the air. It settled on a nearby rock, and it stared at me with piercing eyes. I was distracted from it by a hissing noise, and I turned to watch, transfixed as a serpent slithered across the ground. I tried to shout, to scare it off. But my voice was frozen. I waved my arms, but it drew closer and devoured the eagle then came toward me. I tried to run and felt myself falling into a deep hole. There was nothing to hold on to.

I was ripped from the dream by a knock on my door. I stumbled over to see who it was.

"Hi, Seth," I said groggily, hoping we wouldn't have a repeat of the unpleasantness that had formed between us.

"Kat's not too happy about today. I thought I'd better warn you that she's talkin' like you're becomi' the troublemaker of the bunch."

"But . . . I . . . It wasn't my fault!" I sputtered to defend myself.

He waved his hands. "I know. I know. It was just a friendly observation. Look, Kat wanted some glossies picked up at the nearby copy store. I told her I'd go, but I think it might prove somethin' to her if you went—especially after what happened today. And since I figured you wouldn't want to go alone, I'd be happy to go with you."

I might have been more thrilled at the prospect if Dave had been the one asking. But company was company, and he was right. I'd been more of a hindrance than a help lately, and since it was getting late, I certainly didn't want to go alone. "Sure. Let me get my purse."

"So you really think someone pushed you?" he asked as we got in the elevator.

I didn't really want to discuss it with him and run the risk of him discounting my words again, so I spoke cautiously. "Maybe."

"Did you see anyone or notice anything before it happened?"

"Not really."

We passed through the lobby and emerged onto the busy Reforma. No matter how many times I saw it, I doubted I would stop being impressed. The sky was slightly overcast, which suited my mood. The streets were already starting to crowd with the weekend rush. Which didn't suit me. Suddenly I just wanted to be alone.

"Maybe you were just accidentally bumped," he started in again. "No offense. You seem to be a little, well, accident prone, and it was gettin' kind of crowded up there."

"I don't think so."

"Well, I guess if you didn't see anyone, there's nothing much we can do," he continued, not breaking stride the entire time.

We arrived at the shop, and I hoped that would be the end of the conversation. I found my aversion to technology dissipating as I saw the brochures with pictures we had just taken just a few days before in Tenayuca. It *was* like magic: think it and it's done. But Seth wasn't too pleased.

"Now that I've seen them in this format, these shots are too busy." He pointed to the inside cover. "It detracts from the whole setup. You'd think Dave would know better, but it looks like I'll have to tell him how to do his job." He folded the brochure and handed it back to the clerk. "Shred it."

I sucked in a quick breath at seeing all of our efforts destroyed. Seth must have heard me.

"Hey, we can't risk someone stealin' our ideas. Well, that was a waste of time. So much for hirin' freelance." He stared at me intently. "Because you never know what you're gonna get."

As we headed back, Seth mentioned he thought he'd seen a shortcut through a nearby park. It was nice to step off the busy street and into the peaceful, tree-shrouded area. There were a few benches to sit on, one next to a cascading fountain. There weren't any other people around, and at first I was glad to be alone. But then it occurred to me that I was walking through a deserted area with a man who had a hard time respecting my physical boundaries. My "stupidity" meter went off again, and I prayed we'd be back on the main street soon. However, Seth wasn't showing any sign he was going to take advantage of the situation; in fact, he was still fuming over our failed brochure.

"What a joke," he said under his breath. "If I'd been in charge, things would be going great. None of this waitin' for approval or playin' games. That's what you get when you don't stick with your own kind. Some people just don't get that though. I can't wait until Monday when we're out of here."

It was as if he'd forgotten all about me, and yet for some strange reason, I wasn't sure he was talking about what had just happened back at the copy store anymore.

When I saw Dave pacing the lobby of the hotel though, I cringed as I remembered the shredded brochure. I definitely didn't want to be there when Seth had his "talk" with him. The male ego was a fragile thing, and it would be like watching two sparring elk as they fought to defend themselves. Sure enough, when the two men saw each other, their chests puffed and they readied themselves for battle.

"Where did you go with her?" Dave demanded.

"Why?" Seth mocked. "Afraid I was stealin' her away? We went to look at the layouts for the first color brochure, and I have to tell you, I wasn't as impressed with the final product as I thought I'd be. You may have all those credits behind your name, but yer slippin', pardner."

I felt my stomach clench as I waited for Dave to retaliate. But he didn't.

Instead, he talked to me in Spanish. "Next time," he said, "tell the group when you're taking off. That way, if we, uh, need you for anything, we'll know where you are."

I stammered, "Okay. I . . . I will."

Seth stepped closer to me. "I don't know what you were sayin' there, but she was safe. She was with me."

Now Dave released the scowl he'd been saving before he stomped off.

Wow. Two guys fighting over you?

No one was more surprised than me.

Chapter 22

FRIDAY ENDED UP BEING ANOTHER disaster. I'd warned Kat the night before that the next day was Cinco de Mayo. Fearing that the city would be packed with celebrations, she canceled our plans.

Big mistake.

How was I supposed to know they didn't celebrate their own victory in Mexico the same way we did in the States? In America, it was practically a national holiday, and yet here in Mexico City, they barely acknowledged its existence.

I waited for my boss to erupt like the volcanoes off in the distance. But Kat was surprisingly calm and even suggested we stay at the hotel and do some brainstorming instead. It was as if some worry had been lifted off her shoulders and she was no longer stressing about our next location. I hoped the campaign really was going that well, despite Seth's remarks.

Of course, the only thing I truly cared about that day was my dad. Assuming his procedure would take most of the morning, I was glad we had stayed at the hotel. But by the time we took a lunch break, my parents still hadn't called, so I went up to my room and took the initiative. My mom answered.

"How did things go?" I pounced before she could even get a greeting in.

"Samantha! I'm so glad you called. We just got back—it's as if you knew."

Had it taken the doctors that long? That didn't sound good. "Is he there?"

"Yes, sweetheart. He's a little groggy, but I'll get him on the phone too."

I heard the muffled call of my mother and then the static as my dad picked up the other line. "Hey, princess. It's been quite a day."

I frowned. "You sound tired. Did . . . did everything go all right?"

I could almost imagine him smiling on the other end. "I was their favorite patient, and the doctors at the Huntsman Center said they have no reason to worry that it can't be managed with standard care. By the time my first round of treatment gets started, you'll be home. Well, back in the States, that is."

I felt my eyes tear up, and my voice cracked as I spoke. "I sent you a letter. Silly really, because it probably won't get there until after I'm back. But I wanted . . . I needed to say some things. Let you know in writing what you mean to me."

"Thanks, princess. Well, I'm getting kind of tired. I'll turn you back over to your mom."

My nose started to run, and since the tissue box was empty, I dragged the phone into the bathroom. "Mom," I said when she came back on the line, "maybe I won't be going back to California when this is all over. I'm thinking about what my options might be. Maybe doing something closer to home."

"Why, Samantha? Isn't everything going all right there?"

"I don't know," I said, frustrated. "Kind of. Not like I thought it would. This is a beautiful country, and I've seen so many fascinating things, but I've also seen a side of the people I'm here with that I don't like. Everyone's so competitive, so closed off. I don't know what I'm doing half the time, and the other half I think I'm doing everything wrong."

"It's been that bad?" she asked.

"Yes."

"Why didn't you tell us?"

I sat on the edge of the closed toilet seat. "Well, I didn't want to worry you, and I wanted you to be proud of me and to show you, and probably myself, that I could hack it out here in the real world. But I'm not so sure I *want* to be in the real world."

There was silence for a moment, and then my mom added her thoughts. "I think you have more strength than you realize. You just have to believe in yourself. The world is a frightening place, but we have to find a way to live in it and still remember who we are. Your father and I believe in you."

We talked for a few more minutes about trivial things to lighten the mood. By the time I hung up the phone, I felt like I could smile again. Everything was right with the world. Almost. I may have been convinced that I could do this job, but now I had to convince someone else.

Hopefully my boss was around so I could check in with her. I was still so caught up in my euphoria that everything was all right with my dad that I ran straight into Dave as I headed down the hall. "Sorry," I stammered. "I guess I wasn't watching where I was going."

"That's all right. You're not going out, are you?" He frowned.

"No. I was just checking to see if Kat needed me for anything."

"She's not in her room. But you ought to stay close," he said absentmindedly before walking off.

I frowned and considered my options. Since Kat wasn't around, I wandered around the halls for a little bit before returning to my own room and killing time with a little television. Yikes. Mexican programs were a tad different from ours. Not finding anything that I dared watch at first, I settled for a dubbed-over version of *The Magnificent Seven.* When it ended, I stared aimlessly out the window until I heard a knock on the door. I opened it to find Seth standing there, and I hoped we weren't up for another display of testosterone.

"Well, just a few more days until we're finished. Are you up to celebratin'?"

I started to protest. I wasn't interested in spending a night on the town with anyone, especially him. But he shook his head and even managed a curious grin. "Apparently it's Dave's birthday, and Kat made reservations for us at a nearby restaurant in *honor* of it." I noticed how he slurred the word. "We're meetin' downstairs at six."

Feeling a surge of defiance at how Seth had treated Dave earlier, I smiled brightly. "Of course. I wouldn't miss it."

When it was almost time to go, I changed my clothes again, hoping I fit in with my blouse and skirt. I wished I'd looked for some matching earrings at La Ciudadela after all but had to settle for my one and only piece of jewelry: the bracelet I'd bought in Xochimilco. Considering all the scrapes I was getting into, I almost wondered if it could be my lucky charm to end the streak. After a few fresh bandage replacements, I grabbed a light jacket and confirmed that the contents of my purse were intact and my phone was still charged.

Everyone was ready downstairs—everyone except Seth, that is. He huffed across the lobby ten minutes later, complaining about how his computer had frozen up on him. Before then, I'd been having a hard time not staring at Dave. He was dressed as formally as I think I'd ever seen him: dark blue slacks and a matching blazer, with a white-collared shirt that was striking against his bronzed skin. It seemed a bit much to wear, even though the nights had been a little cool, but I had to admit, he looked handsome in it. Kat resembled a fashion model in her low-cut black cocktail dress and dangling turquoise and silver earrings. I felt dowdy again.

The restaurant was lovely; leave it to Kat to pick out such a place. We must have needed reservations, but somehow, we'd been given a spot right beside a sparkling fountain. My boss was efficient that way. The night's air blended with the gentle scent of the bougainvillea that climbed up the nearby walls like bright splotches of pink paint. We ate by the light of flickering candles. I thought how appropriate it all was—that under the mask of near darkness, you couldn't tell what anyone was thinking.

I couldn't remember what I'd ordered until it was placed in front of me. The chicken *mole* was nicely seasoned, and I smiled contentedly as I wrapped a portion of it in fresh tortillas. The smell alone was divine, but the taste was even better. If only Seth weren't hovering so close to me. Kat was also unnerving me by having a mysterious look of triumph on her face, as if she knew something the others didn't. Dave ate silently, as did Lin and Mike. I hoped my accident and accusation yesterday wouldn't cast any gloom over the party. As far as I could tell, it was forgotten. Which was good. Frankly, I was tired of standing out.

As we ate, the sound of mariachi music poured in from a side entrance. Thinking this was merely the night's entertainment, I sat back and tried to enjoy the music. The group continued to wind their way around the room, singing until they stood by our table. It was then I noticed they had begun to sing the traditional Mexican birthday song, "Las Mañanitas." Our young waitress handed Dave a rose, pecked him on the cheek, and giggled as she departed. I looked hesitantly over at Dave, somehow knowing he hated this kind of attention. He squirmed in his seat while the rest of the sparse audience clapped and sang along. Then, when the song ended, the heavy Mexican woman at the table next to us hobbled over and kissed Dave on the cheek as well.

"What are they doing?" Lin leaned over and asked me.

I knew from my mission that it was a Mexican tradition that the birthday guest was supposed to get a kiss from any members of the opposite gender present. Each one was for a birthday wish, I told her. My heart started pounding in my throat as my explanation brought to mind what this meant. It would be strange if Dave didn't receive this token from those seated at his own table, and I knew Kat wouldn't pass up this opportunity to publicly stake her claim. Several other jubilant participants arose from nearby tables, and then there was a break in the onslaught. With a glance that made Dave look like he was prey in some hunter's trap, Kat rose from her seat. I gulped as a few cheers ensued. People must have thought they were an attractive couple and that they were anxious for a passionate display of affection.

My stomach clenched.

I didn't want to watch Kat cup his chin in her hand and lean close, but I found I couldn't turn away. After all, my boss was taking her time to make sure it was quite a show. Then, just before she found her mark, Dave turned his head slightly so her lips planted just to the side of his mouth. The red stain she left behind immediately blended with the flush that spread across Dave's face as he slowly wiped it away. Meanwhile, Kat's face had become steel, and she sank back down into her chair, lifting a glass of wine to her lips as her fingers trembled with anger.

Lin stood up next and gave him a chaste peck on the lips, smiling as if it were some private joke between them. When I glanced helplessly around the room, several tables started pounding their fists on the table and cheering, "¡Bésalo! ¡Dale un béso!"

With a gulp, I stood up and walked to the other side of the table. As I leaned toward him, it was his scent that reached me first. I took a deep breath and found myself staring into his piercing brown eyes. Would it be sappy to say that the rest of the world melted away? But that must have been what happened, or I would never have been so bold. Our lips met for what was only a brief moment, after which we parted to whistles and catcalls, clapping hands, and more mariachi music. I was back to sitting in the middle of a crowded restaurant. But I knew I couldn't walk away now like nothing had happened.

Needless to say, the rest of the meal didn't go well. I couldn't even enjoy the rose petal ice cream we had for dessert. Pushing around the melting concoction with my spoon, I hoped that looks really couldn't kill.

If they can, Kat is already mentally drafting your obituary and stamping down the dirt on your grave.

Hmm. Jealousy could provoke Kat to do dastardly things. Whether she would use it for the demise of my career, only time would tell. Finally, just when I thought I would scream, Kat addressed us as if nothing had happened.

"So, Lin, what was it you gave Dave for his birthday? Or is it too personal to say?"

My companion at my side laughed. "Hardly personal. After I found out it was Dave's thirtieth birthday today, I thought I'd present him with a hand-carved frame to put one of his favorite pictures in from this trip."

"How thoughtful," Kat mused.

Great. Presents. I hadn't thought about that.

"You should have told us, and we could have planned something a little more grand, Dave." Kat waved her hand as if suddenly the opulent surroundings around us had turned into one of the tin shacks we'd seen as we'd driven out to Anáhuac.

"That's all right," Dave said, fidgeting. "I didn't want to make it a big deal."

Kat grinned her Cheshire cat grin again. "Then we have Lin to thank for bringing it to our attention." She then reached down and pulled out a small package wrapped in silver paper.

Dave took it begrudgingly, and I knew then that things must not have progressed as far between him and the boss as I'd once thought. Maybe there was still hope for me.

You just don't learn your lesson, do you?

Nope. I guess I'm a slow learner.

He ripped back the paper and opened the lid of the carved box, but I knew what was inside before he did. Even then, when the small wooden snake jumped out and nearly "bit" his finger, I jumped. Dave, on the other hand, remained as composed as a stone statue. Kat just laughed softly and signaled for the check.

"Just a little something to remember me by," she purred.

Chapter 23

SOMEHOW I ARRIVED BACK AT the hotel without doing anything else to warrant Kat's wrath. But as I sat at the desk in my room, clutching the familiar blue-covered book in my hands, I lost my confidence at least two or three times. I looked at the shawl on the bed, now minus its wrapping, tossed caution to the wind, and decided to go for it. The fancy paper would work well as wrapping paper for my gift. I just wished I had some ribbon or something other than the dental floss I'd used to hold it together. It seemed even sillier when I wrote the note on the hotel stationery. He was probably going to have a good laugh over it tonight, but so what.

After that kiss, I was already in too deep.

He must have known I'd put my heart into it, regardless of how brief the kiss was. I only wished I could be sure he had returned it.

Does it really matter? That seems to be the least of the obstacles between you.

Arghhh! I hated it when the voice was right. But I still protested that it wasn't impossible. I looked at the facts. He'd had a few cups of coffee, but I hadn't seen him swig a single beer or smoke a single cigarette. And even the colorful language he'd used that one day had been tame compared to what some people threw into their everyday speech. Even I had once let loose with an expletive when the hammer I'd been using hit my thumb. Before my inner voice could add to the opposing list of impossibilities, I groaned and finished its job.

Who was I kidding? I could imagine the homecoming . . .

"Hi, Mom and Dad. Here's my boyfriend I met two weeks ago in Mexico. I know nothing about his background other than he takes photographs and may not be who he says he is."

I crumpled up the note I'd been writing and threw it in the garbage. Then, just to be sure it really was as pathetic as I'd decided, I retrieved it.

Yep. It would have made a hormone-laden high school student proud. I tossed it again. On my second try, I simply wrote:

> Happy Birthday. Here's a book I thought you'd find interesting—it means a lot to me.
>
> I marked a specific chapter for you to read. Let me know if you have any questions.

As I walked trembling to his room, I couldn't figure out how this had been so easy on my mission. Maybe it was because you knew that one day you'd be leaving everyone and everything behind. It let you be bold.

But then I reminded myself that in a few days, I'd be leaving everything here behind. Was that the reason I'd let things progress this far? Because it was the equivalent of having a summer fling: all fantasy and no commitment? I nearly turned around again but then took a deep breath and knocked on Dave's door. My foot started tapping out a nervous rhythm, and I pushed my hair behind my ears as if in seeing my face he might just know how genuine I was being.

There was no answer.

I tried one more time and then accepted that he wasn't there. We'd all come back to the hotel together. Had he gone out again, or was he . . . ? Not wanting to think about it, I quickly set my present down next to the door. Then I scurried back to my room like a cockroach.

That night as I got ready for bed, I was still rehearsing the scene from earlier that day. It almost felt like I'd imagined it all. But then I touched a finger to my lips and remembered the warmth that had been there and sighed. Dutifully, I read my scriptures and said my prayers. But as I lay down, something occurred to me that I should have noticed earlier as I'd thrown away the first draft of my letter to Dave. Something *else* that should have been in the trash. I got up and walked over to look in the wastebasket. With a grimace, I waded through used tissues and a few unhelpful tourist brochures, searching for the elusive note I'd been handed in Tula. When it didn't surface immediately, I dumped the contents of the receptacle on the floor and spread them out—but I still couldn't find it. Sitting back on my haunches, I was puzzled. It had to be there. The maid had come *before* I'd thrown it away—otherwise the rest of this stuff would be gone as well. I checked again. It wasn't there. So where was it?

A disturbing thought formed in my mind. If it was no longer there, that could only mean one thing:

Someone had come into my room and taken it.

* * *

The next day we were all quiet over breakfast. Maybe I wasn't the only one with questions on my mind. Dave ate his *papadzules* as if he weren't interested in the taste, and I found myself only picking at my *pan dulce*. I wanted him to say something about last night because I was too cowardly to do it, but I knew he wouldn't say anything in front of the group. I waited until we dispersed and then managed to catch him alone in the hallway. He seemed like his mind was elsewhere, so to catch his attention, I blurted out, "Oh, did you get that book I left you?"

"Was that from you?" he turned and raised an eyebrow.

Great. Had I forgotten after all that rewriting to sign my name? "Yes, it was." I blushed.

"I didn't have time to read any of it last night—I had a lot to do. What is it anyway?"

"Well, it's called the Book of Mormon." I struggled to put my words together. "And it's a book of scripture that my church believes in. We believe it tells the history of two groups of people who settled here in Mexico and Central America. It contains their genealogy and scriptures and tells of their wars and leaders. Over all, it's a religious book because it contains the words of ancient prophets and testifies of Christ. But there are some fascinating similarities between this book and some of the things you've explained to me about Quetzalcóatl. I thought you'd be interested in reading it. Especially the part I marked."

"Sure." He nodded with a strange look on his face. "I'll try and get to it when I have the time."

I watched him walk away, disappointed.

We spent the rest of the morning redoing the brochures, and then Kat finally suggested we take a few hours for a lunch break. But when she didn't make any suggestions for the group, I realized I'd be stuck down at the restaurant again, and my budget wasn't going to handle that. So I asked Miguel at the front desk—ignoring his look of satisfaction that I knew his name now—if there were any taco stands nearby. He grinned and directed me to cross the street and go a block east then leaned over to whisper breathily in my ear that he couldn't afford to eat here either.

Geez. Did this guy's name translate to "Roger"?

Checking that my phone was on, I figured I could chance being away for a few minutes, especially after I saw Mike sitting in the downstairs lobby and told him where I was going. That ought to satisfy anyone who came looking for me.

The tacos smelled delicious, but I passed on the condiments this time. The Reforma was crowded, considering it was a Saturday afternoon, and though I would have preferred to sit down at a nearby bench under a tree and eat, I asked that they wrap mine so I could take them back. As I started to walk, I realized I really needed to get my eyes checked because someone who looked like Mike was sitting on one of the benches, acting like he was hiding behind a newspaper. I looked again and decided it really was Mike. Was he following me? It was tempting to sit down next to him as if I hadn't seen him and then act surprised. Okay, so it was another strange coincidence. And I could hardly blame him for wanting to enjoy the sunshine as well.

I kept walking until I hit the traffic trying to cross the street. As I waited for a break in cars—hoping jaywalking wasn't an offense here as well—I figured I was going crazy when I saw a man exit through the revolving doors of our hotel. I squinted in the bright sunlight and watched as a dark sedan pulled up and the man got in. He was back to wearing his sunglasses and black shirt, but I knew who it was.

I waited until the car had pulled out of sight and then went inside the hotel. Approaching Miguel, I casually asked, "Was there a man here at the hotel in sunglasses, dressed all in black?"

The desk clerk flashed me his white teeth and leaned forward. "Yes, *señorita*. There was a man like that here."

"Did he want something?" I asked hesitantly. "Uh, something to do with a member of our group?"

Miguel's mouth dropped into a playful frown. "Perhaps. But it is my job to keep the affairs of this hotel, how do you say? *Privado?*"

Now I leaned toward him, hating how low I was going to stoop. "That's too bad. Tomorrow is my last night here, and I'd hoped to see more of your beautiful city before I left."

Now the corners of his mouth leapt up. "There is the most beautiful *restaurante* not far from here. It is very *romantico*."

"Perhaps," I said coyly. "About that man . . ."

His black eyes darted nervously around. "He just left a letter to be sent up to your Ms. Edwards."

"May I see the note?"

"But it was not meant for you!"

I scrambled to think. "I don't want to *read* it, just take a look at it and see if there's something I need to know. After all, I'm her personal assistant, and I'm here to handle her business affairs. If the letter is from the executives here in Mexico, she'll want to know immediately. In fact, I'm on my way back up and could bring it to her."

Miguel frowned but then leaned over and retrieved the note from under the counter. He started to hand it to me and then jerked it back. "I will let you look at it, but then one of my staff will deliver it to her personally. It is, as they say, hotel policy."

Apparently my *femme fatale* persona wasn't all that effective—I bet Kat could teach me a few things. A tad miffed, I grabbed the letter and examined the front. There was a name scrawled on the front in pen:

Sna. Edwards

Other than that, it was blank. But then, as an afterthought, I turned it over and nearly choked. A small embossment had been placed right where the envelope sealed. I looked at it more closely to confirm that it was indeed the image of a coiling serpent. And as I examined the writing more closely, I realized the *S* on this letter for the abbreviated "Señora" reminded me of the *S* on the note at Tula saying the "Serpent" had wanted to meet someone. In fact, it almost looked like a snake itself. I handed the letter back to Miguel as if I'd been burned and then turned away.

"But about tomorrow night?" he yelled after me hopefully.

"Uh, I'll have to see what our plans are," I replied, adopting one of Kat's many smiles.

Feeling dizzy, I walked slowly back to my room, where I nibbled thoughtfully on my tacos. I wished I could have read that note. It might have answered so many questions. Maybe Kat had a secret admirer who had finally become brave enough to express his feelings of love to her in a letter.

You don't really believe that, do you?

No. But it would have been better than the alternative: that my boss might be embroiled in something other than putting together a marketing campaign for the Mexico City tourism bureau.

I lost my appetite. But what should I do? Rejoin the group and try to act as if everything was normal? There was still some time left, and I decided there was only one place I could go to try to make sense of everything—one place I would feel completely safe.

The cab the hotel radioed for me dropped me off right in front of the visitor's center. Sister Remington greeted me with a hug this time, and I was touched that she remembered me. She was excited to tell me that her oldest daughter had just given birth the day before; she wished she could have been there with her, but missions meant sacrifices. I nodded, understanding from my own year and a half away from friends and family. When she asked me how things had been going, I almost chickened out. She smiled patiently as I rambled around the point. But when I started to explain some of the strange things that had happened while on this trip, her expression grew concerned.

"And you say that neither of these notes was signed nor explained in any way, other than some mention of a serpent?" she asked.

I nodded.

She pursed her lips. "I don't like this. Do you still have the first one?"

"Well, I threw it away and then . . ." How did I explain what had happened? "It's gone now."

"It might have been useful to show it to someone, like the authorities maybe."

"I'm sure the police here are just as taxed as the ones at home. They would think it was a harmless prank and probably just file the report away somewhere. If only I had more proof that something strange was going on. But we leave on Monday, and I don't know what to do."

She seemed so genuinely concerned that I suddenly felt bad burdening her with this. But when I apologized, she brushed it off. "Think nothing of it. But I don't like the thought of you going about this by yourself. Isn't there anyone in your group you trust?"

I bit my lip and thought about it. My hope was that only Kat was involved. Then how did I explain Dave's, and even Lin's, odd behavior? Somehow I guessed they were linked to all this; I just didn't know how. And if they really were, Mike had to be thrown into the suspicion pool through mere association. Of course, there was still Seth, but I could almost hear him laughing at me when I told him my flimsy story. I shook my head. "I'm not sure who to trust."

Sister Remington patted my hand and looked up at the *Christus* statue. "That's not entirely true, is it?"

I didn't want to leave but knew I'd better get back. As I stepped outside, I wished I could bring this feeling of peace with me because in all of the worldly commotion, it was easy to lose it. I glanced up at the temple again and would have loved to go inside. Maybe another time. Then I noticed a woman walking nearby, looking up at the edifice as well. She had a silk scarf on her head and, after doing a double blink, I realized how much she looked like Lin. But she turned away and blended into the crowd of numerous other petite, Hispanic women who were ambling around the grounds.

My phone rang just as I stepped to the curb to signal for a ride back, and for some reason I felt paranoid as I stood in the open. I answered it, and a flash of green breezed past me. I scowled that the cab hadn't even slowed down. "Hello?" I said a little impatiently.

"Hey darlin', where'd you mosey off to?"

What is he, your watchdog?

"Uh, nowhere important, Seth. I'm on my way back now. Bye." It was uncharacteristic of me to hang up on him, but another cab had already replaced the rude one and was coming toward me, so I put one foot in the street this time to compel it to stop. The moment I did, a black sedan came whipping toward me from another lane. I wasn't expecting it to come so close—it nearly knocked me off balance and into the oncoming traffic. Wishing my upbringing allowed for a few choice epithets, I tried to gather my senses as I got into the cab.

Safe in my room at the hotel, I thought about what Sister Remington had said. I *did* know who to put my trust in, and I fell onto my knees, humbled by that fact. But I was scared. I didn't want to get involved in whatever was going on. Would it be so wrong to ignore my suspicions and let what was going to happen just happen? Who was I to get in the way? I knew instantly that was a cowardly question. It was one thing to try not to let the world become part of me and another to deny that I was part of that world. If I could make a difference, I had to try, didn't I?

Wiping a tear from my eye, I confronted my fears. This was going to be the most difficult thing I'd ever faced. But as I waited for reassurance, I knew the answer to that final question, and the answer was *yes*.

Chapter 24

WHEN WE ALL REGROUPED FOR dinner, I watched for any change in my boss's demeanor, but aside from a little nervousness dampening what had, for the last few days, been an obvious excitement, nothing seemed too out of the ordinary. And considering that we only had a couple more days left to wrap things up, I was feeling different as well. I was scared and anxious all at the same time—kind of like those few moments before you take a final exam. You know you're going to be tested but not exactly sure in what way.

As we sat in the ritzy restaurant that specialized in Yucatán cuisine, it gave me a chance to see the other members of the group interacting, and it piqued my curiosity. Seth appeared to be back to his usual laid-back self, while Lin and Mike acted like they'd had a lover's spat. I was most curious about the differences I noted in Dave. There was an alertness in his eyes that went beyond his role as a photographer, like he was waiting for something to suddenly appear and didn't want to miss it. He was also bundled in his blazer again, though the air outside was still warm and humid, as if he were trying to shield himself physically from the rest of us. There was a tension in the air that was almost palpable, and I found myself playing with the bracelet on my wrist, circling my thumb over the smooth stones as if it would soothe me. I looked up, caught Dave staring at me, and dropped my hands to my lap.

I was glad when we finished and went outside to meet the hired taxis waiting for us. I took a deep breath and realized I'd almost gotten used to the air, though I'd developed a slight cough. Fortunately, I had assimilated easily to the higher altitude; some of the group had complained from time to time that it zapped their strength. Physical complaints weren't the only thing that could drag you down though. I glanced over at Dave, but he didn't return my look—he was too busy staring at Kat.

I shivered slightly. Not because of any external temperature change but because I had the strange feeling again that I was being watched closely. When I turned and looked, however, I only saw Seth smiling at me. Suddenly I didn't feel well.

Back at the hotel, I spent half an hour pacing in my room. I knew I had to do something more direct, but I didn't know exactly what. I mean, I couldn't exactly walk up to my boss and say, "Hey, it seems to me you've got something else going on here besides our team project. Mind telling me what it is?" And I knew I didn't have enough evidence to approach the local authorities. Maybe that strange note I'd received in Tula would have helped. Maybe if I could have gotten Miguel to give me that letter—but what I had were too many "maybes" and not enough time.

I went to Kat's room, only to find the DO NOT DISTURB sign up. It could have been all the excuse I needed. After all, the last thing I wanted to do was make this more difficult by interrupting something. But I knocked loudly anyway. No one answered. Frowning, I wondered what to do next. My throat had suddenly gone dry, and I needed something to drink, not in the traditional sense, though I could almost understand why a movie character would slug down some Scotch right before facing some unpleasant task. I'd used up all my bottled beverages days ago, so I headed around the corner to the vending machines again. I wished I had an ice bucket as well, thinking whatever I got would taste better if it were bitterly cold and might then excuse the chattering of my teeth.

They were out of all but the caffeinated drinks, which surprised me, considering how many late nights our group had been putting in. I settled on plain water, since even a sugar rush would have affected my jittery mood. I wanted my mind to be clear and alert. Collecting my bottle, I made it to the corner when I heard voices coming from down the hall. Perhaps I should have come out and confronted her instead of ducking behind the ice machine again. Not only would it have shown some backbone, but then I would have seen who she was talking to.

"I can't believe I'm going to meet him," Kat said breathlessly. "After everything. By tomorrow, I can put all this nonsense aside and get back to business. So," she purred, "do you want to come in and help me celebrate?"

I didn't hear an answer to her question, only the clicking of a door being opened and shut—but it wasn't a leap of imagination to think that it was a man she'd been talking to. Peering around the corner, I could see that the hallway was empty. I walked carefully back in the direction of my room. As I did, I stopped and knocked softly on Seth's door. There was no answer. Was he the man with Kat? I stopped at Dave's room as well, and when there was no answer there either, I felt my hopes sink and started to doubt again. What did Kat mean that by tomorrow she could get back to business? Did she mean that because that was the last day of our trip, she could go back to Phizer-Lewis and move on to another project? Or did it imply that something was going to happen tomorrow—something related to everything else that had been going on?

Lin startled me as I stood motionless in front of Dave's door. "Looking for someone?" she asked.

"No," I said dejectedly and went to walk past her.

Her voice echoed after me down the empty hallway. "I told you to be careful what you got yourself into."

My strength gone, I didn't turn around to ask her about her puzzling words but kept walking.

* * *

It was Sunday.

Tomorrow we would be flying home and could put all this behind us. But no matter how I tried, I knew I couldn't rest until I discovered what was going on.

The group had been working frantically since early that morning, trying to determine if we had all the footage we needed for whatever would be worked on back in San Diego. Since I hadn't sat outside Dave's room last night, I had no idea when he'd finally returned. But his bleary-looking eyes this morning told me he hadn't slept well. Hopefully a few late hours of developing photographs were the cause.

When the group started to complain of hunger around two o'clock, I mentioned the taco stand across the street and volunteered to go. But Mike jumped up as if he couldn't wait to get out of the room and said he would. After that, the afternoon dragged on until I was so exhausted I could barely think straight. Seth finally said he had to go back to his room for some peace and quiet, and as I sat listening to Kat and Lin argue over some of the video footage, I thought the escape preferable too. But I saw myself as being on a "by your leave" kind of probation, so I stayed put. Now I couldn't help but try to decipher every gesture, every contact between Dave and Kat. When he brushed her hand reaching for a paper, did it mean something? When she grabbed his coffee cup and drank from it, was it an intimate gesture or a mistake?

Finally we were given a reprieve. No one had suggested dinner together, and it was still early by local standards. When Lin and Mike called it quits as well, I took my cue and blew my remaining budget on the hotel restaurant and then decided to take a siesta. But instead of sleeping, I ended up pacing in my room for a half hour. Just when I'd decided to try resting again, the in-room phone on the desk rang, breaking the silence. Startled, I picked it up.

"Hello?" I said timidly.

There was no answer on the other line. Just a click.

"Hello? Is anyone there?"

I wasn't sure if I was relieved or frightened. My first thought had been that it was my parents calling with some bad news. When no one spoke, I decided it was probably just a wrong number. But it put me on edge, and I nearly jumped out of my skin when my own phone rang a few seconds later.

Trying to calm my nerves, I picked it up. "Hello?"

The voice was impatient and to the point. "It's Kat. Seth did an electronic transfer of some files to the nearby copy store. Go pick them up and come straight back. There should be two files, about two hundred pages each. Think you can do that?"

The advantage of phone conversations was that the other person couldn't see you roll your eyes. I looked at the clock. "Are you sure they're still open?"

"Yes." Kat huffed impatiently. "I made sure of it."

"Oh. Well then, I'll leave right now."

I was already halfway to the door with my purse when she disconnected. In fact, I wasn't even going to waste time on the inconsistent elevator but would take the stairs and be back in such record time that she couldn't help but be amazed. Dashing like an Olympic sprinter, I leapt down the last two stairs and burst through the doorway into the lobby. I noticed Mike sitting on one of the sofas that faced the elevators. I considered stopping to say hello but decided it was more important to take care of Kat's request and gain back what little favor I could.

The copy store was open as she'd said, and it had our order ready. Luckily it had already been paid for. Thanking the clerk, I suddenly realized how heavy a ream of paper was. I turned the bundle horizontally and held it tightly against my chest then scampered back out into the busy Sunday night fray.

Mexico City was alive tonight. Thousands of animated voices from revelers and sightseers blended into an auditory kaleidoscope. The young and energetic were out in full force, enjoying the cooler night air as if sipping a refreshing beverage. I heard the sound of laughter and cars honking. The sound of friends greeting each other. It was strange. Though it had only been two weeks, I had come to know the spirit of the city. In fact, it was interesting that in Spanish there were two forms of the verb *to know*. One implied that you knew a fact, like how many inches were in a foot. The other expressed that you were acquainted with something or someone—that you recognized it. I looked around me and realized that I recognized this city. With all of its faults and tensions, I had started to feel like a part of me belonged here.

As I struggled to move against the crowd, I remembered the shortcut Seth had shown me. Since it was likely not as crowded at this hour, I could easily cut across the small park and slash a few more minutes off my time. As I walked, my footsteps echoed on the cobblestone path. It was darker than I remembered it, especially since the sun had already dipped well below the city skyline. I increased my pace and headed toward the set of stairs that would lead me through a narrow alleyway and back into the reassuring bustle of the city streets again. But just as I reached the end of the path, I heard something that didn't sound quite right.

At first, I thought it was just an echo of my own steps off the nearby wall or maybe even an amorous couple taking advantage of the seclusion. But then I realized it was another set of footsteps. I walked faster. The other steps mirrored my own tempo. I slowed down, and the clapping sound stopped abruptly, like a voice that had been silenced. With frantic breath, I hurried to the steps, not wanting to look back and confirm my suspicions.

The alley was empty, surprisingly devoid of trash like other large cities I'd been in. There was a garbage can up against one wall, and I clumsily knocked against it. The noise amplified in the narrow passageway like a clanging of cymbals in an auditorium. The set of files started to feel like dead weight in my hands, and I thought about throwing them down to run faster. I couldn't hear the other footsteps for a moment and thought maybe I had been imagining them, but then the staccato noise returned. I ran, gasping as I stumbled. Then I screamed as a black figure materialized out of the darkness ahead.

Chapter 25

"*MADRE DE*—" THE OTHER VOICE started to say.

As I stared back at the man in the waiter's uniform, I could barely form an apology. He scowled at me and scurried past, apparently familiar with the same shortcut. I glanced behind me into the dusk and realized that if someone had been there, this waiter had scared him off. Now that I was sure no one was following me—and was starting to doubt there ever had been—I laughed nervously and relaxed. When I got back to the hotel, the bright foyer lights and exuberant conversations helped ward off any remaining fears, and I headed to the elevator. I saw Mike again across the room, but this time Lin was with him. She was shouting and sounded angry, and she kept pointing around the hotel lobby as if to emphasize his apparent shortcomings. Not wanting to be involved in their lovers' quarrel, I changed my course and used the stairs.

I was anxious to get rid of the load I was carrying and hoped Kat was alone. I wouldn't be able to talk to her if there was an audience. But after I stood panting for a few moments in front of her door trying to juggle everything, I realized she wasn't there anymore—or at least was back to not answering.

Frustrated, I stomped back to my room. Why would she send me out for this in such a hurry if she wasn't even going to be there for it when I got back? I threw the boxes down on the bed, and the first slid off onto the floor, breaking the seal that had held it together. With the top of the lid raised partway, it was easy to give it a final nudge and see what was inside. I stared in disbelief. Then I opened the other box and let the contents drop onto the floor. As hundreds of blank pages stared back at me, I felt my knees give way.

As I ran my fingers across the papers, the sound of the footsteps following me through the dark alley came back to me. I crushed one of the blank sheets in my hands and grew angry at the thought. This wasn't an important file Kat needed. Tonight had been a setup. Why? What did I really know?

Enough to make her scared.

So what now?

Find out what Kat's up to, and you'll discover what's going on.

Since I was already on my knees, I decided to do the one sure thing I knew would help—I prayed. When I'd finished, I was certain I heard someone say I already had the key. At first I interpreted that to mean I had the answer. But then I remembered. Rushing to get my purse, I looked inside and realized I'd never given Kat her room key from that day I'd been sick. And since she'd never asked for it, I'd forgotten all about it. I really *did* have the key, and I was going to unlock the mystery of what was going on.

My heart racing and my hands clammy, I inserted the keycard into the slot of my boss's door. When the green light clicked on, I slowly depressed the handle, suddenly afraid that maybe she really was there but had been asleep or busy. The room was dark. I listened a moment and heard nothing.

With no experience in sleuthing to draw upon, I decided to leave the main lights off and only turn on a small lamp next to the bed. It snapped on with more power than I'd anticipated, and I jumped at my own shadow's appearance. I quickened my pace since I had no idea how much time I had. I checked the nightstand by the bed and found nothing unusual, just a couple phone books. Then I checked the closet. Going through her dresser was the most uncomfortable task. As I gingerly picked my way through lacey underwear and silky lingerie, the distance between the world's truth and my own reality grew farther apart.

Satisfied that there was nothing there, I moved on to the desk drawers. I found a lot of papers related to the trip and the work we were doing and wondered if I should take the time to examine them each more closely. I decided against it. Anything that could discredit her wouldn't be kept in plain sight. Even the computer on the desk probably had a pass code, and I wasn't proficient enough to know what I was looking for. Discouraged that I'd found nothing obvious, I went to the bathroom next and suddenly had a thought. I had only seen a few suitcases in the closet, and considering the amount of clothes she had brought, there must be more. I was right. Underneath her bed, I found another large suitcase, a smaller container that looked like a vanity box, and a black briefcase.

Frustrated again, I stared at the three-digit combination on the briefcase. What could it be? It wouldn't be a birthday or other special occasion with only three digits, I knew, but sitting there all night testing out combinations wasn't going to work. I smiled as I realized someone like Kat would have only thought of one thing when deciding upon the code.

Herself.

Yep. As I considered how I would text it on my phone, I turned the individual dials on the case until they spelled out "K-A-T." With a click and a pop, the case opened.

It wasn't the amorous correspondences between Kat and her boss, Brad Lansing, that caught my attention—or the shipping invoices that showed large quantities of office supplies being shipped to the company from Mexico. In the corner of the case was a small slip of paper. I picked it up and started to read.

"*The Serpent has decided to meet you . . .*"

I stopped. With trembling hands, I put the missing, crumpled note that had been taken from my garbage can aside and continued to search. A bulging manila folder caught my eye, and I opened it and found a couple more letters, this time in Spanish. It didn't take much reading before I got the gist of their content. Then, underneath the files, I found the box in brown paper with the serpent insignia. I opened it, dumping the contents into my hand.

Looking down at the small plastic bag in my open palm, I pushed a finger from the other hand into the middle of it, indenting the white powder inside. It was smooth, like baking soda, and I was tempted to open it and smell what was inside.

But who was I kidding. I wouldn't have known what kind of drug it was.

There was someone who would though. I was sure the authorities would be very interested in the note and the letters. But then I realized my first shortcoming at being a spy. I couldn't very well shove everything under my T-shirt and make my way down the elevator and across the lobby without someone noticing. I should have thought to bring something to stow any evidence I found.

Berating myself as I made what seemed like a mile-long journey back to my room, I grabbed my purse and emptied some of its contents onto my bed. My phone would fit in my back pocket, but I'd have to forego my usual necessities. I quickly snuck back to Kat's room.

I hadn't seen anyone in the hallway, and I was even more vigilant in listening for the sound of doors opening and closing this time. I gathered what I'd found then shut the case and repositioned it under the bed. The files made it so I couldn't zip my purse, but it would have to do. It was more important that I got out of there. Fast!

This time I backed out of the room, closing the door as slowly as a bomb expert would defuse a ticking bomb. In fact, the latch settled into place without making a sound. Quite proud of myself, I nearly screamed for the second time that night as I heard a man's voice behind me.

"Lookin' for Kat?"

I jerked around to face Seth, hoping I didn't look like the kid who got caught with her hand in the cookie jar. "Uh, hi. Yeah, I was hoping to give her some files I'd been working on. But I've been knocking, so she must not be here."

He grinned. "She's not. I saw her go out a few hours ago. Dave seems to be missin' as well. It appears that everyone has their own agenda tonight."

I was about to mention that I'd seen Lin and Mike downstairs but thought better of it. "Well, as long as everyone's keeping busy. Have you . . . completed your layouts yet?"

"Just about. There have been a lot of distractions though. Would you like to see what I've been workin' on?"

As he stepped closer, my instinct was to back away. But we were in the open hallway where anyone could come up on us, and I didn't want him to sense anything was wrong. "Well," I replied, "actually, I'm kind of tired. Maybe I'll just go get ready for bed, if that's all right. I'll see them later."

"Oh, come on. I've been workin' so hard, and I know you'd appreciate it. In fact, my project's in Kat's room. We won't take long."

Though every cell of my body shouted *no!* I couldn't see what choice I had. If I made Seth suspicious, he might tell Kat, and she would put two and two together before I could get to the police. "Just for a minute, and then I really just want to go back to my room."

With a grin, Seth opened the door and led me back into the room. It didn't escape me that he had his own card. He walked over to the computer on the dresser, opened it, and waited while it booted up. I walked nearer when I saw that he'd pulled up a file. It was a spreadsheet. Leaning over, I tried to decipher the large numbers running up and down the screen, but they didn't make any sense. Were these figures somehow related to the stats I'd organized on the marketing account? It didn't seem like the same information I'd handled earlier.

"I . . . I don't think I get it," I said as I turned to face him.

He was sitting casually on the bed, and I saw that disturbing look in his eyes again, like when he'd kissed me.

"I'd better go." I shuffled toward the door.

As I reached for the door handle, I heard him ask, "Did you find what you were lookin' for?"

A shiver ran through me, and I clutched my purse more closely to my body. "Uh, what do you mean? I just told you—"

Now his voice was right behind me. "Sam, Sam. You're not an experienced enough liar to be convincing."

I had the sudden impulse to do what I should have done the first time I was alone with him.

Run!

But the viselike grip on my arm and the barrel of what I assumed was a gun digging into my back changed my mind.

Chapter 26

YOU REALLY MESSED UP THIS TIME.

That was an understatement for once.

"Don't do anything stupid," Seth ordered, pressing harder into my back. "I've grown to like you too much to want to see you hurt."

I was past believing that, but I did what he said. Not protesting gave me energy to think about how I could get away from him anyway. Would someone in a neighboring room hear me if I screamed? Or would Seth consider that to be something "stupid"? I knew now I shouldn't have read any of those cheesy mystery novels back in college because my mind started conjuring up all kinds of fates for myself.

"Uh, Seth," I pleaded. "Please just let me go. Here, just take it." I threw my purse onto the floor with the foolish hope he might bend down and take it. He didn't but ordered me instead to pick it back up. I obeyed, but as I reached down, I had an idea. Slowly, I slid my bracelet off my wrist and let it drop soundlessly to the floor. I then covered it with my foot as Seth answered me.

"It's not that simple, Sam. Who are you with anyway? The FBI? CIA?"

The expression on my face must have answered that question.

"Too bad," he said with a shrug. "You might have stood a chance. Now move it!"

When Seth reached out and turned the door handle to lead me into the hall, I breathed a sigh of relief. There was something liberating about being out in the open again, and I reasoned that if we went near the elevators, someone might choose that moment to come out and I could cause a commotion that might get me away from him. But we didn't go that way. We headed down the other hallway toward the stairs.

The lonely, deserted stairs.

He pushed me roughly, still not letting go of my arm as we headed to the stairwell door. I tried to drag my feet as much as possible but to no avail. The sound of the door clicking behind us sounded like the clanging of a prison door shutting.

You would think that after four flights I would have come up with some plan to free myself, but I hadn't. It wasn't until we came out near the lobby that I remembered Lin and Mike. I tried to jerk my head around to see if they were still there and got what would probably end up being a nasty bruise on my arm where Seth clenched it with his free hand. "Think again. And keep moving," he snarled.

As I felt another opportunity slipping away, I realized that even if they were still there, they probably wouldn't have seen us anyway. There were so many potted plants on this side of the room, it was like walking through a jungle. Unnoticed, we made our way to the parking garage. There was a moment of hope when an older woman passed us, most likely on her way to dinner. She nodded politely as she walked by—I bet Seth flashed her one of his killer grins. But the grin had faded by the time we made our way over to where the company van was parked. Somehow he managed to open the back doors and keep me secure at the same time, all while holding the gun menacingly in sight. In what seemed like a split second, he secured both of my wrists in one hand and fumbled around in a toolbox, pulling out a roll of duct tape. I groaned as he fastened my arms behind my back. I'd also seen enough movies to realize my mouth was next.

Face down on the van floor, I heard Seth open the driver-side door and get in. The engine revved, and I could feel the vehicle backing up.

There wasn't much to report on after that. I couldn't see out the windows from the floor, but I could feel the jostling of the van as we drove over bumps in the road. Other than that, there was little to distract me from the discomfort of being in such a position, with my arms straining behind me and my face planted on the dirty floor between the seats. I tried for what was probably ten minutes to turn over before giving up. There was nothing I could do but wait until we stopped.

When we did, my arms were so numb I could barely feel them. As soon as Seth opened the back doors, I moaned, hoping it would elicit sympathy. Instead, he merely hoisted me onto my feet like a newly branded steer and pushed me forward again. We were walking behind a set of residential houses, and we passed under a small archway and into an open courtyard. It was walled off, and I couldn't see any route of escape except for through the back entrance of the house. But not knowing who was in there or where it led, I reluctantly went along.

A little feeling had started coming back into my hands by the time we reached the house, and they prickled as I tensed and relaxed my fingers. I really hoped he wouldn't keep me trussed up like this the entire time. It might do some permanent damage. Then I bit my lip. My comfort was the last thought on Seth's mind, and I was sure that everyone else involved wouldn't concern themselves with it either. He pushed me through the doorway, and I practically fell into the dimly lit room. It was sparsely furnished and had a few pictures of bullfights on the walls, along with a calendar from a local *farmacia*. It wasn't the tacky décor that got my attention though.

It was Kat sitting in the chair across the room.

She looked startled as we burst through the door and didn't give Seth a chance to explain before shouting angrily, "What's *she* doing here?"

"Apparently your hired hand wasn't competent enough to take care of her. Plus, I found her snooping around in your room. Look at that." He tossed my purse toward Kat. When she saw the contents, she scowled.

"And you said she was harmless."

Seth raised both hands in mock defeat. "So I was wrong. Sue me."

I was still getting over the fact that Kat had arranged for someone to "take care of me." I really hoped that meant mug me or, at worst, break my leg so I was out of commission. The alternative was not something I wanted to consider.

"Well, what do we do with her now?" my boss pouted. "We can't take her with us; she'd just be in the way."

"Leave her here. We can deal with her later."

"And if she finds a way to escape? It could ruin everything."

I nearly rolled my eyes as they argued back and forth like a couple of squabbling kids.

"Then I guess we only have one option," Seth said.

That got my attention. I stood there nervously as they decided my fate. Amazingly, it was Kat who granted me a reprieve. I almost started to like her. Almost.

"Hey, I didn't sign up for murder," she said. "Even that stunt at Tula was a bit . . . brutal for my tastes. All I want to do is get this meeting over with and get back on American soil. I can't think about anything else now." She waved one hand with a flourish. "Do whatever you think is best."

Seth frowned. "I'm not going to be the one doing all the dirty work around here."

Kat pursed her lips together in thought. "Then what are our options?"

I gulped as Seth responded. "We'll bring her with us . . . and let the Serpent take care of her."

* * *

After another miserable ride in the van, I thought for sure I was going to pass out or throw up or both. This ride was longer, and if I'd been some kind of genius, I probably could have calculated the time it took and the distance we'd traveled based upon the speed of the car. But I hadn't had a math course since I was a freshman in college, and besides, I was too tired. The sudden lurching of the van as we stopped woke me up from my semiconscious state. I hadn't had any dreams this time—why should I when I was already living a nightmare? I waited for the routine of the doors opening and Seth grabbing me roughly. It took a little longer than last time, but I eventually found myself on my feet, trying to acclimate myself to the scene around me.

I instantly recognized where we were. The pyramids that rose into the sky had a tinge of rose color around them from the disappearing sun; it would have been a beautiful scene under different circumstances. I realized we were just behind the Temple of the Moon in the parking lot on the far north side of the complex. It gave me hope until I looked around and realized there were no other cars and the site was deserted. What time was it anyway? The sun had been setting around eight. I couldn't be sure, but I realized that until tourists started milling around again tomorrow, we were probably all alone.

Alone.

That word suddenly had a new connotation. And it was the last thing in the world I wanted to be.

I was relieved to be on my feet again. I felt like I'd been lying on a rock the entire time. But it hadn't been a rock, and for a moment I had hope—that is, until my backside started chiming.

"What's that?" Seth demanded. He spun me around and began fumbling in my back pocket. When he took out my phone, he scowled.

"Well, well. It looks like lover boy's callin' to check up on you. Here's what we're gonna do. You're gonna reassure him that you're fine and just doin' a little sightseein', *comprende*?" Then, before I could react, he ripped the tape off my mouth. Dang! It hurt worse than that one time I'd had my legs waxed. I flexed my jaw and winced as he thrust the phone at my ear and demanded, "Talk!"

"Hello?" I gasped.

"Sam?"

It was Dave. The version that was minus the accent.

"Where are you? What's going on?" Dave questioned. "When I couldn't find you anywhere at the hotel and then found your bracelet . . . There's a lot going on I wish I could explain, but right now, I'm worried about you. Can you tell me where you are?"

"I'm fine." My voice quivered. "I'm just doing a little sightseeing. There were a few things I missed," I said, trying to follow Seth's instructions. Then I hesitated. After all, how did I know I could trust Dave either? He could still be in on it—maybe Kat and Seth had figured three was a crowd and left him behind.

As my thoughts battled it out, I heard Dave say, "Sam, trust me."

Trusting my instincts, I knew I could. I also knew what to do. "I may hit a few clubs later, so I won't be back until late. You know how much I love the night life here."

There was a pause. "Is Kat there with you?"

"Yes." I tried to grin. "There's a *couple* of places I'm really anxious to see more of."

"So Seth's there too," he said softly. "If you can stay on the line, we'll be able to trace the call—"

"Finish up!" Seth hissed.

"I've g . . . got to go," I stammered, my eyes watering. "I probably won't be here long." Then I added in a methodical tone, "But I'm trying to *look at things differently*."

Seth suddenly grabbed the phone away from my ear and hung up. "Good job. And since we no longer have to keep tabs on you, this has served its purpose," he said, throwing it on the ground and crushing it beneath his foot. My heart sank as I watched the remnants of my lifeline to the world being destroyed. Then, prodding me like I was a stubborn mule, Seth had me walk toward the first row of columns that would lead us into what I knew was the Palace of the Quetzal Butterfly. Kat still didn't look happy about my presence, and I listened to my captors' banter as we walked. Apparently, there was some contention in the ranks, and I wondered if that might be to my advantage.

"You did tell them I was coming along, didn't you?" Seth frowned.

Kat fell silent, and when she finally spoke, she was evasive. "In a way. Naturally, they don't expect me to handle my side of the operation on my own, but I didn't *specifically* mention you being here. Once I've been promoted to creative director at Phizer-Lewis, I'll need some flunk—uh, I mean, *assistant* to help coordinate shipments and such. It will be helpful having someone who actually knows what's going on for a change instead of some mindless jerk who will blindly sign a few papers in exchange for . . ."

My boss glanced slyly in my direction. "Listening ears. Go take care of the baggage while I make sure we're ready for them."

Seth took me up the staircase—the one with the large serpent's head—and we drew close to the decorated antechamber. The shadows cast on the walls made the bas-reliefs seem to come to life. But we didn't stop there. Instead, we continued on to the adjoining Palace of the Jaguars. I knew from my guidebooks that there was a tunnel somewhere that led into what was probably the oldest structure in Teotihuacán: the Substructure of the Feathered Snails. We went down a narrow passageway, and at the end of the tunnel was a small room with a weathered wooden door. I had the feeling this was a more modern addition, however. Seth shoved me, and my knees buckled right before I hit the ground. I took back every nice thought I'd ever had about him and glared my fiercest glare. He only laughed.

"I don't have to warn you to stay put, do I, darlin'?"

He left, closing and locking the door behind him.

As I sat in darkness, pondering my fate, I tried to think about where I'd gone wrong, what I could have done differently. Maybe I shouldn't have tried to take matters into my own hands. But how could I have just sat back and done nothing?

I was past regrets. As I squirmed on the dirt floor, I had to think and think fast. If this meeting happened soon, I was in trouble. Hopefully it was still a ways off. But what good would time do? Even if Dave understood my cryptic words, he'd have to be Superman to swoop in and save me. I found myself pleading humbly once again for help; after all, I had no illusion that I could handle this myself anymore. Heavenly

Father had directed me before, and I had to trust that He would do it again when the time was right. The events of the day were catching up with me, and as I prayed, I found myself half drifting off. My arms were feeling numb again, and there was little besides the occasional chirping of some crickets to keep me alert. Feeling a wave of despair, I collapsed likc a rag doll against the rough stone wall.

In a half-conscious state, I heard the door creak open and saw Seth walking in again. He knelt down beside me and ran a finger down my dirt-caked cheek. I jerked back, and he scowled as he showed me a water bottle and raised a questioning eyebrow. I wanted to be heroic and say I'd rather die of thirst, but, well, I *was* really thirsty. I nodded, and he uncapped the bottle and tilted it over my mouth. Half of it ran down the sides of my face, but it felt good.

He took a swig himself and then stood up, wiping his mouth with the back of his hand. As he turned to leave, I found myself asking, "Why? Why are you doing this?"

He spoke as if he were a parent explaining something complicated to a small child. "It's all about supply and demand, darlin'. We have the demand; they have the supply. And for those of us smart enough to catch on to that, we can make a fortune for a small amount of work. You saw the numbers."

I tried to look as disgusted as I could. "So that's all you care about—money? What about all the people that die or have their lives ruined after taking drugs? Not to mention the fact that these drug gangs are turning this country into a war zone."

His usual jovial countenance turned dark. "This country can"—the words he used felt like a slap—"for all I care. Do you have any idea what it was like growing up in a border town in Texas? Watching all those Mexicans come pouring into our state, taking the jobs away and filling up the schools? My granddad had the right idea in his time: no Negroes, no Mexicans, no *dogs*! If I can make a fast buck off their misery, I'll do it."

I clenched my fists in anger, which helped with the circulation in my hands as well. Never in my life had I come up against such bigotry. I stared at Seth, his face as different as if he'd suddenly put on a grotesque Halloween mask, and I understood the energy that fueled racism. It was ugly, and I was scared. But at the same time, I knew that not everyone felt this way, and I felt kind of sorry for him and the obvious difficulties of his upbringing.

"And you couldn't keep your nose out of our business, could you?" He turned his anger toward me. "Though I still can't figure out how you were smart enough to get that note and make the connection between us and the Serpent."

His question took me off guard. How *did* I end up with the note? Then it dawned on me, though I wasn't sure I was flattered that I'd looked enough like my boss that day to confuse the young boy who'd probably been given a few pesos to deliver it. And as far as knowing they both were in league with the Serpent—since I was sitting here tied up, obviously I wasn't worthy of the credit he was giving me.

"Of course, it's ironic," he said, "that you were the one who started questioning Dave's and Lin's involvement in our group. Helped me win a few brownie points with Kat when I told her I'd done a little background checkin' and some sheep weren't lined up in their pen. If she couldn't do without me before, that clinched it. Well, sit tight, darlin', and I'll let you know if I need you again," he mocked.

* * *

I didn't have to wait long.

When Seth dragged me up the stairs and back toward the courtyard of the palace, the sun was gone, and a thin strip of sky above the horizon had turned blood red. Since Seth was more intent on using his flashlight to illuminate his own way, I stumbled a couple of times on the steps and nearly had my arm jerked out of the socket as he pulled me along.

"Please," I pled. "Undo my hands. Where would I go anyway? Besides, you still have your gun, and I'm not stupid enough to try to run."

Seth just scowled at me. When we joined Kat in the small, arcaded courtyard, I pled my case to her, and I'm not sure if she agreed because she was distracted or because she had a conscience after all, but she told Seth to undo my bonds, adding, "Surely you can handle this one little problem while I deal with everything else."

Thinking it might be wise to rub it in and continue to stir things up between my feuding captors, I gave him an exultant smile as he cut the tape around my wrists. He made sure his gun was prominently placed after that. I stretched my arms forward and heard a popping release in my joints but knew it would take a few minutes before my muscles fully recovered. I tried to pay attention to everything going on around me, ignoring the pain and raw skin on my mouth and wrists from the duct tape. I watched and waited, hoping that a chance for escape would present itself. And soon.

The night was hushed, as if every living thing had somehow been ordered to stay away. The air was thick and dusty. I coughed, and Seth glared at me as if the noise might somehow ruin their plans. And then any plans I'd been concocting faded as I glanced between the two smaller temples and saw a light flickering.

Someone was coming.

Chapter 27

I WATCHED AS TWO MEN appeared, and I instantly recognized the man in black, carrying a flashlight and dutifully lighting the way for the stranger with him. At first appearance, they were exact opposites, one in black, the other wearing what I guessed was a light gray suit that appeared to bob along in the dark without a head until they drew nearer. I saw that the second man's hair was black but had touches of gray around the temples, which gave him an older, more grandfatherly look. But the aura of evil that hung around him made me glad I had no familial connection.

Kat smiled and gave him the traditional greeting of a kiss on each cheek, calling him by his preferred name: *El Serpiente*.

How proper.

No, I groaned. I don't need *you* right now.

Seth obviously felt left out because he stepped forward to make his presence known. He left me standing in the background, and I wondered if this was the moment I'd been waiting for. But no sooner did I take a step back than the older man's eyes darted to me.

"Who are they?" he said with a thick accent. The man in black whispered into his ear, and the Serpent scowled at Kat. "Why did you bring these extra people here? I am starting to rethink our arrangement. Already I have not been impressed with these dramatics and games. I take my work very seriously."

Seth grabbed me by the arm as Kat put on the performance of her life. With a seductive pout, she reached out to the man and touched him lightly on the arm. "You can trust my partner as you would trust me. And as for her, she has only been a slight distraction to us, and the fact that she's here as our hostage should be an indication of our abilities."

"In fact," Seth added, thrusting me forward so I fell on my knees, "she's yours to do with as you please. Consider her a gift."

I should have been extremely insulted at his suggestion. But it was difficult to feel insulted when my body was racked with terror.

The Serpent shrugged. "We shall see. But first, we have much business to discuss, and the night is growing old."

With all the courtliness of a Spanish gentleman, he bowed and directed us into the antechamber of the Butterfly Palace. The eyes of the large stone serpent's head seemed to watch us as we approached, and for a moment, I was transported to another time. I wondered if meetings like this—secretive and under the cover of darkness—took place back in the days when these ancient edifices were built. Were there other secret combinations that had planned nefarious activities within the painted walls of this palace? Did those earlier remnants of the Lamanites value human life as inconsequentially as these people did? I knew the answer to those questions. There have always been wicked men on the earth, and the voices of their victims would cry from the dust if they could.

Was mine about to add to that echo?

I listened as they laid out their plans. It was as organized and calculated a design as our marketing campaign here had been, and as I heard them discuss their "market" and the potential "return on their investments," I could almost imagine that's all it was. But the difference was they were talking about the cocaine that would be imported into Mexico on behalf of the South American drug cartels and eventually filter across the U.S./Mexico border. Apparently Kat had only been a small player up until now. She'd arranged for bulk shipments of marijuana to be sent to Phizer-Lewis with preauthorized shipping invoices—courtesy of an oblivious and love-struck Mr. Lansing. But now she wanted to move on to bigger things. With a bigger payoff.

I was gaining quite an education. I learned how the South American-based organizations relied upon Mexican-based groups to convey their cocaine into the United States. Up until now, the Serpent had only been dealing into Texas, but he wanted to extend farther to the west, and San Diego made the perfect entry point. And Kat wanted to be the contact. As I listened to the Serpent's thick accent, I realized what side he represented. And since the Mexican traffickers wanted to keep a share of the drugs as payment for their services, I knew what the man in black was doing there as well.

This new information taught me two other things as well. The first explained why the man in gray wasn't armed. After all, no one was stupid enough to take on a Columbian drug lord and expect to live to tell about it. The second made clear why they'd let me stay and listen to their plans. Because I wouldn't be around long enough to share it with anyone.

I couldn't help but think of my family. What would my parents do when they found out? Would this traumatic experience make it difficult for my father to regain his health? I hadn't talked to my brothers for months and regretted it now. I realized how important it was to make every day count, and if I made it through this somehow, I'd never take anything for granted again.

Angry voices broke me away from my thoughts. Apparently Seth was disagreeing with Kat over the number of shipments that could be handled. I could hear his cocky voice boasting that if he were in charge, he could handle the increase. After all, he was the one who'd spent hours on his computer configuring the statistics they needed. When Kat protested, the Serpent said in a voice as cold and hard as the stone around us, "¡*Basta*! You both are forgetting who is in charge. The decision has been made, and anyone who does not agree . . . will be dealt with."

"¿*Y la gringa*?" the man in black said cautiously, as if aware he might also be on shaky ground.

His companion naturally responded in Spanish, and since I knew the verb for *dispose*, I realized I had run out of options.

"Wait!" I shouted as the man in black attempted to drag me off.

The Serpent turned around, looking very annoyed, while my captor tightened his grip painfully, as if to warn me I had crossed some invisible line of protocol in speaking out. But his partner finally bid me continue. Not sure at first what I would say, I knew I had to stall for more time, so I sucked in a deep breath and found words coming to my mind.

"Surely you aren't going to trust your entire operation to these screwups, who can't even follow your orders and agree to your terms?"

Kat scowled, and Seth looked like a vicious dog as he lunged at me. But the Serpent's outstretched hand held them back. "Everyone eventually comes to do things my way," he said, his eyes narrowing into slits. "If that is all—" He signaled for his partner to drag me away again.

"But that's not all," I shouted, panic heavy in my voice.

The Serpent smiled. "There is a fine line between bravery and stupidity. You have one minute to convince me which side of the line you're on."

And then I proceeded to try to convince him but this time in perfect Spanish so I wouldn't be interrupted.

After all, Kat had made the mistake of using my phone to make a call to her Mexican contact—in other words, the man in black. I remembered the fear in his voice. Apparently, I wasn't the only one intimidated by the Serpent and knew I could use this to my advantage. So I went on to reveal that I had seen the man in black following our group here at Teotihuacán and then again in Tenayuca. In fact, he really hadn't been all that careful when he'd put the sample of drugs in the serpent statue's mouth.

My tactic worked because when the man in black's anger boiled over and he tried to attack me, the Serpent stopped him with a small silver dagger to the neck. Where he'd been hiding it, I didn't know; it had seemed to magically appear. Kat and Seth were frantically trying to figure out what I'd been saying and what had provoked this attack, but no one, including me, dared move.

"Go on, *querida*," the source of our fears hissed.

So I continued to add to my story, though I doubted it made my would-be attacker happy to hear that I'd also been the one to receive the note at Tula and that I had even come face to face with him at what was supposed to have been the meeting with Kat. I watched the Serpent's face harden like stone as I told him how I'd also seen his partner sneaking out of our hotel and how it took only a little flirting with the desk clerk to find out he had left a letter for my boss with the Serpent insignia on it for all to see.

This piece of information was apparently the final straw.

It was all so sudden that I didn't realize what had happened until the man in black slunk lifelessly to the floor. I stared in horror as I watched the Serpent casually wipe the dagger on a monogrammed handkerchief retrieved from his suit coat pocket. I tried not to look at the stream of red that poured from the man in black's severed carotid artery and pooled in front of the flashlight that had fallen from his grasp. I had never seen anyone killed before. My colleagues were just as stunned as I was, and I suddenly felt as if we were back in this together. Whatever plans they'd been hatching seemed to crumble like the ruins around us, and I could see it in their eyes—especially Kat's. This was no longer an easy means to a rich end. This was a world of madness and greed that none of us understood.

I wasn't the only one who didn't want to give up without a fight. Seth drew his gun from behind his back. But the Serpent just smiled and calmly said, "Do you know what that would mean? Well, do you? Have you friends, children . . . a loving wife? This would not end here, believe me."

Seth slowly lowered the gun in defeat then dropped it and kicked it forward.

"Amateurs," our mutual captor spat. "They send me amateurs. Though you . . ." he wagged a finger at me, "I like. I could find something for you to do."

I couldn't help myself. "No thanks," I replied.

He shrugged as if I'd turned down a glass of water. "Very well. The question is, what should I do with you? I could tie you up in the underground tunnels. Yes, I know about them. I know everything necessary." He pursed his lips. "Perhaps someone would find you in a day or so. Of course, I could arrange for the road to be shut down—construction problem, perhaps—then who knows how long it would be until they found your bodies. But no, I have another idea. Much more appropriate considering the location," he added cryptically. Bending over, he retrieved the gun and signaled with it to the right. "*¡Andamos!*"

The three us stumbled over the rocky ground as the single light flickered indiscriminately behind us. From up high, the terrain appeared to be quite smooth, but there were small crevasses and dips that made it difficult to progress, especially in the dark. Even then, I knew where we were headed. As the Pyramid of the Sun loomed before us, I realized we only had another few hundred yards or so and we would come to the tented area near the Patio of the Four Temples. I thought back to my conversation with Dave as we had peered into the dark excavation hole and talked of the atrocities of ancient times.

"Here we are," our captor announced when we arrived. "What a shame that the government of this country does not see fit to spend its money on saving its ancient treasures, only on stopping the profitable business of my network. See," he clucked disappointedly, "the work has been abandoned, leaving behind this ugly pit. Of course, it will be easy to hire a few loyal workers to see that it is filled in."

He sighed. "The only question now is, which one of you will be first?"

Chapter 28

With an unearthly howl, Seth launched himself at the Serpent. I knew I should have been concerned about what would happen to my colleagues, but instead, I saw the opportunity I'd been waiting for.

I bolted across the dusty ground and saw the Pyramid of the Sun's ghostly shape rising before me. But where should I go? There was the restaurant beyond its perimeter; perhaps there would be a guard or a security system I could disrupt. But between the grove of trees and multiple levels of structures, it would be easy to lose my way. I had to think fast, but the more I tried, the more I found I couldn't. *What should I do?*

Let go and reach out.

I felt humbled. This was the greatest lesson I'd learned so far, that I didn't have to figure this out on my own.

With newfound determination, I started running north on the Avenue of the Dead. When I heard the sound of repeated shots being fired, it stopped me in my tracks for a moment. But then I accepted that I couldn't wait to see what happened—I had to keep moving. Hopefully, with my age and stamina, I could outrun my pursuer. Creating an image in my mind, I continued toward the looming shadow, though I couldn't move too swiftly because of the uneven ground. Even though I remembered there was a raised area in the center of the open square, the first incline took me by surprise. With the wind knocked out of me and my knees battered and bruised, I had a difficult time starting up again. I was a little more wary now and better prepared for the next incline. I hoped I would hit some flat, paved ground again so I could head off at a brisk run. Then a second series of shots echoed in the distance, and I stumbled. I'd like to say I bravely got up again at this point, but the truth was, I stayed on my knees for a moment and cried like a baby. When my sobs subsided, I got to my feet again. Looking back through the trees, I saw the bobbing of a light headed in my direction.

The Serpent was coming.

That inspired me to start running again.

Now I could see the distinct rows of structures that lined the street, and though I stumbled off course a few times, I could finally make out the smaller pyramid's base, and I rushed toward it. My gaze searched beyond its stone walls, and I could see the stars and a waning moon hovering on the horizon behind the fortress, though they scarcely illuminated the scenery around me. Once I reached the pyramid wall, I would have only a couple options: I could hide in one of the numerous tunnels of the Butterfly Palace or even make my way back to the parking lot. I considered the second option but thought twice. I wished that hot-wiring cars had been a college course. Besides, the pyramid was still a hundred yards away, and I'd have a few hundred more yards after that in pitch darkness to try to find our van. If I had been a world-class sprinter, I could have easily made it, but this was a far cry from an easy jog along a sandy beach. My lungs had started burning, and I realized that between no dinner and only a little water, my strength was quickly fading. I paused long enough to glance behind me and see if the light was still there. It was and getting even closer.

Now silence seemed as imperative as speed, and I slowed my pace and tried to still my breathing. Aside from an occasional flickering light behind me, everything was silent and black. Haunting, really. But not as haunting as the voice that called out to me.

"You can run, *señorita*, but you will never be able to hide from me!"

I started to run again, kicking a stone noisily across the dusty path, and saw the light shift directions and bounce in a staccato rhythm in my direction. Now being quiet didn't seem important either, so I dashed toward what I hoped would be safety in the tunnels. But it wasn't going to be that easy.

When I tripped over the man in black's body, I was thrown to the ground. I had to bite down on my lip to keep from screaming. A moan did escape my lips as I looked at the still figure lying in the puddle of his own blood. Shuffling away from him, I shook off the image and got back up. I tried to remember the direction Seth had taken me. Was it two rights and then a left? Or just one right and two lefts? My hands were sweating so badly they were soon caked in mud as I felt my way along the dimly lit walls. But I finally found the room, though it would do me little good to hide inside. At least I had my bearings, and I continued on.

I continued to feel my way along the passageway. After a while, I paused to listen. Had he seen me come in? At first it was quiet, and I felt my breathing return to a somewhat normal pace as I allowed myself to rest for a few moments. I still couldn't wrap my mind around the fact that this was happening to me. It seemed unreal. All of it. Maybe I was dreaming again, and I would wake up. But I seemed to be stuck in it, and it seemed to be reality, and for the moment, my plan seemed to be working and I was alone. Would it stay that way? How long could I sit here and wait before he gave up?

Then I heard a thud echoing through the narrow corridors behind me, and I realized a man like that would never give up. My chest tightened as I struggled to find a breath.

The Serpent was in the tunnels with me.

I'd been trying to keep a mental map in my head as I rounded corners and made my way in the dark. With one more left turn, I decided that I was going north. The sound was definitely behind me, which gave me some hope that if I could find my way out of the tunnels, I would be directly beside the Pyramid of the Moon. What I'd do then, I didn't know. I was taking this one step at a time. The air was growing dank and musty. I stifled a cough and shuffled my feet along, trying to stir up as little dust as possible. I heard the creaking noise of a door and realized the Serpent must have come to the room where Seth had kept me. That meant he was only a few turns away—and then he would find me.

I continued through the maze and almost felt like I'd never find my way out. Maybe there was no escape, and I'd be trapped in here forever.

Stop it!

I couldn't let myself despair. I had to continue on. I pushed a little farther ahead, and I wondered if it was just my imagination or if I could finally see the outline of my hands as they inched along the walls. And was the air getting fresher? My pace quickened until I saw another set of steps up ahead. They were crumbling, but I ran to them, climbed up, and found myself collapsing on the ground outside.

But this was no time to rest.

It was so dark. Making it to the parking lot was definitely out of the question; I just needed to put some distance between him and me. I scrambled over to the main steps and made it to the first landing of the pyramid just as more adrenaline kicked in. I had to decide if I was going to keep climbing or inch my way along the narrow perimeter of that first level. The sound of rocks skittering on the ground beneath me forced me up. Apparently he'd found the exit as well.

Then a bullet ricocheted about twenty feet away from me.

I pushed my body harder.

By the next landing, whatever second wind I'd found had vanished. To move faster, I leaned over and started scampering up the giant-sized steps like a monkey. My thighs burned. My hands could feel every pebble and stone, and I was sure I already had a dozen cuts. The arduous climb began to sap my endurance. I knew I was slowing down.

"That's right, *querida*. Up and up you go, like a butterfly—a quetzal butterfly! But I know how to keep butterflies from flying away."

When a bullet came whizzing by me, hitting the nearby rocks and pelting me with shards, I shrieked.

"I have only got one left, *querida*, but I will make it count."

That stopped me. My bravery didn't extend to guns, and I turned around and called out for him not to shoot.

He slithered close enough to the pyramid for me to see him in the light of his flashlight, and I felt like a tiny animal, cornered and waiting for him to strike. He began walking up the steps, and I stood paralyzed until he was right next to me. "You should have learned from your friends' examples and not made me exert myself so much," he panted. "Now I am angry." His polished veneer slipped as he swore at me and slapped my face.

Stunned, I still had to ask, "What did you do to them? Are they . . . dead?"

He cocked an eyebrow as if it were a foolish question. "That was my intent. After I take care of you, however, I shall return and make sure of it." He tucked the gun into his pocket and took out the dagger— apparently his weapon of choice—and the light from the flashlight glinted off it. "The question now is, where should I start?"

Keep him talking.

"Uh . . . what happens when the authorities find three dead American bodies here? They'll trace us back to you."

This amused him. "If the authorities were competent, they would have captured me already. How many opportunities have they had, and still I slip through their fingers." He ran his thumb over the tip of the blade. "Yes, I play games with them, but they do not know the rules, so I win."

"You won't win forever," I said in a near whisper. "Sooner or later, everyone loses."

He grabbed me violently around the neck with one hand and pulled me forward, his blade scraping along the line of my jaw. "This may be true for some, *querida*, but tonight I will be the winner. And I have decided that whatever I do to you, I will make sure it goes slowly . . . very slowly." He snarled, and flecks of spit splattered my face.

Don't bet on it!

I don't know where the inner rage came from. I swear, I had never felt anything like that before. But as I simultaneously screamed and gave the Serpent a giant shove, it was enough to catch him off guard, though not enough to send him tumbling down the stairs. Now I really was running for my life, and I ignored the pain in my thighs and the way the skin on my knees was being pummeled to shreds with each stumble. I could hear my pursuer's frantic panting behind me, and I drew upon everything I had to climb higher and higher. Even when I realized I was putting some distance between us, I didn't slow down.

My vision clouded as I began to cry. Perhaps there was one more prayer in me. *Please help me, Father.*

I climbed higher and higher, and I knew I was only a few dozen steps from the top. What I'd do then, I didn't know—perhaps I *would* sprout wings and fly! My heart was pounding, and I could hear a *thud-thudding* in my ears, like the sound of a ceiling fan off balance. It was faint at first but grew louder and louder as I climbed. And then the sky exploded with light!

With dust flying in my face, I could barely make out the helicopter hovering above the pyramid. I coughed, tried to cover my eyes from both the wind and the blinding glare of the searchlight, and continued to ascend. But toward what? Was this the rescue I'd prayed for or the means of the Serpent's own eventual escape? I heard coughing close behind me and wasn't sure if, regardless of the answer, I was going to make it. The tumult disoriented me, and I stumbled off the main stairway and found myself sprawled behind an adjacent narrow ledge. My hands dug into the rock, and I struggled to keep from toppling over the side.

The pounding of the helicopter's engine was getting closer, and as I turned, I saw the Serpent scurrying up the stairs after me, the gun in his hand again. There was nothing I could do but try to hold on as he drew nearer. Sweat was dripping from his face, and I saw that his eyes had a wild look about them.

Then I heard someone above us shout, "Let her go, Matamoros. There's no way out."

I squinted and thought for sure I was hallucinating when Dave peered down from the top of the steps at us, holding a gun pointed to my right.

My pursuer hesitated a moment, looking around with the first sign of insecurity I'd seen. I cast my eyes about as well and saw dozens of lights moving like dancing fireflies across the ground below. I couldn't believe it—I was pretty sure the Serpent had finally lost.

"This is my last warning."

Instantly, I heard gunfire, and when I saw Dave's body lurch back like he'd hit an invisible wall, I realized that the Serpent knew he'd lost and cared only about revenge now. In horror, I watched as he drew out his silver dagger again and started inching his way across the crumbling platform toward me. Any praying I could have done had already been done, and I took one last calming breath and prepared for the blow that would take me down.

But this time, it was my turn to win. The agitation of the helicopter's rotors as it finally landed kicked up a huge cloud of debris from the top of the crumbling ruin. I clung to the pyramid and was able to duck behind the protective outcropping of rock. The Serpent wasn't as lucky. He panicked as he saw the whirlwind coming closer and backed away from it, flailing his arms and eventually letting the dagger fall to the ground. Then he screamed and lost his balance, tumbling down the stairs and into the darkness like a collapsed puppet with its strings cut. A choked sob escaped my own lips as I clamped my eyes shut.

"Give me your hand!" a voice called out.

I glanced up and saw Dave's illuminated figure leaning toward me in the hazy light. But he'd been shot. Was he a mirage, a vision? My senses whirling, I only knew I was out of strength. "I can't . . ."

"You have to trust me. Let go and *reach out!*"

Somehow I managed to pry the fingers of my right hand loose, and I reached for him.

Chapter 29

As I SAT ALONE IN the interrogation room at the police station, I realized it was five in the morning and about seven hours had passed since my horrifying ordeal.

By the time the *ambulancia* had transported me (against my wishes—after all, they were only minor cuts) to the hospital and then the squad car had taken me to the police station, I could see the thin line of dawn forming on the horizon. All the formalities of the process had kept my mind from focusing too much on what had happened. Which was good, because I didn't want to remember the look on the Serpent's face as he came toward me. And I prayed that I would forget the sounds of the gunshots and everything that had taken place outside the Palace of the Quetzal Butterfly. I hadn't been able to avoid seeing Seth's and the man in black's bodies being loaded into the coroner's van, and now those images were imprinted on my mind.

Of course there were a few things I wanted to remember. It was almost worth the terror I'd experienced to see the look of anguish on Kat's face as she was loaded into a police car, shoulder bandaged, having realized everything she'd been planning had failed. But that triumph was nothing compared to the feeling of a strong hand pulling me up to safety from the ledge of the pyramid. As we stood there with the helicopter resting on its makeshift platform, I saw Dave unzip the front of his DEA jacket to reveal the compact bulletproof vest underneath. I traced the outline of the bullet hole directly over his chest with my finger, and he grabbed my hand and brought my fingers to his lips. The look in his eyes had nearly thrown me off balance again, and I sucked in a quick breath as he leaned in closer. But he only laughed softly.

"It seems we always have an audience."

I sighed and thought of the pilot and the other dozen or so Mexican *policia*, DEA, and FBI agents who swarmed around on the ground below. Everywhere was chaos, but I knew I would remember this moment forever.

I snapped back to the present when a large Mexican police officer in a stained uniform came through the door and hobbled over to where I was sitting, plopping my purse with a thud down on the table. He must not have realized I could understand Spanish because he grunted and gestured at the door. I took that to mean I was free to go, and grimacing slightly from the newly inflicted wounds on my body, I stood up and gladly left. As I looked up and down the fluorescent-lit hallway, I saw the woman I knew as Lin coming toward me. She nodded and signaled for me to wait while she handed a file to a nearby officer.

"I guess I ought to introduce myself officially." She stuck out her hand, and I took it. "Amanda Wong, San Diego Field Division of the DEA, special agent-in-charge."

"Uh, hi . . . Amanda."

"It seems like you're good to go?"

I shrugged. "I suppose. Thanks for telling them I wasn't part of it."

Her expression was controlled and missing some of the warmth she'd previously shown me. Of course, maybe that had been just part of the act. "I told them the truth. Is there anything else you need?"

How about the answers to a few questions?

True enough, I wanted to know how I got mixed up in all of this. What was going to happen to my boss? Was I safe now? But what I really wanted to ask her about was Mitchell Davies—the man I had known as Dave Ayala these past two weeks. After he'd helped me down the pyramid steps, an official-looking man had taken him aside, and I hadn't been able to talk to him since.

She stared at me with a telling look on her face. "An unmarked police car is waiting for you outside. Everything should be ready for you back at the hotel—though I apologize that your room had to be searched. We'll have an escort wait outside your door until you're packed. After that, a private car will pick you up and take you to the airport. If you need anything, give me a call." She handed me a business card with a chain-link border and a solitary phone number printed in the middle. "My private number. Just in case you need anything." As I turned to walk away, I heard her say, "The two of you looked right together. It seems I was wrong about a lot of things."

I was smiling as I left the station. I couldn't blame Amanda for being protective now that I knew Mitchell was her partner on this case. Having had a little time to think about everything, I couldn't even blame her for questioning my involvement in all this.

Back at the hotel, I rode up the elevator with my escort, wondering if it was rude of me not to try to make trivial conversation. I was too exhausted to formulate any more coherent thoughts. Even when I saw the yellow tape across the doors of Seth's and Kat's hotel rooms, it only slightly registered what it meant. My own door was open, and an officer was sitting inside. He stood and nodded his head slightly and then followed his companion outside, leaving me alone to pack. I glanced around the room, realizing I would have been completely unaware that police officers had been here searching through my suitcases and private things. Everything appeared to be right where I'd left it. And yet, nothing seemed the same.

Because *I* was different.

I packed my clothes, carefully putting the shawl and presents I'd bought on top. I scooped up my makeup and toiletries from the bathroom and wondered if someone had opened each one. With teary eyes, I glanced around one more time and realized that was it. It was time to go.

The officer immediately turned around as I opened the door. He took my bags from me, and I followed closely behind him down the hall and into the elevator. When the doors opened downstairs, I cast a quick look around and saw that Miguel wasn't at the front desk this morning. But I did see what I now knew was a friendly face sitting in a nearby chair. He jumped up when I came over but had a sheepish grin on his face, like a little kid who'd let someone down.

"Hi, Mike." I smiled, letting him know I didn't blame him for anything. After all, he really *was* just a cameraman who had been in the right position to get his real girlfriend a job at Phizer-Lewis so she could investigate more closely the suspicious shipments coming in. And even though Amanda had put him unofficially in charge of tailing me from time to time and watching the elevators the night before, my own bizarre behavior had unintentionally made those tasks difficult.

"Hey, kiddo. Quite the adventure last night, huh? I'm glad you're all right and hope you have a good flight home."

I grinned, realizing this was the most we'd really spoken to each other. "Thanks. It will be good to get back."

The hulk of a man patted me reassuringly on the shoulder. "Take care of yourself."

I promised I would, and my escort and I left.

I don't know why I kept looking for Mitchell at the airport, waiting for the experience to end like the scene of a movie where the hero comes rushing in just as the girl heads down the runway and he grabs her, telling her not to go. Mine ended up being like a comedy, where I tripped several times over my carry-on as I kept trying to look back.

Seated next to the window again, I watched as the haze gradually dissipated and the dawn-lit air turned blue and clear over jagged hills and deep canyons, brown and burnt by the approaching summer's sun. When I fell asleep this time, I was blessed not to have any more nightmares, just a distant longing for something I felt I'd left behind.

Chapter 30

WITH A MILD RELUCTANCE, I headed out to work the following Wednesday morning. Was it only a little less than three weeks ago that I'd found out I would be heading to Mexico? No. At least three lifetimes had passed since then. And I felt older for it.

After having been interrogated at the local DEA headquarters the day before, I was told by another special agent that I should have nothing to worry about. There was nothing about my presence or my name that would be associated with this case. As far as everyone was concerned, any evidence that I was there had been erased. Even the deaths of Francisco Guadalupe, a small-town Mexican drug dealer, and Juan Diego Matamoros, a South American drug trafficker, had been kept under wraps. And because of the remote location and unusual circumstances, none of this would have to become public information. (Of course, I now understood what those UFO sightings I'd read about on the Internet could be based on.) Needless to say, Seth wouldn't be bothering me anymore, though I felt sad it had ended that way for him. And since Kat would be in jail for a very long time, I wouldn't have her to worry about either. Still, I wasn't totally convinced it was over but tried to have faith that this time the authorities were doing everything they could to keep me safe.

I walked tentatively through the doors of Phizer-Lewis, having been instructed to tell my coworkers the most basic of details. Both executives had already been updated on the situation and would back me up that Ms. Edwards and Mr. Proctor had opted to take employment elsewhere. As for the duped Mr. Lansing, well, he had been sent on a long sabbatical. A few of my coworkers welcomed me back to the office, and I pasted on my smile. Janice only wanted to know about the hot

Latin men, so I humored her a little. Otherwise, it was back to business as usual.

There was one thing, however, that the police had not informed me about.

"Did you hear about Roger?" Janice lifted her eyebrows.

"No, what?" I asked nervously.

Janice grinned. "It appears he's been fired for helping himself to some of the company's personnel files. I heard he also used to hang around the office late at night to see what employees had left behind—from purses to cell phones."

"That explains a lot." I scowled.

"I've already put in a request for reimbursement from the company on those phone charges. Apparently there's a fund being set up through the State Victims' Injury Act."

You don't say.

"It seems like management's dropping like flies around here," she continued. "Maybe that will leave room for some of us to climb the corporate ladder."

"Huh? Yeah," I answered tiredly.

"You don't look like you got very much sleep on that trip. Did they overwork you or something? I'll bet you anything . . ."

I let Janice ramble on as I considered that things were going to keep changing around here. I couldn't continue to work here at an entry-level position anymore, and I had no idea if the company was ever going to offer me a promotion after everything that had happened.

But . . . I didn't have to wait very long to find out what their plans were. When an electronic memo popped up on my computer screen stating that Mr. Lewis wanted to see me, I gulped. I grabbed my purse and headed up the stairs, past the conference room, and on to Mr. Lewis's office. When I arrived, I saw he was on the phone in an intense discussion. He saw me and motioned me in while he continued to speak.

"I don't care what their usual percentage is. We signed a contract, and tell them we'll see them in court if they don't abide by it!"

He slammed the phone down without so much as a good-bye. My heart dropped into my stomach.

"Yes. Ms. Evans. Thank you for coming." He leaned back in his chair and placed his hands together in a praying stance under his chin. "Before I begin, I want you to know we had no idea about the, uh, situation that was going to occur. For all we knew, this was a legitimate operation, and you were never going to be in harm's way."

I started to wonder if Mr. Lewis thought I was going to sue the company or something. I figured it wouldn't hurt to reassure him. "I know that. I don't hold anyone at the company responsible."

He let out the breath he'd been holding. "Naturally we've covered all your expenses, and if you make us aware of any others, we'd be happy to pay for them as well. Now," he shuffled around some papers, "regarding your future with us. We would like to offer you a full-time staff position here as a copywriter that will include a five-year contract, full benefits, and other entitlements as will be outlined in your employment summary. As you can see . . ."

As he went on, I realized I was being given everything I'd wanted when I first started. Everything the old me had wanted. Now, I wasn't so sure.

"Uh, Mr. Lewis," I interrupted. "I haven't decided what I want to do at this point. You can understand how working here might be, well, uncomfortable for me. I appreciate your offer, but I'll have to ask for time to think about it."

He wrinkled his brow as if this hadn't been what he'd expected. "Very well." He shifted the papers to one side, and I caught sight of the layout beneath them.

"What is that, if I may ask?" I pointed to the object in question.

"This? Ms. Edwards FedExed me a few of the final ideas she'd been working on, and we think they're brilliant and capture the essence of what we were looking for. It's unfortunate we can't use them now. We don't want that kind of association."

I stepped closer and saw several of the photographs from the trip juxtaposed around a bold heading:

Mexico: The Land of Two Cultures

Then I turned the print ad around and read, "Imagine a country where two cultures have been blended into one . . ." As my own words stared back at me, I couldn't help but smile. Regardless of the fact that Seth had stolen my ideas, seeing them like that was an amazing feeling. Besides, Mr. Lewis had said it was brilliant. Maybe I did have what it took after all.

"I'll keep in touch, Mr. Lewis." I confidently waved as I left his office.

Things were definitely improving. At least, I didn't think they could get much worse.

As I drove home, I felt a jolt of spontaneity come over me. This had, by far, been the most interesting week of my life, and I was going to celebrate. After a few more miles, I found myself outside Donovan's Steak House. Okay, it was a splurge considering I could find myself unemployed by the end of the week. But I felt I deserved it.

The hostess asked if I had a reservation, and I hoped that being early on a weekday would garner me a seat even without one. It did.

When asked how many were in my party, I laughed. "One!"

They seated me at a small table near the window. I ordered the best filet mignon on the menu, with baby roasted potatoes and steamed vegetables. For dessert, I dined on "Death by Chocolate." Ah . . . considering how close I'd come to the real thing, I realized chocolate was the only way I wanted to go. I reluctantly finished up, paid the bill, and threw down a twenty-dollar tip as my good deed for the day. I couldn't eat another bite, but my heart was empty as I walked back to my car. I willed myself to be patient.

I opened the door to my apartment and dropped my purse on the kitchen table. The place was quiet. I hadn't seen Terri at all during the previous two days I'd been home, which was good. Even she probably would have sensed that something had happened to me in Mexico. But now, as I stared around the empty room, I felt myself desperate for company, even if it was the noisy energy of my roommate. It would have kept me from having to think. To decide.

Now what do you do?

I don't know.

As I stood pondering that question, my phone rang. For a brief moment, I thought it might be Mitchell. Instead, it was just the canned voice of a customer service representative calling from the fraud department at Bank First USA.

Great. What do they want?

"Ms. Evans? In a random review of charges on your new account, we noticed some irregularities. You have several charges from vendors you do not usually frequent. We are calling to make sure you are still in possession of your credit card."

I wanted to laugh out loud but merely smiled at this turn of events. "Yes. I have my card, and if the charges you are referring to are for a five-star restaurant, a posh boutique, and some foreign locations—they definitely belong to me."

He confirmed the charges, and I hung up. Yes. Life was definitely changing. I felt like this was just going to be the start.

* * *

The next morning I woke up a little groggy and was *not* prepared for Terri to pounce on me as I walked toward the bathroom.

"Oh, Sam, you'll never believe what's happened to me!" she squealed through the mud mask on her face.

I probably could. I waited for her to go on about some new guy she'd met while I was gone.

Terri led me over to the sofa to sit down. "I came back to the apartment the Thursday after you'd left. Oh. You must tell me all about your trip; it sounds so exciting! Anyway, I got back after my weekend with Angelo. Sam, wait until you see this hottie . . ." A dramatic eye roll got her back on track. "Okay. I came home and the phone rang, right? I picked it up, and there was a girl on the other line. She said her name was Shiloh, that she was fourteen years old . . . and that she was my daughter."

Now that *did* surprise me.

Terri had paused for dramatic flair before continuing. "There's something I never told you, Sam. When I was fifteen, I got pregnant and had a baby, which I gave up for adoption. They asked me if I wanted the files sealed, and at first I was going to. But then I wondered if one day I'd want to know about her   what she was like, who she'd become. So I've always kept in touch with the agency. But my baby . . . Shiloh . . . she went to a nice couple from Seattle named the Hancocks. They gave her everything I couldn't at the time because I wasn't ready to be a mother." Tears formed in her eyes. "Now she wants to get to know me. She wants to know her birth mother."

I found my own eyes clouding up. I clutched my roommate's hand while she chokingly said, "When I first heard from her, it scared me to death. I didn't think I had anything to offer her. Then I grabbed a copy of that Mormon's book you gave me. I don't know why. It was just the only thing I could think of."

I smiled at the mistake.

"I turned to that part you marked for me, where that prophet—Moroni, right?—said that if we ask God, He'll tell us the truth of everything.

So I got down on my knees like I've watched you do. You should have seen me, Sam. You probably would have laughed." I doubted that. "Then I asked God what I should do about my daughter. And it came to me. I've got a cousin in Bellingham who owns a little strip mall. I called her, and she said I could come up there and start my own business if I wanted to. I'd only be a few hours' drive from where my daughter lives."

Terri stood up and walked over to the kitchen window, reminding me of another confused figure not so many days ago. "I've got to get out of the city. It hasn't been good for me—the partying and guys. I need to settle down and start thinking about where I'm going, what I'm supposed to do with my life. But I have the strongest feeling that it involves being closer to my daughter."

I felt a strong impression of my own that she was right. "I think your daughter is going to be very lucky to know you. You have such unconditional love and the ability to accept people for who they are. She'll sense that, and it will help her come to you when there's a problem. Just be there for her."

"I will." She paused to wipe her eyes. "You know what this means, don't you?"

"That I've lost the most exciting roommate I've ever had?"

"That and the fact that I'm going to have to sell the place."

We hugged, and I reassured her that I would be fine when that happened and perhaps would come visit her someday. But I sensed other big changes of my own coming, of which this was just a part.

Chapter 31

I DOUBLE-CHECKED MY LIST TO make sure everything was ready. My car was gassed up, the final utility bill paid, and I'd even put the garbage can out two days early. I looked over at my bags sitting by the door, packed and waiting for my long drive home. I still had a day, but it was nice to be ready.

Naturally, my parents had been ecstatic when I told them last week that I had decided not to take the full-time job at Phizer-Lewis and instead wanted to do some interviewing at a few companies in Provo and Salt Lake. It would be good to be home and finally let them know what had happened. That wasn't something I could do over the phone: tell my parents that I had been kidnapped and nearly killed. (I still couldn't believe that was almost a month ago.) And with my dad struggling to get through his first course of chemotherapy, I needed to spend some time with him. Time had suddenly become a very precious thing.

Fortunately, Terri had found new owners to take over right before she left for Seattle last Friday. The young couple was going to enjoy living here. I sighed. It was a great starter home. Everything seemed to be falling into place.

Almost.

My mind kept replaying the events of those first few days of the trip, before I was burdened by any disturbing events and had felt those first stirrings of attraction. I pulled out the pictures Mitchell had given me, and I tried to recapture every smile, every nuance between us. Fighting the urge to discount it as mere wishful thinking—after all, I'd misjudged people before—I knew there had been something there.

The strains of ColdPlay filled the air. As I took the gleaming black iPhone out of my purse to see who was calling, I smiled. (I know. But my other one *was* outdated, and every time I saw this one, I remembered how its "cousin" had saved my life.) For a brief second, I thought it might be Mitchell, but it was just my parents making sure I had everything I needed to leave the next day. I told them I did, but that wasn't entirely true. With the phone in my hand though, I knew what I had to do. I'd been putting it off, waiting for Mitchell to make the first move. My hand trembled as I dialed information.

"Telequest local and national directory. What city please?"

"San Diego," my voice managed to squeak out.

"And the name . . . ?"

"Mitchell Davies."

The voice on the line hesitated a moment, typing in the request before answering, "I'm sorry. But that name is not listed for that area. Is there anything else I can help you with?"

"No, thank you," I murmured and hung up.

Since I hadn't thought to ask exactly where he lived, it was a long shot to begin with. Though it felt better knowing I'd tried.

Well, that's that then.

As I placed my phone back in my purse, I saw the card Lin, I mean, Amanda had given me. She'd said to call her if I needed anything. Was this what she meant? Probably not. But I'd learned over the past two weeks that when faced with losing everything, it made you more aware of what you had to gain. Someone picked up on the second ring.

"Hello?"

I gulped. "Amanda?"

Can you hear a smile over the phone? I thought I could hear hers. "I was wondering if you would call. How have you been doing?"

I briefly explained what had happened during the past month, along with my current plans. Then we finally got down to business because she knew why I had called. "I saw him a few days ago in a cooperative meeting regarding border security. Our success in Mexico has caused a surge of funding for our Priority Targeting Initiative in other hot spots as well. I wish I could go into more detail, but suffice it to say, we've got something big in the works."

"Does that mean you're going undercover again?" I asked, fearing she wouldn't be the only one involved.

"Umm, wish I could tell you more, but . . ."

"I know. The less I know the better. Don't think I haven't learned my lesson." I crossed my fingers. "So I guess you can't tell me if *he's* going, too?"

"Actually I can fill you in a little bit. Mitch is coordinating a different investigation right now, something closer to home and with no undercover work from what I understand—maybe we scared him off down in Mexico, making that his first deep undercover job. But after we became suspicious that it was Ms. Edwards and not Mr. Lansing as the U.S. contact, we realized we needed a man who could—how should I put this?—ensure that we could get close to her." I gulped, not sure if I wanted any more information. "I was afraid the Mexican agent we'd already coordinated things with wouldn't pique Kat's interest. Mitch fit the profile of everything we needed and was able to immediately get on a private flight to Mexico. And that was that."

Then she paused before saying, "He blames himself for what happened, or almost happened, down there."

"He does?"

"Yeah. Look, it's not my place to say, but I think you should know a few things. Mitch has been trying to come to terms with it all, but I still see him struggling. Of course, considering I was the case agent, I'm the one who should take the responsibility for our failures. I'd already made Kat jealous, snooping around Doug Lansing, so I had to back off. I would have turned my attention to Seth if we hadn't already guessed she had the hots for him as well. We just didn't realize she'd already made Seth her partner on the drug deal because keeping her men in the dark was more her M.O. Of course, we knew Mike was on our side. And then there was you."

"I know. And I kept getting in your way."

"Well, I have to admit when it came to what we thought of you, Mitch was on his own for a while. He wouldn't accept that you were working with them, and I wasn't willing to risk trusting you until it was almost too late, and that nearly ruined everything." She sighed. "We knew we were getting close, but after all that time, we still hadn't been able to figure out where the actual meeting was taking place. But that phone call Mitch made to you, and the information you were able to give, saved us," Amanda continued. "I doubt any agent could have kept a cooler head. Maybe you ought to think about joining the Agency."

I groaned. "I think I've had enough of that kind of excitement to last me a lifetime. But thanks for telling me all this."

"I guess we're not all cut out for this business." She added, "Still, I owe you a big favor."

"Well . . ." I smiled. Then I explained exactly what favor I wanted.

"I think I can make that happen. But before I do, you ought to know something. Mitch got some flack from the assistant regional director for his . . . how should I put it? . . . lack of focus on the job. Plus he's been hurt before—so go easy on him."

I sighed. "And let me guess—you're going to consider that last tidbit classified information and not tell me by what or whom?"

"Sorry, Sam. But I figure if you can handle Mexico, you can handle about anything."

I groaned again. "You're not trying to make me rethink this are you?"

"No," she said. "Just hang in there. He's worth it."

I said good-bye and hung up the phone. This was a big step. Once again, I was going to have to trust my instincts—and risk it all.

Chapter 32

THE WARM BREEZE SLIDING OFF the ocean played with the hem of my designer sundress and the curls of my salon-coiffed hair. I hopped off the wall, afraid I might be wrinkling the dress, though at the price I paid for it during my splurge mentality last month, it should have ironed itself. But it was worth it, and I knew I looked good. Under ordinary circumstances, I suppose that statement would have been vain—but this was no ordinary occasion. I stared back at the parking lot and watched a few rollerbladers go by. Looking past them, I thought I saw a dark-haired figure approaching. But then I realized the figure was wearing a wet suit and carrying a surfboard. I checked my purse and my phone one more time. Yes, it was on, and Amanda had assured me the GPS signal on my new phone could be easily tracked.

After an hour had passed, I kicked off my sandals and walked along the beach. The sand felt soft and supportive beneath my feet, and I dug my toes in as I headed toward the water-soaked shoreline. The mist had started to dissipate, and I could see to the end of the nearby pier. Morning joggers joined the surfing enthusiasts who were trying to catch the remaining high tide. The water caught the edge of my toes, and I stepped back to make sure an unexpected wave didn't get my dress wet. I shivered a little now that my legs were damp, hoping the sun would break through soon and warm the sand. Hoping by then . . .

But the rhythmic waves continued, and I could have been lulled by them if I weren't so anxious. I prayed that I wouldn't end up looking foolish after all this. Well, even if I did, I would still go home tomorrow as planned and put this all behind me.

"A hundred meters is still a large area to track, especially in this fog," said a deep voice behind me.

Thank you technology! I felt a shiver of excitement but tried to act casual as I turned around and said, "Then we'll have to work on your tracking skills."

Mitchell Davies stood beside me, wearing his trademark jeans and some sunglasses. He had his hands in his pockets, as if still trying to contain his feelings. "I've lost you a few times before. What made you think I could find you now?"

"I had faith in you . . . Mitchell," I answered, trying his new name out.

"My friends call me Mitch," he said with a slight smile. He paused and then started tentatively. "I've thought about calling you. I've just had a lot of paperwork to catch up on. Like my trainer always said, 'If it isn't written down, it didn't happen.'" He ended with a nervous laugh. "Actually that's not entirely true. I, uh, had a little explaining to do about you to my superiors."

"I know. Amanda told me."

"What else did she tell you?" he asked warily.

"Actually I'm not interested in what she had to say, but I am interested in what you want to share."

He gestured with his hand, and we walked along the beach awhile before he finally started to open up. "Before Mexico, I'd only done a few stings, where I had to act like I was a user or a dealer to catch some petty street criminal. But I've had friends who did some deep undercover work. I never knew how they could spend months, sometimes years, pretending to be someone they weren't. Especially when it meant that in order to accomplish their final goal, they had to accept that they might be asked to do things they wouldn't normally do. It seemed to me like too much of a price to pay just to bring down one more bad guy.

"But when SOD approached me and told me they'd been overseeing Operation Serpent and had a chance to stop a major drug trafficking operation that was funneling cocaine across the border and onto *my* city streets, it took on a new meaning. As a street cop, I'd seen too many kids OD and drop out of life. I thought it would be my chance to do something big."

The water had lapped up over Mitch's shoes, but I think he was too far into the past to notice. "It was easy at first. I was supposed to get to know the other members of the group and determine who else I thought was involved and, with Amanda's help, stay close to them—real close. We caught on right away that Kat was the ringleader, but I wasn't sure about you or Seth. At first I thought there was something between the two of you, but then I'd catch you watching me, and I didn't know how to read it. You were like two people, and I wasn't sure which one to believe in. Were you the consummate liar or simply an innocent girl? I had to decide. When I did, the toughest part was convincing my superiors that you had nothing to do with it."

"How did you do that?" I asked incredulously. "When I think back over the evidence you had piling up against me, I think I would have convicted myself. I mean, first you find Guadalupe's number on my phone . . ."

"I know. And then we saw you that first Saturday night and you looked, well, strung out, and even I doubted my instincts."

I groaned. "I'll never eat guacamole again! I don't blame Amanda for building a case that I was a poor student who had been sucked into making some quick cash."

"It didn't add up to me though. I followed you that next day when you went off by yourself to Chapultepec Park to see if you were trying to score another hit, but it was inconclusive."

"Is that why you had my room searched?"

Mitch blushed. "Sorry. We also confiscated that letter you sent to your dad. But don't worry, it's been forwarded on now."

I let my jaw hang open in amazement. "How did you find out about that? Wait, Miguel?"

He shrugged. "Mexican *policia*." Then he grinned. "I think he had a crush on you."

I scowled back. "Anything else I should know?"

"Uh, well, we eventually got a warrant from the local authorities to have your room bugged, hoping it would make things clearer, but it wasn't enough to prove your innocence. Especially since the transcriber kept presenting us with the most interesting transcripts. Your letter explained the 'Big Boss' pseudonym for your dad, but I still can't get over our mix-up about what an LDS meetinghouse was."

I burst out laughing and could barely speak. "I know! The original transcriptionist thought I'd said *LSD* instead of *LDS*, the abbreviation for the church I belong to."

He laughed too. "Well, like I said, it was all a confusing mess. But it was a good thing it was Seth and not us who found that note about how the Serpent wanted to meet you, or who knows. Still, regardless of what I thought I heard or saw, I decided to take a chance on you. But that meant I was supposed to let Amanda deal with you and never leave Kat's side."

Now we were at the crux of it all. "It looked like you were doing a good job," I said with a little too much edge in my voice. I found the courage to ask him if he was the man who went into her room that night when Kat was in the mood to "celebrate."

He ran a hand through his dark hair. "No, it didn't progress that far, but it came close. Too close for my peace of mind. Seth was probably the man who went in with her that night—and, I believe, any number of other nights." The relief I felt was almost tangible, but dredging things up had only brought back more regrets for Mitch.

"I can't forget how scared I was after that incident at Tula, when I not only had to deal with Kat but also had your safety to worry about. If I'd had my way, we would have gotten you out of Mexico, but that would have looked suspicious, so we tried everything else we could to keep you safe."

"Is that why Amanda and Mike kept following me?"

I saw the look of disbelief on his face. "Who are you? Are you sure you're not a covert agent with the FBI?"

"I guess you'll have to stick around and find out." I grinned. Then I added more seriously, "I have my own bad memories. I'll never forget what it was like thinking the Serpent had killed you and that I was next. But then, there you were—alive and looking down at me."

Mitch nodded his head. "You can thank Amanda for that. After you were pushed, we realized things were getting ugly, and she insisted I wear the vest. Even though it was made of some new top-secret material and was only a few millimeters thick, I felt as if everyone knew I was wearing it. But in the end, it saved my life. Of course," he smiled slyly, "it was really the second-best birthday present I got that day. I can't wait until my real thirtieth birthday."

I blushed at the memory.

After a pause, he grew serious again. "Yeah." He frowned. "It was a nightmare down there."

"But don't you see," I said, "you found me when it mattered most, so doesn't that count for anything? You don't have to feel guilty. Amanda told me everything, and I understand that you were a little, well, out of your element."

"Thanks for the excuse."

I glanced up at him and studied his strong jaw as he stared off into the distance. "That wasn't an excuse. Who believed in me when no one else did and understood what I was trying to say when I was at the pyramids?"

But he wasn't willing to relent. "Who lost track of Kat at the pivotal moment and should have caught on to Seth's involvement earlier? I should have stayed by your side the second I knew you weren't involved. It was my job to protect you."

"So I was just a job, then?" I looked at the ground and bit my lip.

"Sam." His hand on my chin tilted my face up. "If you were just a job, I wouldn't be here."

Then he kissed me. Not long enough or passionately enough, I have to admit, but I understood that we were still walking on shaky ground. I looked around at the people on the beach and smiled. "It looks like we still have an audience."

"Then I guess we'll have to work on that," he said, his face still close to mine.

With a grin, I started walking again. "So how about answering a few of *my* questions?"

"Like what?" He picked up his pace to catch up to me.

"Well, like telling me about the real David Ayala. Was he that guy whose photography studio we visited?"

Mitchell sighed. "Yes. We knew we had to find some basis in reality for my cover, and I'd known Dave for years—ever since we were at a photography seminar together. He was willing to do me a favor. Unfortunately, it appears Seth got suspicious of me and tracked him down. Then Kat paid him a visit . . . and you know how *persuasive* she can be."

I grimaced at the thought and changed the subject. "So you're not really from Mexico?"

"No." There was a pause, and I wondered if I'd hit another raw nerve. But he answered. "I've lived in either L.A. or San Diego all of my life. My mom's family was from Guadalajara, and they came across the border when she was twelve. Yes, illegally. Growing up, though, there was always the pressure to move away from that side of my heritage because my dad is Scotch-Irish, and his family has roots in California going back more than a hundred and fifty years to the mining days. I think my dad wanted to forget the circumstances surrounding my mother's family because we rarely had anything to do with her relatives.

I guess we embarrassed him," he said with bitterness in his words. "Of course, my mom tried to teach me to love my heritage. She'd have *pan dulce* waiting for me when I got home from school, and we'd always speak Spanish when we were alone."

"I'm glad. It's part of who you are."

"I suppose. Maybe that's why I had such a hard time in Mexico. Not only was I trying to be two people, but I *felt* like two people. I was always trying to see the beauty of the country while knowing what I was there for. Somehow, you helped me with that."

"How did I do that?"

"By being true to who *you* were." He stopped and stared out at the ocean again. "Is that because of this religion of yours? I finished that book you gave me. It was . . . interesting. Especially that part about how Jesus was supposed to have come here to America. I'd never heard of that before, but after everything I saw down there, it makes sense."

He read the whole Book of Mormon?

Wow. "Would you like to learn more about what I believe?"

He looked over at me and smiled sadly. "Maybe. I've always thought that following a religion was pointless after everything I've seen. How can there be a God when such horrible things happen?"

I nodded. It was the number one question I'd encountered on my mission. But I sensed this wasn't the time to get into a deep, religious discussion. "All right," I continued, trying to change the subject and hoping that eventually I'd find out everything I wanted to know. But I was willing to go easy on him for now. "As to my next question. Are you really a photographer?"

He shrugged. "Amateur, if anything. Sure, I'd love to take pictures for a living, but photography's like writing or painting, I suppose—not many find success in it. So I made it a hobby and instead enrolled in the police academy when I was out of college. Then two years ago, I completed my training at Quantico to become a special agent. My job takes up so much of my time that it's been difficult to do anything else. But I still dabble in it from time to time."

"You should," I encouraged. "You have a real talent."

He smiled. "Maybe I'll start trying again. You know what my favorite picture was from down there?"

I shook my head.

"The one of you up on the Pyramid of the Moon, your face all innocent and full of excitement just to be there."

"I'll never think of that place the same way again." I shivered at the memory, and Mitch, understanding, reached out and laid a hand on my arm. As he did, the sleeve on his arm rode up and I saw the old, puckered scar and finally realized it had to be from a gunshot wound. One day I hoped he'd tell me the story.

"So," he took charge of the questioning again, "what are your plans now?"

I told him about my decision to go home and look for a job closer to my family, watching his face carefully for any sign of disappointment. I thought I caught a trace.

"Our division here has an opening for a contract linguist," he said softly. "I checked into it a few days back."

"You did?" So he *had* been thinking about me. "What would I do?"

"Well, you'd work directly with original documents related to ongoing investigations, determine the relevance of the material, and then analyze and put the information into context. You might even be asked to assist with interviews, interrogations, and polygraph examinations."

"You mean, I might be in the same room as terrorists and dealers? I don't know."

Mitch shrugged. "Think it over. I've never seen a civilian handle a situation like the one that happened in Mexico so competently. You're a natural and could do a lot of good."

"And how was I going to find out about this good I could do if you were too chicken to come tell me?" I ignored his look of protest. "Yes, chicken! So how did Amanda get you to come here anyway?"

He groaned. "She told me we'd received a tip on someone in danger. In danger of having her *heart broken*. I think Amanda crossed the corny line with that one."

"I won't take the credit for that." I waved my hand in protest. "She came up with that all on her own. I think Mike's really bringing out her soft side. So then, Agent Davies. What's the typical protocol in a situation like that?"

"Well," he said as his mouth curled up, though he tried to suppress his grin, "we assess the circumstances, see if it's in our jurisdiction, and then decide how we can help."

"What's your assessment then?"

He leaned in and kissed me—satisfactorily this time!—and then I added, "It seems I've got a few new options to consider. Of course," I frowned slightly, "I do need to spend time with my family." I told him about the situation with my dad. "Plus, they need to know what happened, and I have to be there in person to tell them."

Mitch shuffled his feet in the sand. "Would you like some help? After all, I've been trained to deal with this sort of thing."

I tilted my head coyly. "I'll think about it. Though it would be completely on a professional basis, right?" I added playfully.

"Naturally, ma'am," he said as he saluted me. Then he took me in his arms. "There's one more thing you ought to know about me, Sam."

Suddenly I didn't mind the nickname anymore. "What?" I asked nervously, hoping there wasn't anything else too shocking that he hadn't told me. He took off his sunglasses, and I gasped. "Your eyes are really blue?" And they were. Blue like the ocean all around us.

"So you aren't disappointed, are you?" he asked. "I'm giving you a lot of new things to deal with."

I relaxed and looked into the blue eyes of the man who may have saved me in more ways than one, silently hoping this wasn't the end for us. "Then it's a good thing I'm learning to look at things differently," I answered back as a warming sun broke through the clouds.

He smiled. "That makes two of us."

Author's Notes

OVER THE LAST SEVERAL YEARS, the war on drugs has taken on a new meaning in Mexico. When Felipe Calderón became Mexico's president in 2006, he bravely made it part of his mission to eradicate the drug cartels from his nation's borders. Though he's enlisted the help of more than 50,000 of his own country's soldiers and 40,000 federal police over the past six years to curb cartel activity, violence has escalated to unheard of levels. Between 2006 and 2008 alone, drug violence killed more than 10,000 people. To date, that number has risen to more than 40,000. Sadly, it appears his mission has resulted in a bloody battle, with the government authorities fighting the drug cartels who seek to move billions of dollars worth of their product into the U.S. through Mexico every year. In fact, Mexico is the largest transshipment point of South American cocaine destined for the United States and continues to be the preferred corridor to smuggle a variety of illicit drugs.

The United States has made its own investment in this war with the creation and management of numerous organizations designed to control the flow of drugs across its border. In 1991, the DEA established the Special Operations Division (SOD), a program that uses technology and intelligence to coordinate efforts between the DEA, the FBI, and other government agencies. Their mission is to target the command, control, and communication of major drug trafficking organizations.

Though this novel is not based upon factual accounts or real persons, I wrote it in hopes that it will bring to light this tragic circumstance that is slowly eroding the foundation of a country steeped in rich culture and history. I can only imagine what will be lost if it continues. But the guilt can't be placed entirely upon Mexico's shoulders because as Seth puts it in this novel, "It's all about supply and *demand*."

About the Author

K. C. GRANT WAS BORN IN rural Idaho but has made Utah her home for most of her life. She lives in northern Utah with her family. After serving a full-time, Spanish-speaking mission, she returned to Weber State University, where she received her bachelor of arts with a double major in English and Spanish. She has traveled extensively throughout Mexico and studied briefly at a local college in the state of Michoacán. Over the years, she has been a frequent contributor to several family/home-oriented magazines, such as *LDSLiving, Natural Life, The Washington Family,* and *BackHome* and has also written for the *Deseret News* and KSL. She is an active member of both the League of Utah Writers (where she was a chapter president for three years), LDStorymakers, and the Association for Mormon Letters. This is her third novel.

To learn more about the author, visit her website at www.kcgrant.com.